Best Wishes

Billy Graham

Dead Men Don't Talk

Chapter 1

It never failed to amuse Jake Russo why so many people left their cars unlocked, especially with the keys still in the ignition.
Sliding into the driver's seat he started the engine of the Buick and slowly reversed down the driveway. At 1am there were not many house lights still showing. Gradually increasing speed he turned the street corner passing the rental car he had picked up earlier. Less than fifteen minutes later Jake Russo was out of the suburb and heading for the city centre.

At thirty five he had long since mastered the art of equability. This present job was no exception. Had he not already planned it with his meticulous penchant for detail, which was why he had never so much as received a parking ticket throughout his life of crime.

Jake stared ahead at the sudden appearance of the tailback of assorted stationary vehicles, blue lights flashing from the police cars parked on either side and calmly turned down a side street: he would have to find another way out of town.

A quick look back at the line of cars with their trunks open told him that the Law were not after small fry, not at this time of the morning, and although the car he had stolen from the driveway would as yet not have been missed by its owner the last thing he wanted was to be questioned by flash- light bearing cops in all probability there as a result of a tip off and only too eager to make their name by apprehending some unfortunate marijuana pusher.

Another ten minutes brought him to the street of his destination, slowly cruising by the row of tall elegant mansions, each manifestly different from one another, until reaching the last but one, this although standing as elegant as its neighbours was easily distinguished by its lack of security guards or CCTV cameras.

Jake cursed. It served the stupid old bastard right to have thought his reputation would save him from anyone bold, or should that be stupid enough to invade his premises, and the ferocious repercussions should they have the misfortune to fall into the hands of old Simon Ferris. Personally the thought did not in the least scare him. He had planned this only too well.

Russo halted, turned off the engine and quietly exited the car.

As usual the iron gates stood unlocked. Russo gently pushed one open and let himself into the grounds, losing himself amongst the trees and bushes aligning the walls. His eyes on the one lit ground floor window, he waited.

A glance at his watch told him Simon Ferris, head of that family should emerge from the house at almost any moment, having observed the old man's habit over the past five days, and he had no reason to believe this evening should be different.

Russo was right. A shaft of light cut across the doorstep and on to the gravel pathway when the door opened, and an incoherent murmur of voices followed by the sharp barking of a tiny dog reached the patient onlooker across the darkened lawn.

Involuntarily Russo stepped back a little into the bushes, while the little dog happy to be free ran back and forth a little way from its master.

His eyes on man and dog Russo waited.

Following the path bordering the lawn the duo came on. Another five minutes and they would have reached where he stood.

Calmly Russo slid the revolver from his shoulder holster his eyes never leaving his victim as he fitted the silencer. As if sensing his presence, growling the little dog drew to a halt, its sudden barking disturbing the tranquillity of the evening.

Cautiously, suspiciously the little dog slowly approached where Russo stood hidden, its instincts telling the animal that there was danger here. It gave another bark louder this time, and the old man halted. He was too late, Jake Russo's first shot took him between the eyes his second silenced the dog.

Holstering the gun Russo left the safety of the bushes and bending down dragged the lifeless body towards the gate. There, he laid it down to take a look out at the street, and seeing that it was still deserted dragged the corpse to where he had parked the borrowed Buick.

Russo let out a deep breath at the unexpected weight of the old man. A squeal of tyres in the distance urged him to hurry and he quickly stooped to open the trunk.

Only on few occasions was Jake Russo ever at a loss and this was one of them. Draping the dead body over the edge of the trunk he stared at a white sheet partially covering what appeared to be the dead body of a young woman. "Jesus! Of all the cars in town I had to pick this one!" Now slightly rattled albeit for only the second time that he could recall, he bundled the old man into the trunk. "Now you two can get acquainted while I get myself the hell out of here." The irony in his voice outmatching any thought of humour.

It had been his intention to drive through the town suburbs to the hills beyond where he'd planned to unceremoniously dump the lifeless body of one Simon Ferris, collect his fee and be on the midday flight back home but that was when there was only one body to dispose of, not two!
Jake swore again he'd have to detour even more, thanks to the city's renowned police force still at work catching dealers. Poor bastards, he himself had made a few dollars from that side of the business in his early days.

The solitude of the surrounding countryside as he neared the foothills helped him to reorganise his thoughts. The first of his plan remained unchanged; dump the old man somewhere up the mountainside, then return his borrowed car to the vicinity of its owner, walk to his rented car then collect his contract money from Jack Kane. The only exception to this was one additional body.
He'd concluded it would not be wise to dump them both together, though, he chuckled how would the city's finest work that one out? One Mafia type, together with? As yet he did not know who or what, that was the problem.

The name on the house door of his borrowed car had read Charles Simpson. What he had seen of the man was that he was married with one small girl about six year old. The wife, pretty, definitely his type, then again who was not? So how had the dead young girl come to be in the trunk of his Buick? His final analysis omitted the possibility of Mister Simpson not knowing that the body was there at all. No, Mr Simpson did know and probably awaited the opportunity of doing what he in turn was doing for him. Why he had killed the girl was of no concern of his, his only consolation was that Simpson would not alert the police to the theft of his car, after all he could scarcely inform them of its theft with the addendum "by the way there is a dead body in the trunk."

It was close on 3am before Jake Russo was on the hill path leading to a parking place some distance above. At this hour the odds were that all young lovers would have long since vacated the site. Fortunately he had slowed the car down to a crawl when it unexpectedly hit a deep rut and he was thrown forward, his head inches away from hitting the windscreen. Cursing his bad luck Jake slammed the car into reverse, dust flying into the night from the rear wheels, revving again and again until he was free, and before the dust had settled around the Buick had the trunk open and was unceremoniously dragging Simon Ferris to his temporary resting place.

For a moment Jake halted, straightened his aching back muscles and took a swift look round. The place was deserted, only the incessant noise of chirping cicadas' filled the night air.
He looked down, it was quite a steep drop to the first line of bushes. He stooped, hauled the dead old man to his feet, swung him round and heaved him over the side, and as he

watched, it appeared that even the cicadas' were silent as if they too were absorbed in the descent of the body before continuing their nocturnal deliberations.
Now there was only a cloud of dust to betray where the old man had come to rest amongst the thick undergrowth. He turned, it was only a matter of time before the body was discovered. Of course this had always been the plan. Now for the next unexpected part.

Jake Russo gunned the Buick a further six miles along the highway swinging off the road on to another dust filled mountain track, which he had intended earlier for his old victim, until eventually deciding on the latter, now this one would have to do for the youngster in the trunk.
This track was narrower than the previous one, but not so for dust. Although he had the windows rolled up he still choked at some invading particles.

At length he reached the spot he'd previously marked out for Simon Ferris. Jake Russo sat back ran his handkerchief over the sweat on his face and waited for the dust outside the Buick to settle.
A few minutes later he was outside and opening the trunk staring down at the body of the dead girl, grunting, "swine" that anyone should kill someone so young.
Russo drew back the white bed sheet. The girl's eyes were closed, the only sign of what had happened to her a mark on her forehead, though he thought there could be further evidence elsewhere. He pulled down the sheet, the girl was dressed in jeans and a white blouse, now blood stained.
Jake Russo put both hands under the body, and what for him was a gentle lifting of the girl out of the trunk, together with a strange reluctance at what he had to do,

again grunted "swine" at whoever had done this to such a lovely young girl as this.

Jake carried the lifeless body a little way into the undergrowth gently setting it down under a tree.

He'd leave the girl her jewellery, only robbers stole from the bodies, or serial killers taking bits and pieces for souvenirs, a habit that usually led to their downfall.

A few minutes later Jake Russo had covered the body as best he could with stones. Now she would remain here until discovered by some unsuspecting hill walker, or eventually by the police themselves. Jake walked back to the car. Now to pay Jack Kane a visit and receive his contract money.

At the same time as Jake Russo was on his way to meet his benefactor, Charlie Simpson lay alone in the downstairs spare room. He had told Jenny his wife that he had a cold coming on, maybe flu, so in order not to pass it on to her or their daughter he'd sleep in the spare room, this excuse had given him the freedom to silently leave the house and dispose of poor Mary Dewer.

Charlie lay there staring up at the ceiling. How had it all come to this? He of all people a murderer?

It was only bad...evil people who killed, not self respecting married men such as himself.

Self respecting? Charlie silently spat out the words amid his self loathing.

He breathed in, remembering how it had all started.

"Mister Simpson," Irene Kerr the department supervisor pushed his office door a little open.

"Come in Irene. You looked troubled." He beckoned her with a wave of his hand.

Not that he was alarmed by her look, Irene always looked troubled but he could not have run the department without the overweight middle aged woman who took everything in her stride, unlike himself who was prone to panic should a serious problem arise.

Irene stepped inside. "Those urgent reports you asked for are not yet finished. They should have been by this time, but we are two computer operators short." She studied her watch, her voice rising a little. "And we only have four hours before the courier arrives."
Charlie laid down his pen. "Can you take any others off the work they are on that is not as important, Irene?"
The woman thought for a moment. "Could do I suppose. There is one girl working on draft schedules."
"Good. Have her stop what she's doing and start immediately on the reports." Charlie lifted his pen, "Ask her if she'd be willing to stay back if necessary."
"OK boss, will do."

Charlie lifted his head from the document he was reading. It was two hours since Irene had informed him about the reports, instead it was a girl scarcely out of her teens who stood in the doorway.
"Mister Simpson," she started nervously, "I have finished most of the reports you wanted."
Charlie choked back a reply, for the youngster who stood there was probably the best looking girl he had seen in a long time. He waved that she should come in.

"Thanks….I don't know your name," he smiled apologetically.

"Mary Dewer, sir." The blonde girl took a hasty step into the office.

"Thank you, Mary." Charlie glanced at his watch. "How long will it take you to finish the remainder?"

"About another hour sir."

"Good. Can you hold on until I OK them? Not that I expect you to have made any mistakes," he quickly assured her, "But….."

Mary smiled. "Yes. I quite understand."

As she turned, Charlie got out, "Does your folks know you are working late? I shouldn't want them to worry."

"No sir, that's all been taken care of."

Charlie watched her return to the computer section through the glass partition of his office, incapable of understanding why his heart was pounding as it was.

"Christ," he swore, "she must just be out of her teens, early twenties at most."

Charlie picked up his pen again, surprised that his hand was shaking. He swore again, chastising himself for his thoughts. Was he not a happily married man with a six year old daughter? And this girl must be at least fifteen years his junior. Behave yourself man. This time his curse was at his office supervisor for choosing Mary Dewer.

It was in fact close on two hours before all the reports were completed, just in time to catch the evening courier. Thankfully they were all correct.

Charlie left his office and walked towards the now deserted computer section.

Mary Dewer rose when she saw him coming. "Was everything satisfactory Mister Simpson?" she asked nervously. "I guess they must be when I saw the courier leave."

"Yes thank you Mary. You did an excellent job."

"Then I take it that you won't require my services further this evening?" Mary reached for her coat.

'If only you knew how much,' Charlie thought. Instead he said, "No, thank you I think I have detained you long enough. How will you get home? You have your own transport I take it?"

Mary gave a little laugh, "On my salary." She saw her boss frown. "Sorry," she apologised, "That was uncalled for. I did not mean anything by it." She was making a hash of it. "I know it has nothing to do with you."

Charlie nodded. "Understood. Then how do you get home?"

"By tube."

"To where?"

"Broadmeadows."

It had to be nowhere near his own home, and although a little voice was telling him to leave it there, he could not help from hearing himself say. "Good. I can offer you a lift."

"But you don't live anywhere near there." She stopped, "Or so I believe."

"Maybe so, but it is the least I can do at this late hour."

Curling a lip, Mary nodded. "If you are sure?"

"Sure as I will ever be," he smiled reassuringly.

Lying in bed Charlie heaved a deep sigh. He'd give himself another half hour then do what he had to do, unable to say to himself 'bury the body that's in the car.'

He knew he should have left it there, not offered the girl another lift home the next night, but he could not wait for the work day to end to be with her again, smell her perfume, her presence. It was like being a teenager all over again.

With the greatest of willpower he called a halt. Already Irene was becoming suspicious his calling the girl into his office on the most trivial of excuses. Just when he thought he had gotten over his schoolboy crush, fate lent a hand, or to be precise to Mary Dewer.

The office was in turmoil, or the computer part of it, a rail strike had brought all public transport to a halt, buses ran at full capacity, hire of taxi cabs non existent.

Charlie took a few steps out of his office. "OK here's what we do." No one took a shred of notice. He tried again, louder this time. "I said this is what we do!"

Suddenly everyone stopped what they were doing.

"Hands up who have a car that could take someone home?"

The question raised a few hands. Charlie went on from there.

A half hour later Dickson the general manager strode into the department. "Got it fixed have you Charlie?" he asked, an eye on those ready to leave, and silently counting the cost of lost production.

"I believe so sir. Some have agreed to go out of their way to take four home."

"Good." The stern old man swung towards the door. "Then there's no need for me here, I might as well be on my way."

"All by yourself, no doubt," Charlie muttered under his breath.

He took a look around at a few on their way to the escalator, their laughter reaching him as he stood there. A movement from the back of a row of computers caught his attention it was Mary Dewer

making her way towards the escalator.

"You all right Miss Dewer? Got a ride home?"

The girl blushed. "Not quite sir, no one lives in my part of town."

No. he should not do it, everything in his brain said no to what he was about to propose. "I'll take you, Miss Dewer, give me a minute to finalize a few things."

And that was how it all began.

Russo now only two streets away from where he had left his parked rental car chuckled at the thought of what must be going through the head of Mister C Simpson should he have found his car missing from his driveway, and who had taken it.

Russo swung into the street drawing up a little way from his rented car. He was not worried about leaving his DNA behind, sure the cops who in time were certain to examine the car would find his prints but as he had no record would have nothing to compare them with. Fingerprints? Sure, but the same applied there though he had taken the precaution of wearing gloves. Besides, another eight hours and he was out of this big city and on his way back home. Fifteen minutes later Jake Russo drove up to Jack Kane's considerable sized mansion, in many ways similar to that of his last victim.

He got out and walked to the front door. Although it was a little past 5am there was still one light showing from a downstairs window. Jake rang the bell, stood back and waited.
It was Jack Kane himself who answered the door. Saying nothing he stood back to let his visitor pass, closing the door and following him into what appeared to be a large comfortable study.

"Drink?" Kane held up the bottle of Scotch.
Jake shook his head. "Better not, I'm driving."
"Quite," Kane agreed filling up his own glass, and sitting down opposite Russo in an armchair by the wall. "So, did you get the job done?" There was only the slightest sound of nervousness in his voice as he asked the question.
Making himself comfortable in the big chair Jake sat back. "Went like clockwork. No hitches."
He was on no account going to mention the dead girl. "Ditched Ferris."
Kane quickly held up a hand stopping Jake from continuing. "Where or how I do not wish to know. The least I know of your business the better it is for me. Except," he hesitated, "he will be found quite soon I hope?"
"Sure to, where I dumped him." Jake Russo yawned. "So as I should like a little shut eye before my departure from your marvellous city, I'd be obliged if we settled up now."
Kane took a sip of his drink. "Well that's what I'd like to talk over with you." Russo's face darkened. "No, no Russo, there's no problem paying." Kane stood up, "it's just that I have another proposition that might interest you."

"No thanks, Jack. One of the things that has kept me safe is not to hang around in the same place after the job is done." He was thinking of how he had come in contact with the body, both bodies, any tell tale signs he might have left in Mister Simpson's Buick, but more essential, his intended cleaning of his rental car before leaving it at the airport.

"I could make it worth your while?"

Jake shook his head, growing a little angry. "We made a deal Jack. Just pay me what you owe and let me get the hell out of here."

Kane moved behind his desk and sat down. "I could easily refuse to pay you."

"I shouldn't if I were you, there's plenty of room beside the late Mister Ferris."

Kane sat back in his chair. "OK I will level with you. There is another 30k in it for you if you do one more job for me."

Jake made a face. "Must be very important to up the anti."

Kane's face relaxed a little in the belief he had caught Jake Russo's interest. "It is. I will let you know the target in a few days. I have one or two details to take care of before then." Kane rose indicating the discussion was at an end.

"You still at the same place the one I set up for you?"

"Yes." Russo got up.

"Is it all right? I could have it changed if you like?"

"No it's comfortable enough and the food's good."

Kane offered his hand. "Glad you have agreed to do this little job for me, Jake."

"And if I hadn't?"

Kane shrugged. "Then I might just decide not to pay you for the Ferris job."

Russo sought to remain calm though inwardly seething at the man's audacity. "As I said before there's plenty of room beside Ferris. But this aside should I refuse your kind offer, who would you have replace me? Those you hired for your last job are still inside."

Kane threw his hands in the air. "OK, sixty grand and don't try screwing me for more."

Jake walked to the door, already regretting that he had accepted the offer. Now he thought, he should have been more careful and not have taken it for granted that he'd be out of town and hopefully also out of reach of the local cops.

Jake Russo drove his borrowed car back to where he had left his rental. Though there was now no need to hurry as he'd not be making that midday flight, he still wanted to be well on his way to his hotel before a certain Mister Simpson discovered the disappearance of his Buick. Or had he already done so? One thing was for sure, he'd not inform the cops.

The street where Russo had parked his rented car was only just round the corner from where Simpson lived. Sliding the Buick to a halt behind his car Russo took a last look round the interior, ensuring that he'd not left any incriminating evidence behind, his tired face breaking into a smile at the thought of the man's turmoil when discovering the Buick's disappearance. Or had he not as yet? If not he better be quick for it would soon be light.

It was as Jake Russo reached the end of the street that Charlie Simpson tip toed to his front door, where he stood for moment listening for any sound from either of the upstairs bedrooms; there was none.

Charlie stepped out on to his driveway his thoughts on the shovel he'd have to fetch from the garage. Nothing else. He had to be careful. He looked up, his car was not there! Charlie Simson panicked, his mind churning out a kaleidoscope of reasons why his car was not where he had left it.

Joyriders! Had joyriders taken it, and if so would they look in the trunk and find Mary?

Then what next, inform the police on the pretext of finding his car abandoned or were they likely not to take the chance and walk away. Whatever the outcome he was doomed, the Buick would eventually be traced back to him.

Shaking, Charlie walked to the curb and looked up and down his deserted street, it being too much to believe that his car might be left there. It was not.

Charlie walked back up his driveway. So if no joyriders then who? All that was left was blackmailers. He'd have to wait. His immediate dilemma was in explaining the Buick's disappearance to his wife.

Charlie usually left for his office around 8am, except today, today he'd have to travel by tube.

Charlie gave his watch a dismal glance and downed his coffee. He had no appetite for anything else.

"Charlie! Leaving early? Something big on at the office? Has that old fool Dickson got you running around like mad again?" Yawning, his wife Jenny came into the kitchen.

"What have you had for breakfast?" She asked tying the cords of her dressing gown.

"Not too hungry Jenny, still have a bit of flu' on me."

"Then you should not be going in to the office at all.
You'll get no thanks for it." Jenny poured herself a coffee.
"Besides, should you have flu you might just spread it
around." Jenny made a face, "Then who would be the
popular one?"
Charlie had almost forgotten his excuse for sleeping in the
downstairs spare room.
"Do you have to leave so early? It's scarcely seven."
Now came his first lie, something he'd never made a habit
of, that was before his affair with Mary Dewer, since then
there had been more than he could care to remember. His
coming home taking little Alice on his knee asking how
she had got on at school that day. Loathing himself while
watching his wife prepare the evening meal. How happy
they had been throughout their marriage until now, he
corrected himself, *before* his meeting and desire for Mary
Dewer.

Charlie returned to the present. "The car's in the repair
shop. I had them call last night."
Jenny sat down at the table absently clutching her coffee
cup. "I did not hear anyone." She looked up at her husband
awaiting his explanation.
Charlie put down his cup. "No, it was late when they
called. I asked them to be as quiet as possible and not wake
the neighbours. I called them earlier but that was as quick
as they could make it."
He lifted his briefcase. "I knew there was something far
wrong with it when I tried to start it after I brought it
home."
"There's always something to bite into our savings," Jenny
sighed. "Will it cost much?"

At the door Charlie shrugged. "Knowing our luck probably quite a lot. Now I have to go, Jenny or I'll miss my train." Jenny followed him to the front door. "I suppose you will be late home?"
Charlie waved. "I suppose so."

Charlie Simpson walked round the corner of his street, drawing to a halt in disbelief at the sight of his parked Buick. For a moment he just stood there oblivious to whatever else may be happening around him in that quiet street.
Trembling, Charlie took a step towards the vehicle. He stopped. The keys were still in the ignition. He would never leave them there again.

To say that Charlie Simpson was convulsed with fear would be a gross understatement, petrified would be more an apt description. Yet he had to do it, do it before anyone rounded the corner and started to ask awkward question such as why he was just standing there staring at his car. Was he ill? Should they call a doctor etc. etc.?
His stomach churning with fear Charlie drew in a deep breath and stepped to open the trunk, lifting it an inch at a time, steeling himself to look inside.
Charlie did not know what to do or where to look. There was no dead Mary Dewer inside!

All the way to his office Charlie pondered on every possible scenario, of which blackmail was uppermost. No one was going to do him a favour by disposing of the body without receiving something in return. He couldn't hide the fact that whoever it was, knew who he was and where he lived. Now to get through this first day, and how many more he murmured.

"Mr Simpson, Mary Dewer has not called in sick." Irene Kerr's voice reached him from the open office door.

Charlie looked up wrinkling his brows. "Who?"

"Mary Dewer from the computer section. You know the one that worked on the reports for you?" Irene nudged his memory. "The one you took home on the day of the rail strike."

"Oh that girl," Charlie pretended to remember, studying the woman who stood in the doorway for any sign of suspicion that he knew very well who she meant.

"Was she working on anything important, Irene?"

"Not really. Just thought I'd let you know of her absence. Her supervisor told me, and I'm passing it on as usual."

Charlie nodded. "Thanks Irene. I appreciate that."

When Irene had gone Charlie sat back in his chair. Had he fooled the woman? Did she know anything of their affair? Irene was the soul of discretion, but women liked to gossip. Had in fact Mary told anyone? More so in the office. It was not impossible that a girl of Mary's age should boast of having the boss eating out of her hand, especially to others of her own age. God help him if she had when they found her body. Then his world would really start falling apart. He swore, not only his world but that of his family.

Chapter 2

It was three days since he had disposed of the bodies. Jake Russo threw the newspaper down in disgust and looked out of his hotel window. Nothing as yet, not a word. He had expected someone to have come across old Ferris by this time. As to the girl? Perhaps not as yet, she'd be a little harder to find.

A little on edge Jake grunted. Now more than ever angry at himself at taking this latest job, it ending his practice to move on after a hit and be well on his way to another part of the country as soon as possible, for no matter how meticulous he was it was always possible to leave some detail behind, no matter how miniscule.

It was evident that over the years he would at some time leave his fingerprints and DNA somewhere. The cops were not stupid, their system would throw up the same details of his numerous jobs, who that person was as yet they did not know, but staying on in this city increased the chances of their finding out. The only thing left to him was to wait for Jack Kane to name the target. Bad as the waiting was for him, what must it be like for Charlie Simpson.
Three days, three days in which he'd not left his hotel room. He'd go crazy if he stayed in any longer.

The tables on the boulevard were almost full when Jake decided he badly needed that fresh air.
It was good to be out and amongst carefree people. Walking along, Jake took a look around him dodging the occasional body hurrying past, aware of the incessant chatter of those at their meals. All innocent law abiding citizens. Jake smirked, guessing that everyone without

question had something to hide. Perhaps not so bad as himself but there was always something, from infidelity to tax evasion to God knows what else.
Jake found an empty table, one in which he could see into the interior of the restaurant besides that of the street. He picked up the menu from off the table aware of the coming and goings of the tray carrying waiters charging by.

A sudden loud burst of laughter from a table had him look in that direction, his gaze moving to a table close by where a middle aged well dressed man sat together with a woman of similar years and a younger woman close to Jake's own age. Here there was no laughter, here the faces were drawn, solemn, obviously from some family tragedy.

There was a scream and the younger female from the 'solemn' table flew to her feet. It took Jake only a second to realise that the man heading for the street had lifted the girl's purse. Instinctively he was after him. Jake caught up, swung him round, a punch relieving the robber of his spoils.
Reluctantly Jake let the man escape, he could not afford to have the police involved in this. Stupid asshole he thought of himself, why not just sit there and mind your own business.

All around, diners were on their feet, a few only now aware of what had just happened.
Jake returned to the 'solemn' table holding out the purse to the younger woman. "Yours I believe," he smiled at her.
"Thank you. I don't know what I would have done without it," she responded with only a glimmer of a smile, as if she at least owed him this.

"Well done sir." The middle aged man had risen to his feet holding out his hand. "What it must be like to be young again. Had it been left to me that villain would be over the state line by now." He offered Jake a smile.

"Sorry he got away."

"No matter you saved Faye's purse."

"Mister Sagan I am so sorry," the perspiring tubby manager apologised, hurrying towards them throwing his hands in the air in despair, "This has never happened before in Maxims".

"It is all right, Marco, no damage done." Sagan assured him.

Sagan turned again to Jake. "Peter Sagan's my name, let me introduce you to my wife Nancy and Faye my niece….Mister eh?"

"Russo, Jake Russo," Jake said without hesitation, experience having taught him, that to lie about ones name, only led to later repercussions, followed by inquisitive snoopers making it their business to explore even further. "Pleased to meet you all."

"You a stranger here Mister Russo?" the elder woman asked.

Jake nodded, cursing ever having gone after the purse snatcher. "From the East, you would never have heard of the town, it's so small we use the city limits at either end as goal posts."

There was a wholehearted laugh from Peter Sagan while the women merely smiled.

Sagan's cell phone rang and apologising took a step away from the table.

"Peter's contacted the Police Commissioner about our niece's disappearance," Nancy Sagan soberly informed Russo.

Russo nodded as if he fully understood.

"Got to go love wanted down town." Sagan stepped back to the table. "Nice to have met you Mister Russo. Maybe next time I will have time to thank you for what you did for my niece."

Nancy rose flashing Russo a smile of apology. "When you have to go, you have to go."

Faye too, rose to follow her elders.

Sagan turned back. "No need for you to come Faye, we will tell you all you need to know. Stay and keep Mister Russo company over his meal."

Russo experienced a difference of emotions. One: he wanted the girl to stay as he had not spoken socially to anyone outside of his reason for being in the city. Two: it was much safer if she were to leave. He looked up at her and saw her hesitation. "I won't be offended should you decide not to stay." Her standing there vaguely reminding him of someone, but for the moment he could not recall who.

Faye pulled out a seat and sat down opposite Russo.

A waiter appeared and he ordered a coffee, and one for his guest. Minutes ago he had been hungry, looking forward to a good meal, now that appetite had gone and he could barely face a coffee.

"So how do you like our great city?" Faye started the conversation.

Russo lifted his coffee cup to his lips sipping slowly to give himself time to think. Her next question dependant upon his immediate answer. "Very nice. Pity I wont have time to take it all in."

Faye sipped her own coffee. "Why, what's the rush? Don't tell me business?"

"Got it in one," Jake smiled. "Computers."

"Very up market." She became solemn. "That's the work Mary… my sister used to do."

"Used to?"

Faye played with her napkin. "She's missing. Missing from Sunday. That's why Uncle Peter had to leave, he's meeting the Police Commissioner." She gave a wily smile. "Uncle has a great deal of influence in the city." Her smile broadened, "who would not, who owns half of it.

Now that no one has seen or heard from Mary for over three days the police are treating it as a missing person's case. At first they tried to tell us that she may have just run off with someone. Young folk do they say. But I know my sister, her home had nothing missing. Her credit cards, money, clothes were all there. Nor would she have left a job she loved as a computer operator at Martin's. Besides, she enjoyed working for her boss Charlie Simpson."

At the mention of the name Faye mistook the look on Jake Russo's face for one of surprise at her sisters unexplained disappearance, when instead the surprise was that this young woman sitting opposite him was the sister of the girl he had disposed of from the back of her boss's car.

Of all the restaurants and all the tables on the boulevard he had to choose this one. Jake ran a spoon round the inside of his cup, now more than ever convinced he should get himself out of this city and the quicker the better.

Jake Russo shared a cab with Faye Dewer until she alighted outside of what was probably the most expensive hotel in the city. And to his surprise handed him her personal card with the promise that he should call her before he quit the city.

Standing at the window of his room Jake poured himself a Scotch. To leave now was the smart thing to do, but in doing so he forfeited the money from the Ferris job besides pissing off Jack Kane at his reneguing of the present contract, whatever that might be.

Jake was not long in finding out who this was to be. Answering a knock on the door, he opened it to two heavily built men,.
"You Jake Russo?" one asked gruffly.
Jake replied that he was.
"Mister Kane says I have to hand you this personally, it's what you've been waiting for."
He handed Jake a buff coloured envelope. The man's silent partner confirming the delivery with a nod.

Thanking Jack Kane's messenger, Jake closed the door, finished his drink and sat down at the small table in front of his room window his only window. Whatever intentions he had of skipping town it was now too late. Pensively Jake opened the folder, a few photos and a foolscap sheet of paper spilled out on to the small table. He picked up the sheet, headed Target. For the first time in a while Jake Russo's hands shook as he read the name Peter Sagan.

Charlie always knew they'd call. Through the glass partition he picked out the two strangers making their way towards his office. Apprehensively he waited. Although he had played this forthcoming scene over and over when lying awake at night it still left him unsure on how to react. Best take it as it comes was his final thought as they reached the door.

"Mister Simpson, Mister Charles Simpson?" one asked showing his badge. "I'm Detective Lieutenant Sam Andrews, and this is my partner Detective Sergeant Sims." Charlie stood up hoping they would not hear his knees knocking behind his desk. "Come in officers.
How may I help you? Please take a seat." Charlie gestured. Seated Andrews asked, "We are conducting inquires regarding Mary Dewer, one of your Company employees." Silently Charlie waited.
"She has been missing from home since last Saturday or Sunday."
"Yes. I understand she has not been at work this week. Irene, Miss Kerr my supervisor has informed me she has not called in as required by the Company."

"Is it usual for her not to do so would you say, Mr Simpson?"
Charlie thought for a moment. "I don't think so. I really don't know."
Andrews raised his brows. "You are her boss are you not?"
"Oh yes, quite. But you see, Miss Dewer (he had almost said Mary) is employed down in I.T. It is up to my supervisor…"
"Miss Kerr?" Sims confirmed.
"Yes. Irene deals with that side of things." Charlie forced a laugh on the pretext at not appearing to be over concerned by one employee's failure to follow Company procedure.

"So you have no reason to offer why this particular employee is not at work as usual?"

"Or not at home?" Sims added.

"No officers. As to your question about Miss Dewer's absence from home, I know nothing of her private life." The lie had come easier than he'd expected. "However, perhaps one or two who she works beside could help you there." Charlie gave a stilted laugh, "You know how young girls love to talk."

"Oh we do, Mister Simpson, we do," Andrews assured him, rising. "We'll do just that."

Almost the entire journey home Charlie mulled over and over his interview with the detectives earlier in the day, his mood alternating from a high to downright fear. His lie about not knowing anything regarding Mary's home life had come easily to him. His fear was, that Mary had confided their affair with someone in the office, and if so those two cops would instantly know he had lied, which in turn would make him a suspect. Charlie gripped the steering wheel tighter, and stared out the windshield. But if any of her chums had known this and told those cops, surely they would have returned to his office to query what he had said at their earlier interview?

No, Mary had not told anyone, at least not in the office. Charlie sighed, his heart pounding. Now for further deception, one which he had little stomach for, and that was with his wife and child.

"Anything exciting happen in the office today, Charlie?" Jenny asked, her full attention on the stew she was stirring. Sitting at the kitchen table Charlie scanned the evening paper. Mumbling 'no,' then thinking better of it, swung round in his chair to face his wife. "Well, now that you ask, yes there was. One of the computer operators seems to be missing."

Jenny tested the flavour of the stew with a sip. "Don't you have spare ones hanging around?" she laughed.

A little annoyed at his wife's humour, his answer was a little strained. "She's been missing since Saturday or Sunday. We were all interviewed by the cops. Of course I believe the girl kept to herself more than the others did."

"Did you know her well?" was Jenny's next question.

"What do you mean, did I know her well?" Charlie's answer was abrupt.

"I mean in the office. Did she do any important work for you?"

"Only one day when we were short staffed. She worked late to help me finish some documents, and I drove her home."

He looked up at his wife standing by the stove. "We made mad passionate love." Charlie buried his head in his newspaper, awaiting his wife's reaction.

"Must have been some passion, you were not so very late home, should it be the night I remember," Jenny giggled.

He should not have said what he had said, it was cruel, too cruel to joke like this with his unsuspecting trustful wife.

"What's her name?"

Charlie pretended to read his paper. "Who?"

Jenny was enjoying teasing her husband, poor Charlie, so innocent. "The girl you had mad passionate love with. Who was she?"

Charlie thought for a moment as having forgotten, eventually saying, "Oh her name, Mary Dewer."

Captain Gordon glared at Andrews and Sims from across his desk, not that either deserved the glare, but this was their Captain's way of frightening the proverbial crap out of those whom he did not believe had fulfilled their duty to the utmost.

"So you came up empty, much like the contents of you heads."

"There wasn't much to go on skipper, the girl's only just reached the Missing Persons."

Gordon cut him short. "You tell me that now?" Gordon's mocking voice switched to one of anger. "I have had the Commissioner down on me all day. It appears this missing girl," he glanced at the file on his desk, "Mary Dewer is the niece of one Peter Sagan." He halted for affect, mockingly asking, "You both have heard the name I believe?"

Both officers took the sarcasm with a drop of their heads.

Peter Sagan was reputed to own half of the city. Kane and Ferris the other half, the only difference being that Sagan was accepted as a business man where as the other two were regarded as close to the criminal element.

"At the moment Sagan is out of town on a business deal but keeps in touch regarding his niece's disappearance through Commissioner Jackson." Gordon halted to stare belligerently at his two officers. "Hence the Commissioner to me. Now get out there and do some detective work. Try by starting with Mary Dewer's house!"

Four days later Gordon had to confront another two of his officers.

"Well, you two it's up to you." he halted for affect while the officers stared at him, waiting for him to go on. "The body of Simon Ferris has been found up in the foot hills out of town. The bullet in his forehead suggests, a professional hit. By early evening it will be all over the media. I'm giving you both the case. Do not make an ass of it, or you might find yourselves back directing traffic."

"Have we anything to go on, Captain?" Mark Sale asked.

"Only that forensic say he has been dead for the best part of a week."

"Strange his son did not report him missing," Bob Stewart raised his eyebrows.

"Maybe he did not know his father was dead." Sale suggested without conviction.

Gordon shook his head and sighed in resignation. "They both live in the same house, Sergeant."

"It's a big house," Sale murmured in his own defence.

"Not that big, Sale," Stewart corrected his partner.

"OK both of you get over there and find out as much as you can. I suspect the reason for Nat Ferris not reporting his father's demise was to give himself time to check up on a few of the old man's, shall we say 'business' acquaintances."

Jake Russo summoned, or commanded might be a better word by Jack Kane, was shown into that man's study by the same person who had handed him the details concerning Peter Sagan. Once inside Kane glared at Russo, asking angrily from behind his desk.

"What's the delay, Russo? I gave you the information on Sagan days ago."

"Maybe he's got the hots for Sagan's niece?" It was the second man who had called on him, that laughed at his own joke.

Russo stopped the man's laughter with an icy stare.

Surprise in his voice, Kane asked, "Is this so, Russo? I heard you had met her but are you on more than nodding terms? Is this the reason for the delay?"

Russo sat himself down comfortably on a leather chair a little to the right of Kane's desk.
"I suppose your gorilla here who's been tailing me for last two days told you." Jake fixed his eyes on the man sitting across the room, who was now in no mood to laugh at Russo's expense.

"Only protecting my investment." Kane lied. "So why the Dewer chick?"
Prepared for the question, Russo's answer was intentionally sarcastic. "How much closer to Sagan do you think I can get, if not through Faye Dewer? You must also know your favourite rival is not in town. Perhaps you'd be happy if I were to hit him where he is at present?"
Kane's eyes lit up. "Not a bad idea. It would take any suspicion off me if he were hit somewhere else. You too, Russo, then you could be on your way home, wherever home might be."

Jake cursed himself for his suggestion. True, it was not beyond the realm of possibility, but to do so meant having to give up seeing Faye again, and at present she was his main source of getting near his intended victim. Jake cursed himself again. Until now he'd never mixed business with pleasure? Granted, only a little pleasure at present. Jake Russo had no compunction at using the girl.
"I could, if you are prepared to wait longer while I discover where Sagan lives, his new habits, his reasons for being where he is. Etc."

"OK point taken. But why are you taking so long, if not because of Sagan's niece?"

Russo let out an exaggerated sigh. "Unlike Ferris, Peter Sagan does not live in an unguarded mansion, he lives on the top floor, the entire top floor of a condominium of which he just happens to own. The building, which of course you are aware of sits off the main thoroughfare surrounded by high walls, CCTV cameras and a dozen or so security guards, on every gate. Getting to know Faye Dewer might be my way of getting past all of these obstructions, if she were to reintroduce me to her uncle. Remember that man believes he owes me one for retrieving his niece's so important purse."

Although Kane accepted Russo's explanation he was more than a little anxious now that Simon Ferris's body had been found, the papers having decided he had been taken out by a rival gang. Although not mentioned by name he was in the frame.

It might only be a matter of time before he himself became a target, should old Ferris's son have anything to do with it. Then again it was feasible that Sagan too, might be considered a possibility.

To Russo, Kane took overlong to continue the conversation.

"Now that they've found old Ferris, Nat might come after me, should he believe I had something to do with it."

"Which you have." Russo said quietly. "You must have known this would happen, Jack, should I have terminated Peter Sagan."

Kane toyed with his pen on the desk, his staring eyes oblivious to everyone and everything in the room.

"Of course I knew where the blame would fall, more so with Sagan also out of the picture."

Suddenly he looked up, once more back in control. "I set up the Boricuas to take the fall. I had them invade Ferris's turf. Of course they have the idea that the tip off for the heist came from Sagan."

"It might not work boss," Russo's gorilla ventured. "Nat Ferris might not think that mob capable of attempting a takeover."

"That's why I had the Boricuas do a hoist in Ferris territory Dan."

So the gorilla has a name, Russo thought.

"Would it not be best to let Sagan live a little longer boss, if only to keep him in the frame?" Dan asked.

So Dan had a brain as well, Russo thought, damning him. He turned his look to Kane. Should he OK Dan's suggestion he might be here longer, a lot longer than he'd like. Maybe find himself caught in the middle of a gang war. A prospect he did not much care for.

"Could be you have something there Dan. With Sagan still alive it might have Nat Ferris think again before he comes after whoever he thinks killed his old man."

Kane swung his look to Russo. "I think Dan may well be right, Jake. Delay your hit on Sagan for the time being." His face broke into a grin, "Give yourself a little more time to investigate a little further." Kane's innuendo not lost on the rest of the company in the room.

Alex Ferris, grandson of the late Simon Ferris, turned his back away from the screaming naked man hanging from the rafter beam, the smell of burning flesh thick in his nostrils.

Again a high pitched scream filled the cellar, and he turned quickly back. "Do you think this is the right thing to do Pa? Is there not another way?"

It would not do to appear to be shaken by what he was witnessing, nor even more so, weak in front of his father's henchmen, who to his disgust seemed to be enjoying the tortured man's agony.

Nat ignored his son's question. Instead he took a step closer to the hanging man his face only inches away from that of the sobbing man.

"Tell me who was behind the heist and I will put an end to this," he pointed to where a grinning man stood blow torch in hand. "I know it was not your boss, he's too thick in the head to have thought of it himself. So who tipped him off? Who told him where the goods would be, eh? Who was it? Kane? Sagan?"

The man's head came up, fear and hatred in his eyes, he spat into his torturer's face "Fu.. Ferris."

Nat took a step back wiping the spittle running down his cheek, nodding to his man.

Alex turned away again as burning flesh filled the air, the scream louder this time as the flame was put to the man's back, Nat nodding to his henchman to prolong the burning.

A minute passed, an hour to the tortured man Alex thought. Nat Ferris grabbed the moaning man by his hair and forced his head back. With his face close to his victim whispered "Tell me and I will end this. OK?"

The man's mumbled answer inaudible to Alex.

Apparently satisfied, Nat turned to the man standing next to him, "Phone," he snapped his fingers.

The henchman tossed the cell phone to his boss, and Nat turned again to the hanging man. "Tell me the number." Again there was a mumbled answer from the victim, then the phone rang followed by a slight pause and someone answering.

Nat was smiling as he spoke into the cell phone. "We have somebody here who would like to speak with you." Nat held the phone up to the tortured man, "Speak in English you Boricuas" he warned him.

"Carlos. They want to know where the word on the job came from." The man choked struggling to speak, his face contorted in pain. "They have me brother. I can't take much more."

Nat spoke into the phone. "Best that you tell me, if you want your brother back in one piece, or as near as dammit."

Even a little distance away Alex heard the roar of anger out of the cell phone. "Ferris I will kill you if you hurt my brother!"

Nat was not intimidated. "Cut the bull. Just tell me who did the job in my territory and you can have your brother back, Carlos. I know you Boricuas didn't do the job, you haven't the brains."

There was a moment's silence, before the trembling angry voice on the other end said, "It was Sagan, Peter Sagan. He gave me all I needed to know about the heist."

Nat Ferris snapped the phone shut before the angry man could ask any more about his brother.

"Well well well. It was dear upstanding citizen Peter Sagan." Nat chuckled. "Pillar of society. Thought he'd cause a little trouble between us and the Boricuas. Asshole, he did not reckon on us catching one." He smiled to where the tortured hanging man mumbled and cursed in pain.

"What do we do now, boss?" the henchman jerked a thumb at their victim.

His foot on the first stone step of the cellar, Ferris drew a finger across his throat. "Put the poor bugger out of his misery. Then send him back," he took another step on the stair "First class. Didn't I tell Carlos he could have his brother back." His laughter echoing around the stone cellar.

Razor in hand the henchman stepped to the hanging man.

Unable to believe this of his father, Alex roared at him "Must you Pa? It can only make things worse. Carlos will only come after you, us, for what you have done to his brother."

Nat turned on the stair to face his son. "I know. Would you not do the same if it was me hanging there?" he nodded to where the condemned man's head was held back by the hair "That's why I have to do what I have to do. Killing him makes it one less looking for revenge. However," he sighed, "First we must deal with Peter Sagan."

Chapter 3

At first Charlie did not take much notice of what the good looking young woman TV presenter was saying in the early morning bulletin, until the name Mary Dewer arrested his attention. Putting down his coffee cup on the kitchen table his hands shaking Charlie forced himself to listen.

"What have you had for breakfast?" Jenny yawned into the kitchen drawing her morning coat more closer around her. Angrily Charlie waved her silent, pointing to the TV screen.

"The body was found on the hillside south of the town. Mary Dewer was the second niece of magnate Peter Sagan," the announcer was saying.

"Is that not the girl who works in your office?" Jenny, her eyes on the screen poured herself a coffee.

"Yes."

Charlie sighed, sooner or later it had to happen. Now for endless inquiries.

Was it a good thing that Mary being found so quickly softened the blow that little sooner? Or live in hope that she might never be found for years or maybe not at all. But above all the question was who buried her there? And what would his next move be. Whoever it was knew where he lived, and must surely reckon it was him that had killed Mary. Charlie closed his eyes blurring out the scene of that fateful night. He hadn't killed Mary, he was not a murderer it was an accident. Unfortunately the Law would not see it that way, but above all neither would Peter Sagan.

At the same time as Charlie Simpson heard the news on TV so too had Jake Russo.

Russo thought quickly, picking up his phone he dialled Fay Dewer. "Hello Faye, just phoned to say I'll be out of town for the most part of a week, something big has come up and my boss tells me I have to be on it right away, or bang goes my job. I'll keep in touch and let you know when I'll be back." He halted for a second to continue cheerily. "Let me know where we can have dinner together when I get back. OK?"

Jake heard the sobs on the other end, then the tearful voice saying, "You don't know? You have not heard the news?"

"What news Faye? You are not making sense, you sound upset. What's wrong?" Jake hoped he sounded convincingly innocent.

A sob followed his question, "It's Mary.... They've found poor Mary. She's been murdered Jake! Murdered!"

"What? You are telling me your sister has been murdered?" Jake thought he sounded good, but he must not overdo it. "Look Faye I will cancel my trip. Do you want me over there to be with you?"

More sobbing "No Jake. Your job is at stake. I will be fine. Uncle Peter is already on his way back. He will see I am OK."

Jake offered up a prayer of relief. Had Faye said she wanted him with her, his plan would have gone down the Swanee.

Jake let the girl go on to relieve herself of her grief, her tension. At last telling her not to worry now that her uncle was on his way back, he put the phone down.

It was only a short train ride to the town Jake thought it safe enough to stay. Once settled he phoned Jack Kane from a public booth.

"Hello Jack it's me."

There was silence for second or two, before Jake heard him ask angrily. "Where the hell are you? Do you know anything about the hit on the Dewer dame?"

"Why should I know anything about that, Jack. I was not paid to take out young females."

"OK. So where are you? I need you here for back up, just on the off chance a certain girl's uncle thinks I had something to do with it."

"Exactly Jack, that's why I skipped town for a little while. It's not unusual for undercover police to be around the graveyard at the burial, with the possibility of the killer being there, that's one frame I do not want to be in when they discreetly take their photos. If I had hung around Faye Dewer was certain to ask me to attend the funeral and would think it strange should I have a notion to refuse."

There was a slight chuckle at the other end. "OK. Good thinking. Keep me posted." The line went dead, Jack Kane had hung up.

Charlie estimated there had to be around one hundred people when they laid Mary Dewer to rest.

He looked skywards unable to watch the lowering of the coffin into the grave. Mary's final resting place. God! How had it come to this? So young and beautiful, but not so innocent as he had first thought. OK, she was this at first, that was before she became more demanding.

Charlie was seeing it all again. It had started that night.

"When are going to take me out Charlie?" Mary pouted sitting up in bed.

"You know I cannot do that." He pulled on his pants. "We have to be careful, Mary."

"Careful! Careful! That's all I ever hear from you these days. It was different in the beginning. How you used to make excuses to *her* about working late. You remember? Those out of town restaurants you took me to." Mary's voice rose angrily her eyes flashing hatred across the bedroom. "Oh yes Charlie Simpson, quite the cavalier were you not? That's before you had what you wanted." Charlie reached for his shirt. "That's not true and you know it. Yes, I admit I wanted you, wanted you from the very first day I set eyes on you."
"I remember that first day too," she stared up at him. "Not that first day in the office. No, I mean that first day, here." She pointed to the bed. "You thought you were the first, me being young and all,"she threw her head back, her laughter mocking him at the way she had said it.

It was true, thinking after their first love making of how he had taken advantage of an innocent girl. His self loathing, his betrayal of Jenny, his returning home to her bed, talking over what improvements he was going to make to the house, building a garden swing for little Alice. Even now he could feel the bile rise in his throat at the thought of what he had done.

Yet for all this he'd be here next week making the same empty promises. It had to end but how was the question. He could never break it off and still see her each day in the office. Should he do so he'd never know how she would react. Maybe angry enough to let someone or even everyone know of their affair. A woman scorned?

Charlie slipped on his coat, looking down at the lovely figure sitting there. "OK next week for sure. I'll take you to that restaurant I first took you to."

Mary was far from satisfied. "This is how it's to be, always afraid of a chance meeting by someone you know that could end it all. I want more than that, Charlie."

"I can't Mary. Can't you see that? Already I pay half the rent here; give you money for clothes. I cannot take too much out of our joint account without Jenny becoming suspicious. You can see that can't you?"

"Then get a divorce. You will if you love me as much as you say you do."

The suggestion halted Charlie in his tracks. The proposal out of the question. "Don't be absurd, Mary." He should not have said that, it had only made this girl worse.

"Why not? Are you ashamed of me? Or that people will call you a cradle snatcher?"

Charlie threw his hands up in exasperation. "Let's be sensible about this Mary. Financially it would ruin me. The alimony would leave me with nothing. We'd literally be living on your income." Then mockingly, "No more fancy restaurants, Mary. You'd see less of them than you do now. Besides there would be one all mighty battle over who gets custody of Alice."

"Does not the mother usually win? Besides I want children of my own."

It was enough for Charlie the callous way she had said it that decided he must end it. He'd do it when next they met, how best to tell this lovely but greedy half naked girl lying there that it was all over.

"Dust to dust ashes to ashes…"

The pastor's words brought Charlie back to the present. Not all who had attended Mary's burial had returned to the hotel. The room though large sounded empty, mourners sipping tea, or in most cases something stronger, whispering or talking in hushed tones, or just standing there at a loss at not knowing anyone to chat to.

Charlie took Irene Kerr gently by the arm and guided her to the tea urn followed by two of Mary's friends whom she had worked beside.
"We will just stay a little while, just enough to pay our respects, then leave," Charlie suggested. "Then I will run you all home. No need to return to the office today."
Both girls offered Charlie an appreciative little smile.
"You too Irene."
"But.." Irene stammered. "what about those accounts?"
"Tomorrow will do. We'll catch up tomorrow. I'll look into the office once I have dropped you three off."
Charlie laid down his coffee cup on the white linen table cloth. "Come on, lets pay our respects to Mary's sister and Uncle Peter."

It was as far as he got before the explosion threw him sideways amid screams and shouts of hysteria. Dazed, Charlie struggled to his knees, through the thick rising smoke his two fellow workers stumbled to their feet. He looked at his hands, ran a hand down his face, grateful he'd not been hurt and searched around, saw Irene stagger to her feet with a bloodstained handkerchief held to her cheek.

Everywhere scenes of devastation. An elderly man lay on his back staring in disbelief up at the ceiling. A woman snatched a napkin from a table dropped by his side applying a tourniquet to what was left of the old man's arm.

A young boy appeared from beneath an upturned table his trembling lips crying for his mother.

Red wine spilled from a bottle on to the lifeless body of a woman lying on the floor. Somewhere people arrived to help. Charlie staggered across the floor to where Irene, and the two girls stood sobbing and hugging one another. All the while the incessant screaming of those in pain.

"Are you all right, Irene?" Charlie asked, thinking what a stupid thing to say.

The woman nodded. "I don't think it's too bad," she said applying a little more pressure to her cheek.

One of the girls gently drew the handkerchief away. "It's a cut, Miss Kerr. You should be all right. We'll get someone to have a look at it." she looked hopefully around.

Charlie heard a man's voice call out something inaudible. It came from Peter Sagan trying to bring some order to the chaos.

A fire had started at the end of the room, a few not hurt were busily beating it out with whatever they could find. A young man ran to help someone trapped beneath a table, Charlie took him to be an undercover policeman searching for anyone in connection with the death of Mary Dewer, something that seemed right now to be of little consequence.

Charlie found an unbroken chair for Irene to sit on, while he looked frantically around, for help.

The door leading to the kitchen flew open and uniformed figures rushed in. Help had arrived.

It was close on ten o'clock before the police had all they wanted from the bomb victims. Charlie had seen Irene Kerr, Susie and Jo to their homes, ordering all three to remain at home next day, Irene as he expected protesting about the work needing done in the office. He, calmly persisting that she stay at home.

Eventually Charlie drew into his street and into his driveway, Jenny stood anxiously at the door.
Charlie got out of the car waving that he was all right.
Jenny her resolve not to break down ran to meet him.
"Oh, Charlie what happened? Are you really all right?"
Charlie hugged her and led her back into the house. "Right as rain. Could do with a stiff one though."
Jenny left him in the living room and ran to open a bottle of Scotch. "You said over the phone Irene was hurt. Is it bad?"
"No, not really. The doc assured her it wouldn't need stitches," he called to her, "But you know Irene, joked about it not spoiling her good looks," he chuckled.

"I thought you'd never get back tonight."Jenny handed him the Scotch and slid down on the settee beside him. "It must have been awful."
Charlie nodded and sipped his drink. "I thought the cops were never going to end their questions Jenny. There was no saying we would like to ask you a few questions, this time."
"The TV said there were seven dead. They said they could not disclose names until the police had informed their next

of kin."Jenny shuddered. "Had you not phoned me Charlie I would have worried myself sick waiting for the phone to ring or the police to call at the door." She squeezed his hand, "Thank God you are OK."

Charlie did not sleep well, if at all that night. The horrific scene of devastation searing through his brain, all of it too visual to be dulled by sleep.

Next morning he arrived late at the office, fully expecting a disobedient office supervisor to be there. She was not, apparently Irene had taken his advice and stayed at home, as had the two girls who had accompanied him to the funeral.

Dickson the General Manager having heard of his arrival summoned him to his office, offering his sympathy at what had happened to his staff, and no doubt to find out first hand what had really taken place, adding how he would have been there himself had not a last minute business call prevented him. He had let out a deep breath then with the words "or perhaps I could have been a victim myself."

Charlie came away from the office with even less respect for the man than he had before. No doubt to enforce the reason for his absence a call to Peter Sagan would surely follow Charlie thought as he descended in the elevator to his own office, after all, business was business and Peter Sagan was responsible for over 40% of their annual turnover.

It was a long day at the office, and he had really not done any work, finding himself looking into space or reliving the bombing, and when he had knuckled down to do some work inevitably his door would open to someone calling to ask about Susie, Jo and their supervisor.

No doubt Mary Dewer's murder and the further tragedy at her funeral had affected them, brought them closer together. Charlie was almost sick, he stood up, shaking at the thought, of what it would be like when they found out it was one of their own who was the murderer?
It was enough for today. So thinking, Charlie lifted his coat from its hanger, switched off his office light and made for the elevator. Now to face his wife and daughter. When would it all end?

Sam Andrews put down the phone. "Skipper wants us upstairs." He stood up. "In the commissioners office, pronto, Joe," he addressed his partner with a look of annoyance.
Joe looked up at his lieutenant, threw down his pen and pushed back his chair. "I suppose we are in deep shit if the big boss himself craves our presence."

Peter Sagan stood centre stage, already in full flow when the two detectives entered the room.
Grateful for the interruption Commissioner Jackson seated behind his oval desk gestured the pair to take a seat. He held up a hand. "A moment, Peter, let's hear what my officers have to say.
Now, officers can you bring us up to date on the Mary Dewer case."
Andrews as senior officer took it upon himself to answer. "We searched the victim's home."
"Did you not do that before?" Sagan commented sarcastically.

Andrews took time to glance at his senior, before turning his attention back to Sagan. "When we did your niece was reported as a missing person, Mr Sagan. The second time we searched the house it was regarded as a crime scene." For a moment Andrews answer appeared to silence if not satisfy Sagan's belligerence.

"Please continue officer." Jackson urged.

"A thorough search revealed four sets of fingerprints excluding those of the deceased. As yet we have not come up with any that match." Andrews went on relishing what he was about to disclose hoping it would silence the big contemptuous ass sitting so smugly across the room. "Besides the victim, we found four sets of prints and DNA in the bedroom."

To everyone's surprise Sagan remain silent.

Andrews continued. "We also found an envelope containing twelve hundred dollars. The bedroom wardrobe revealed several dresses, shoes and other expensive items such as jewellery. All well beyond the means of a working girl."

This time Sagan broke his silence with a mighty roar. "What are you insinuating Officer?"

Andrews coloured. "I'm not insinuating anything sir, I am merely reporting what was found."

"Officer," Sagan regained his composure, "the reason for all of these items could well be the monthly cheque I gave Mary for her house and her sister Faye's hotel as well as spending money."

For the first time Sagan's face broke into a smile. "I offered both employment in my own organisation, but you know what youngsters are like these days, want to be independent to do their own thing."

"Thank you for that, Peter," Jackson sounded relieved. He leaned forward on his desk. "Now officers we come to the main facts of your investigation. "How did Mary Dewer die? Was she murdered in her own house, or elsewhere?" Andrews cleared his throat. "She was killed in her home, sir. We…" he corrected himself, "Forensic found a speck of blood on the corner of the glass coffee table. It is their opinion as there were strangulation marks on her neck, that after the assault she fell unconscious and hit her head on the table."

"She was not dead before she hit the coffee table?" Sagan choked.

"No sir."

"So it was hitting the edge of the coffee table that killed her?" Jackson asked

Andrews nodded, his voice soft, "Yes sir."

"So my niece knew her attacker who will probably say her death was an accident, and plead manslaughter when you find him." Sagan's voice held nothing but contempt.

Captain Gordon spoke for the first time. "No, Mr Sagan. Although your niece's death might not have been premeditated, whoever did kill her compounded the act by removing and attempting to conceal the body."

Sagan accepted the explanation with a nod. "Very well gentlemen. Can I ask what you have discovered concerning the atrocious attack at the funeral?" Sagan's voice had regained it's former precedence.

Gordon answered. "At present it is a matter for the Bomb Squad. Also as the crime is outwith our jurisdiction the case is now in the hands of precinct 14."

Jackson rose, "Thank you officers. I believe that is all we need to know for the present." He turned to look across the room at Gordon, "I would be obliged if you could wait behind Captain."

In the elevator, Andrews let out a sigh of relief. "Thank Christ that's over. I thought that we were in for an interrogation by that asshole Sagan."

Angrily Sims pushed the button for the second floor. "What's the betting he's already on his way to the 14th precinct?"

Andrews focused on the dial above the door watching the floor numbers flash past.

"The commissioner will be on the phone to warn them before Sagan has left the building."

Sims smirked. "Hope you are right." The elevator jerked to a halt and he stepped out ahead of Andrews.

"I noticed you didn't say anything about those photos we found in the girl's home?"

Walking side by side down the corridor to their office, Andrews cautioned his partner. "Some things are best left as they are at present. Forewarned is forearmed, and I do not want Sagan even to get as much as a whiff of what we have found. At least not yet. But I think Faye Dewer might provide the answers when we pay her a call."

Jake Russo dialled Faye Dewer's number from a pay phone, idly watching the hustle and bustle on the busy street as he waited. Eventually he heard Faye's voice.

"Hello Faye it's me, Gulliver, back from his travels," he began cheerily. "So they let you out of hospital? You OK? I was shocked when I heard the news about the explosion. Sorry I could not reach you earlier."

"Oh it's you Jake," Faye answered pleasantly. "Yes I was discharged two days ago. It's mostly my arm. They say it will take time to heal."

Jake took his eyes off the passing traffic. "Are you at home? Can I come and see you?"

"That will be nice, Jake."

"Is today all right, say in about an hour or so, then you can tell me all about it."

"That will be cool, Jake I'll wait for you. May even have a drink ready."

"So the wanderer has returned."

Jack Kane greeted Russo.

"Yip," Russo slid into the seat opposite in the small cafe Kane used close to his own home. "So you have your little war Jack." He waited until Kane had finished eating.

"Hopefully not so little Jake. Ferris believes it was Sagan that did the job on him." Kane sat back a smug look on his face. "So Nat hits Sagan when he least expects it." His smile broadened, "at his niece's wake."

Russo unlike Kane was not amused. "You sure it was Ferris?"

Kane nodded. "Street says Nat caught one of the Boricuas mob on the job, worked him over and found out that the poor bugger's boss, who in fact was his brother thought that the word about the job had come from Sagan." Kane chuckled. "Of course it came from me. Now Ferris and Sagan will go after each other and I, my friend will be the only one left to pick up the pieces."

"Until the Boricuas find out," Russo added sarcastically.

Kane leaned forward drawing his cigar case out of his inside coat pocket. "Even if they do, they do not have the muscle to do one damned thing about it. After all it was

Nat Ferris who did his brother." He pointed his cigar at Russo, "And not in the best of fashions so I believe. So where do you go from here? Jake?"

Russo chose not to answer the question until he learned a little more. "If it was Ferris who blew up the hotel reception room, why did he not just burst in with a couple of gunmen and go after Peter Sagan himself instead of blowing a few innocent people all over the wall?"
"And run the risk of one of his men getting himself killed, or even worse, taken, then Sagan would in fact know it was Ferris that was behind it." Kane lit his cigar, "As it is although he believes it to be Ferris he is not certain. After all it may well have been the Boricuas working either for him or themselves."
"And you Jack, why not you?"
"I have pretty well covered my tracks there."
"You better hope so. Should Nat Ferris ever suspect you of taking out his old man?"
Russo's warning had not the least impact on Kane.
"*You* took out the old man, Jake, remember? Speaking of which when are you going to do the same to Peter Sagan?"
Russo shrugged and stood up to leave. "Why should I when there are at least one family with a score to settle."
By the look on Kane's face Russo thought he had gone too far. "Because, Jake Russo that's the contract you have with me. No hit. No money."

Sagan waited until Gordon too had left the office before asking Jackson. "You think there is any connection between the hotel bombing and my niece's death Harry?"
Jackson stood up and crossed to the window looking down at the flow of traffic nine floors below, answered without

turning. "It's too early to know all the facts but at present the answer is no."

Sagan splayed his hands as Jackson faced him. "Then why was Mary murdered Harry? She was just a normal girl living a normal life, and your officer said there was over twelve hundred dollars in an envelope so it wasn't robbery."

"Depends where the envelope was, Peter. As to the bombing I should think you may have more of an idea who was behind that little incident than me. Wouldn't you say?"

For a moment Sagan hesitated before replying. "In my like of work you are sure to make enemies, don't you think?"

"Depends what line of work that is, Peter. Is it not?" The commissioner smiled.

When Sagan left the Commissioner's office it was not to Precinct 14 as Andrews had predicted, instead it was to one of his several offices down town where he threw himself down behind his desk bellowing out superfluous orders to those unfortunate enough to be passing at the time.

Jackson's attitude to his last question had rattled him. How dare he act as though he did not have a hand in it himself. Not that Jackson was corrupt, only inclined to look the other way when it suited him, and usually it was he who caused him to do just that.

Sagan left his office to wander down a corridor, nodding at those passing who offered him a cheerless smile. These were the people who really knew the real Peter Sagan, not the cheerful happy do gooder as his public saw him, but a brutal cunning man, who would stop at nothing to get what he wanted and usually did.

Sagan threw himself down on a settee in the empty executive lounge. Things were not planning out as he had hoped. Perhaps it had been a mistake telling the Boricuas when and where Ferris's latest drug deal was going down. Now he had Nat Ferris on his tail, the bombing had confirmed that well enough. One ace he did have up his sleeve and that was that Carlos was after Ferris for what that man had done to his brother. Unwittingly he had made an ally of the Boricuas.

Sagan drummed his fingers on the settee arm. It was time to leave town again to keep himself safe. Yes this is what he'd do, leave Mason to keep an eye of things until his return or should that be their return for he must take Nancy and Faye with him. Peter Sagan was still not convinced that Mary's murder was not connected to either Ferris or the Boricuas, though he did not rule out the possibility of Jack Kane being involved, more so for his silence of late, no he must tell Mason to put a few men on to watching Mister Jack Kane as well.

Jake Russo came out of the florist a block away from Faye Dewer's luxury hotel, hoping she would like the flowers he'd chosen. It was as he was about to cross the street that the two men got out of the black car and walked to the hotel entrance. Russo drew up, instinct telling him that they were nothing other than cops, with the odds that they were about to call on a certain lady he knew.
Jake exhaled. Another few minutes and he would have been in Faye's room, most likely sipping wine when they

knocked at the door. He turned, looked around, spied a coffee bar and walked towards it. He'd wait there until they were gone.

The waitress smiled cheekily as he sat himself down on the bar stool. "For me? How sweet. My favourite flowers, and we have only just met."
"You should be so lucky." Jake blew out a breath of impatience. How long before the cops left? And why were they here? Could be either to ask questions about Mary Dewer, or the bombing, or maybe both.

"What will it be, sweetie pie?" The waitress grinned.
"No pie, just coffee, black."
She indicated the flowers on the bar, "Dumped were we?" her smile still hovered.
"No, I brought them along for my funeral as it looks though I will die of thirst before I get a cup of coffee around here."
"Nasty nasty," the girl laughed at Russo's humour.
The waitress turned to pour out the coffee giving him time to glance down the street. The black sedan was still there.

Andrews stood back when the door opened holding up his badge. "Good afternoon, sorry to disturb you. Miss Dewer is it not?"
Faye nodded.
"Could we have a word?"
"This is not a good time officer, I was about to leave," she lied.
"Sorry about that lady, but it is about your sister's murder," Sims supported his partner.

Reluctantly Faye took a step back to let the officers enter, hoping as she did so, that Jake would not arrive too soon. "So how may I help you officers?" Faye made herself comfortable across from where the policemen were seated. Sims pointed to Faye's arm, "Nasty. Was that the bombing?"

"Yes."

"Is it painful?" Andrews followed up.

"Could do without it, officer."

Andrews especially noticed the woman's impatience, thinking how peculiar it was, considering they were here to find out who had murdered her sister.

"We have a few photos that we found in your sister's home, hoping you might identify one or two for us." Faye leaned forward as Andrews spread a row of photos on the coffee table. She nodded."I know most of them."

"Any of these, the men I mean,"Andrews corrected himself, "who may have been a frequent visitor to her home?"

Faye shook her head."As far as I know, Mary was not seeing anyone in particular. If that's what you mean? If she was, she would have confided in me. We were very close."

Andrews sat back. "No one at all?"

"Such as?" Faye drew Andrews a far from friendly look.

Andrews responded, "Such as an older man, maybe even a married one. One she thought it best to keep secret."

Faye's voice rose. "What are you implying officer? Should my sister have been seeing someone in particular it certainly was not to hide anyone she was ashamed to be seen with."

"Quite." Andrews coughed an apology.

Sims thought it time to come to his partner's assistance by lifting the nearest photo and holding it up for the woman to study. "This guy with you and your sister? Looks like it was taken at college."

Faye waved a dismissive hand. "That was years ago. I have not seen Arnold Reiter in years, neither I suspect had my sister."

"Yet it was on her dressing table in her bedroom." Sims held the photo closer for the woman's inspection. If your sister had not seen this guy since college days as you say, why should it be on her dressing table?"

Faye shrugged. "Your guess is as good as mine, officer."

"You did not know it was there?" Andrews asked.

"As I said inspector, I had no knowledge of how it came to be there. I am as surprised as you are."

"This Arnold Reiter, do you know where we might find him?"

"The last I know, he lived on 49th I don't know the number I'm afraid. It's in a rundown block of apartments. He could well have moved since college days. He could be most anywhere by now." Faye ended with a sigh of impatience.

The partners came away from their interview, neither completely happy by Faye Dewer's attitude towards their questions.

"This guy Reiter, should we pay him a social call?" Sims drew the car keys out of his pocket.

Andrews opened the car door. "May as well, we have nothing else to go on. Those other photos were not much help, although we'll have to chase them up anyway." He slid into the passenger seat, adding with little enthusiasm, "You never know they might lead to something."

It was in fact three coffees' later before the sedan moved off. Jake gave it a few minutes before retrieving his flowers from off the bar top.

"Not leaving before we really get acquainted?" The waitress feigned disappointment.

"'Fraid so. Next time, I'll come back with flowers to suit your taste."

The waitress threw up her hands in mock horror. "Don't tell me. Dandelions?"

Russo threw the dollar notes down on the bar top, saying as he turned "I bet you are a Dandy lying."

Hearing as he reached the door, "Cheeky. Have a nice day."

Jake reached the sidewalk opposite the hotel one step off the curb when the taxi cab squealed to a halt, and Peter Sagan got out making for the hotel at a dignified trot. Again Russo cursed his bad luck and stepped back on to the curb, his thoughts that maybe today was not a good day to visit Faye Dewer. Perhaps he should call her and find out, before these flowers like himself began to wilt for want of a welcome drink.

Ten minutes passed and no sign of Peter Sagan re-emerging. Jake decided to call Faye on his cell phone, waiting a further four minutes before Faye's voice eventually answered.

"Should I call off our little drink for another day?"

Faye's reply was little more than a whisper, "I think it best that you give me a rain check on that Sybil, my uncle wants me to accompany him on a business trip."

Sybil? Jake thought, plainly the woman did not want her uncle to know who it was that was calling.

"I take it you cannot speak freely?"

"Yes."

"How long is your trip? Or don't you know?"

"Oh I don't know Sybil, perhaps three or four spoonful would do. Depends on how sweet you are.

Then you always did care for something sweet." Jake heard the titter at the other end. A slight pause then, "OK Sybil you do just that, call me when I get back. Or if you miss all those sweet dishes, call me up when I am away, you hear?" Then the phone went dead, leaving Jake to imagine the questions Peter Sagan was asking his niece at that very moment as to who was calling. And by the hurried way Sagan had left the cab the trip out of town was more than just urgent.

Chapter 4

Andrews and his partner had thought it best to wait until evening to call upon those in Mary Dewer's college photographs, believing those same people might now be home from work.

First call brought no result, the young man in that photo providing an alibi for the night of the murder. Second interview was something similar.

"Third time lucky." Sims rang the apartment doorbell, to have it answered by a man in his early twenties.

"Arnold Reiter?"

"Yes."

Sims held up his ID. "I am Detective Sergeant Sims, and this is my senior, Detective Lieutenant Andrews. May we have a word please? It is connection with the death of Mary Dewer who I believe was known to you."

For a moment Sims thought he saw the shabbily dressed young man shrink a little at the mention of the girl's name. Hesitantly Reiter pulled open the door a little more. "Then you best come in."

To the officers the apartment was as shabby as its owner: Not unclean but untidy, newspapers cluttered most of the chairs, Reiter hastening to gather some together in order to give his unexpected or even unwelcome visitors a place to sit.

"Well Mister Reiter." Andrews extracted an edition of the local newspaper from under his right hip and eased himself into the two seater settee. "It is Arnold Reiter, is it not?" he asked pleasantly.

"Yes it is. Arnold Raymond Reiter to be exact."

"Good. Can I call you Arnold, or is it Arnie?" This last equally as pleasant from Andrews.

"I prefer Arnold," was the defensive answer.

"OK Arnold. As you will be well aware the body of a young woman who you knew as Mary Dewer was found buried in the mountainside a few miles out of town." Reiter splayed his hands. "What has this got to do with me? I only knew Mary Dewer from college."

"You have not seen her since? Spoken to her? Met her by accident, so to speak."

"No."

"Are you sure? Think about it. It might help with our inquiries."

Reiter thought for a moment. "Maybe in the street on way to work." The words came a little nervously. "We waited at the same stop. But not for the same bus."

"So you never exchanged words, not as much as a good morning?"

"No. She was usually running to catch the bus before it drew away." He gave a little smile. "Folk that noticed used to wave as she climbed aboard, always out of breath she was." Reiter's smile broadened at the memory.

"Then can you explain, Mr Reiter how the photograph of you and Mary Dewer came to be on her dressing table, if as you say you have not spoken to her since you last attended college?"

Arnold Reiter shrank back in his chair his face void of colour. "What.. what do you mean? She would not have my picture there, she would have nothing to do with me in college." He halted, a smirk on his face. "Peter Sagan's niece thought herself something with all the guys chasing after her. Maybe you should ask them, not me."

"We will, Arnold." Andrews swept an open newspaper off the coffee table laying down the framed photograph of him and Mary Dewer. "This mean anything to you, Arnold?" Reiter choked. He nodded. "That was a long time ago. I asked if she would have her photo taken with me as it was our last day at college, graduation day to be precise."

"And obviously she agreed."

Reiter's anger showed. "Yes she did. Out of sympathy, humiliated me in front of the whole class.

"That was not so long ago. You are the same age as her, so you only finished college three years ago," Sims suggested.

"Yes, but I never forgot that day."

"Remembered it enough to get your own back, maybe?" Andrews supported his partner.

"If you are insinuating that I killed her and put that picture…" Reiter's hand shook as he pointed at the photograph, "Then you are very much mistaken."

"Where were you the night of the murder?" Andrews asked.

Hunched in his chair Reiter uttered. "I cannot remember. I don't think I know what day it was."

"It was Sunday May 16th."

Reiter gave a slight shrug. "Most likely at home watching TV. There's a programme on wild life in Alaska that I like."

"Just by yourself were you?"

"Yes. Is that a crime?"

"Depends." Andrews followed by his partner stood up. "Thanks for your co operation Mr Reiter. I think we have all we want for now. We can see ourselves out."

Sims swept a hand round the untidy room. "And leave you to your newspapers."

"Well what do make of that?" Andrews asked on his way to the car.

"Obviously hiding something."

Andrews halted by the car. "Funny that Faye Dewer did not mention seeing the photo on the dressing table when we were finished with the house."

"Maybe she overlooked it. Was too busy putting a few of her sister's cherished items together."

Andrews grunted. "Maybe, yet I don't think so, Joe."

The car was three blocks from Reiter's apartment before Joe Sims spoke again. "Where do we go from here? We have nothing to tie Reiter to the murder."

Sims halted the car at the traffic lights. "We could pay him another call. Maybe shake him up a little."

"You think he's our man, Joe?"

Sims drew away from the lights. "Pretty sure."

"How do you think he did it then, get his victim to the mountains. Hire a cab? He cannot have his own wheels as he rides the bus to work each day. That's when he sees Mary Dewer."

"Point taken, partner." Sims slowed to turn a corner, righted the wheel, asking. "Can we get a search warrant do you think?"

"On what grounds? The only thing that's going for us at present is that he has no alibi. So why a warrant, Joe?"

"Only a gut feeling, that and the fact that most of those newspapers that I had a sly look at showed pictures of the Mary Dewer crime scene. Yet he said he could not remember the date or even the day."

"As you say, Joe he could well be our man. We'll pay him another visit same time tomorrow, hopefully with your search warrant."

Charlie Simpson sat by the fire in his own living room, a glass of Scotch in his hand: his third that night. It was becoming a habit, a habit that he had no control over. It was his only source of solace.

"Daddy! Daddy! See what I drew at school today." Little Alice thrust the sheet of paper into his lap slightly spilling his drink.

"Look out you stupid little girl!" he hurled at her, wiping at the wet spirit on his pants.

Taken aback and frightened by her beloved father' s uncharacteristic action, howling, Alice her drawing now forgotten spun on her heel for the safety of her mother and the kitchen away from this horrible man who had shouted at her.

It took the best part of half an hour to calm her daughter. Hugging the little girl her mother led her back to her room.

"Daddy was angry at me he shouted at me. I don't think he loves me mummy," she sobbed.

"Of course he does sweetie. It's just that daddy is tired he has a lot of work to do at the office. He'll come in and see you in a little while, and tell you he's sorry." She squeezed the sobbing little girl's hand, giving her a reassuring smile. "Now come on, under the clothes. Do you want Mr Teddy with you?"

Jenny reached across to the bedside table lifting the toy bear and sliding it under the bedclothes by Alice's side. "Now go to sleep. You have school in the morning. I will tell bad daddy to come and kiss you good night."

"Well, did you make it up with your daughter, big bad daddy?" Jenny asked slumping down in the settee across from her Scotch drinking husband. "Honestly Charlie I do not know what has come over you these last few weeks, snapping at Alice and me for nothing in particular. It is as though you cannot wait to come home to take your bad temper out on us both."

Jenny was close to tears. "You never used to be like this Charlie. Seldom a cross word between us and a little girl you adored." She pointed to his glass, "Now the first thing you do is reach for that damned bottle, instead of little Alice." Jenny sobbed shifting her gaze to the TV set, though oblivious to what was on the screen. "Is it your work, Charlie? Is that it?"

Charlie could have laughed at that. Here at home the cause of his troubles and change of demeanour was deemed to be his work, whereas at work his staff thought it was his home life, when neither was the answer.

Charlie sat back sipping his drink, his thoughts a million miles away. Almost four weeks now since they found Mary, he could not bring himself to say four weeks since he had killed her, murder being too harsh unfeeling a word to describe what he had done.

The daily suspense was too much, waiting for the law to call at his office, or the inevitable knock on the door here at home for the usual idiom of may we have a few words Mister Simpson.

Charlie took another sip of his drink, his wife's words somewhere in the background.

"They are working you too hard Charlie. Ever since that girl died you have never been the same."

"What has Mary Dewer got to do with this? What are you implying?" Charlie snapped.

Jenny swung back from the screen to her husband sitting there with a look on his face that she had never seen before. "I am not implying anything Charlie." Suddenly she felt frightened. "It's just that the girl's murder has affected you."

Charlie realised his mistake at snapping at his wife over the name. He gulped his drink down and rose. His little faux pas could be the beginning of Jenny's suspicion of him and Mary, unless he satisfied her curiosity here and now. Feigning anger was not hard to do. Standing there he put his empty glass down on the coffee table. "Maybe it has not occurred to you, that my change of temper, character, demeanour whatever you chose to call it may be because of a little episode known as a bombing, that I, and three people that I work beside might have been killed or maimed, and to us for no apparent reason." Charlie choked anger, "Or had you forgotten, Jenny?"

Jenny's tearful apology was scarcely audible as Charlie strode out of the room, his thought of had he got away with it, and how he must be more careful in future.

Andrews and Sims returned to pay Reiter a visit at the same time as before, this time however there was no response to their knock on the door.

"Maybe late night shopping," Sims suggested, staring at the door as though waiting for it to magically open.

"Pity since we did succeed in securing that search warrant," Andrews consoled himself.

"I wonder?" Sims reached hopefully behind a pot plant close by. "Eureka!" he held up a key for his partner's inspection.

"Beginners luck," Andrews affirmed in a tone suggesting this had never happened before.

"Hello! Anyone at home?" Sims pushed the door open, taking a step inside.

Andrews turned up his nose. "Could do with a bit of fresh air, or a clean, or both."

Sims looked around. "Same dirty dishes since last night. Not very house proud is our Mister Arnold Reiter."

"You can say that again,"Andrews agreed, opening the single bedroom door, muttering a few niceties at the unmade bed and untidy room. "Same in here."

While Andrews stood at the bedroom door, Sims opened what appeared to be a clothes closet, letting out a string of oaths followed by a sharp whistle of astonishment. "You had better see this Lieutenant," he suggested taking a step back to let his senior have a look.

Puzzled by his partner's actions Andrews stepped to the closet door taking one look inside, then back to Sims. "This puts a different complexion on things Joe."

"Obsessed would be the word I would use, Sam."

Together both men stared at the three closet walls filled with photos of Mary Dewer.

Sam Andrews took a step closer, his partner at his shoulder, staring at a range of large coloured photos together with smaller monochrome ones of the deceased. "Seems our boy has been busy with his camera, Joe. What do you say? Not all of these were taken during his college days, or I am very much mistaken."

"At least they are decent, Sam."

"Couldn't be much else, seeing as the deceased would have nothing to do with him."

"Except?" Sims reached to touch one almost hidden at the foot of the wall. "Mary in a bathing suit. Must have followed her to the beach."

"A stalker as well." Andrews suggested. "At least looking at these they are all of one person, Mary Dewer."

"What do we do, partner, wait for him to come home?" His senior nodded. "Doesn't seemed to have done a runner. No appearance of having packed any essentials as far as I can see."

"You never know this might be his way of getting out of doing his Spring cleaning," Joe Sims laughed.

Arnold Reiter did not come home that night, Andrews calling in a patrol car to have it stationed outside on the off chance of their suspect returning during the wee small hours, when he had not, that officer issued an APB.

In fact Reiter had been less than a block away when he spied the two officers enter his apartment building. Understanding why the police should have returned so soon, panicking he boarded the first passing bus, destination immaterial.

Arnold Reiter...suspect, spent a cold sleepless night in a park not so far away from his home. He dared not stretch out on one of the numerous wooden benches but rather, hid amongst the undergrowth fringing the park, it being irrelevant whether caught as a murderer or pervert.

Next day was the longest Arnold had ever known. Constantly on the move halting to quickly move again should someone's stare last beyond a few seconds.

He bought a hot dog eating it as he strode along the
sidewalk avoiding those clumsily rushing past on their way
to work, wishing vehemently that he was one of them.
He needed a drink, a coffee. A coffee shop a little distance
away caught his attention, unfortunately there were no
tables outside. He was desperate, the coffee now an
obsession, plus, he was hungry again.

Taking a chance Arnold squeezed passed someone leaving.
He sat down at a table recently vacated, lifting the menu
more to help hide his face that what it had to offer.
The waitress came, he ordered, watching her when she left
and what she would do. Had she recognised him? Was his
picture in the papers as a murder suspect? What were his
friends, his fellow workers thinking of him?
When it came, Arnold cupped his coffee in both hands,
gulping, disappointed that it did not taste as good as he
imagined it to be. He could not do this. Go on day after
day indefinitely for the remainder of his life He should not
have run away, it only added to the suspicion of his
murdering Mary Dewer. He could not do that, he
worshipped her or rather had. Even though she had treated
him like dirt at college. It was the photos: Cops would take
a different meaning out of those...brand him as an
obsessive maniac or something similar.

The news of Arnold Reiter as a person of interest to the
police accompanied by a photograph hit the newspapers
that same evening with a warning that if sighted that on no
account should he be approached.
Now he was dangerous not to be approached, he who had
never won an argument less a fight.

Arnold shrugged into his hooded jacket as best he could to approach the ATM. He needed money, enough until he decided what was best done.

Wednesday, his third day on the run. Arnold sat amongst the trees above his favourite park. Looking down he visualised those college days when he watched the ball games, the laughter of those playing and spectating. He was never really part of it. No coordination was his trouble the same with the girls. His appearance did not help either. No one knew about his home life. A father who constantly beat him and his mother. Never the right clothes to wear, the sniggers when he passed on the campus. Did any of them realise how hard his mother worked to send him to college to give him an education that she never had? His holding down a job after college, shifting crates in the docks for some big shot, until the Union objected and he had to leave. Finding out later that the Big shot was a certain Peter Sagan uncle of a certain Mary Dewer, and if he remembered correctly sister of Faye Dewer.
The vision fading Arnold Reiter rose. Those days were gone. What now was left to him? He'd withdraw the remainder of his money and hope no one would see or trace him before he once more disappeared into the night.

Sitting at his office desk the newspaper shook in Charlie Simpson's hands. The cops were after someone by the name of Arnold Reiter in connection of the murder of Mary Dewer. Charlie let the paper drop on to his desk. Poor bugger. What had he to do with Mary's death? How had they come to suspect him in the first place? Why was he hiding when Charlie knew he was innocent? But above all should he himself contact the police, anonymously of course, inform them that they had the wrong guy? Charlie stared out of his office. He could not do that, it was too risky, his call could be traced, besides why should they believe him? The Cops were sure to have a dozen crackpots calling with the same information or confessing to Mary's murder. No, it was best that he leave it at present, wait for further developments. Charlie drew some papers towards him. Anyhow when they did catch the poor bugger they would soon discover that he was innocent, then the hunt for the real killer would continue. The real killer! Him.

On the opposite side of the city, Jake Russo also sat reading the morning newspaper his thoughts on what Charlie Simpson should be thinking right now. Would he give himself up? Wait until this Reiter guy was apprehended? Or just sit shaking and let fate take its course?

"Jake, a word if you don't mind." Kane held his office door open waiting.
Deliberately taking his time Russo entered the office. Agitatedly Kane hurled at him from behind his desk, "You have to hit Sagan now, no more waiting for you to make love or whatever you do to Faye Dewer."

Russo threw Dan the rooms only other occupant a cold stare and made himself comfortable in his favourite chair, hearing Kane go on.
"It's five weeks since you promised to do the hit, and all I ever get from you is how more difficult it is than the Ferris job." Kane's voice had almost reached hysteria. He took a quick glance to where Dan sat, contemplating if he should

include him in what he had to say, deciding that he should
he went on, "Guardin is on my back."

Jake Russo had learned never to show any emotion, good
or bad, this time he had, Paul Guardin was the most feared
Mafia boss in the state.
"How the hell did you get yourself mixed up with a guy
like Guardin, Jack?" Russo blew out a breath in disbelief.
"I owe him big time. I'd have been OK had you wasted
Sagan before he had time to horn in on my west coast
investments. Now it's too late."
"How late, boss?" Dan asked, Russo detecting a note of
apprehension in his voice.
Kane made a gesture. "I have… had," he corrected
himself, "two casinos on the coast, and before I was aware
of what had happened Sagan's men had taken them over."
"How come boss?" Dan interjected. "Our men would not
just stand idly by and let it happen."
"They would if the money was right," Russo suggested.
Kane nodded in agreement. "Jake's right, Dan. Now all my
men work for Sagan. All legal and proper of course," he
ended bitterly.

Dan shook his head in disbelief. "I would never have
thought this of Jeff Blake, you paid him well over top
dollar boss. He had a job for life running those two
casinos."
"Well Dan, he now runs them for Mr Peter Sagan."
"Say the word boss, and me and the guys will pay him a
visit. You'll get your property back quick time."
"Thanks Dan, but just now I cannot afford a war, at least
not one I'd be involved in, not after planning one between
Sagan and hothead Nat Ferris. Except with Sagan out of

the frame I could once again take over what I've lost and more. Pay back the Big Man what I owe him."

Kane turned to Russo. "Is there any way you can get to Sagan, Jake? I need him dead, then I can get back my two casinos."

Russo sat back in his chair. "My plan was and still is, to have Faye Dewer invite me to Sagan's condo, however I'd have to wait until she has, otherwise it would be suspicious to ask her to invite me to meet her uncle."

"Why?" Dan asked, "I thought he owed you one."

Jake looked across the room at the speaker. "OK but what excuse do I give for wanting to meet him? Say excuse me I should like to meet you to gun you down, should that be OK with you."

Neither saw the humour in Russo's comment. Kane asking, "Is there another way in? You told me you were working on one."

Russo nodded. "I was. I only got as far as learning that there was a garbage disposal unit at the rear of the condo that may be used as an entrance to the back stairs. Plans that I obtained showed Sagan's apartment could be reached from there. The difficulty is in getting past the front gate, which in my case I had hoped would be with me sitting next to Sagan's niece. However failing this I explored the back fence, it's not electrified and the CCTV cameras I believe are too far apart to pick up someone clipping the wire and crawling through, and in the dark could reach the swimming pool the sides of which are lit up only by strobe lighting."

Suddenly interested Kane sat forward in his chair behind his desk. "So where do we go from here Jake? Is there a chance that should you and the niece not meet soon, you might somehow get under that wire?"

"Give her your famous chat line when you do meet Russo, it might save you from getting your pants caught on the wire," Dan chuckled, winking at Russo.

Choosing to ignore the man's obvious sarcasm, Jake's answer was blunt and to the point. "Sagan is back in the city but as yet Faye has not contacted me, so I don't know where she is at present, not having returned my calls."

"We shouldn't wait boss. I say we hit the casinos. Send Sagan a message that he cannot just take what he likes from you." Dan said bitterly walking to the drinks cabinet. "Boss?" He held up a whisky decanter.

Kane nodded, "A large one, make that two, and one for our friend here."

The bottom of the wire fence was as he had expected. For a moment he crouched there listening. All quiet except for the odd sudden flutter of a bird in flight. Wire cutters put a swift end to the already rusting wire bending it upwards until there was a gap wide enough for him to crawl through.

Once on the other side crouched, he ran along the side of the swimming pool; no strobe lights invaded the darkness. A final cautionary look up at the building in front of him for any inquisitive CCTV camera told him where it lurked like a nocturnal bird of prey. Flattening himself against the building wall he shuffled slowly and quietly along its smooth white surface until coming to what he understood to be the entrance to the garbage disposal unit.

The first of his keys did not work, the second too failed. Had he got it wrong?

A sudden noise followed by laughter from one of the floors above had him stop. Sweating he tried again. This time the key turned in the lock. He was in!

The passageway was short, a door at the end unlocked, he opened it and stepped into a corridor where another door he suspected led to the back stairway. He was right.

Music drifted down to him from somewhere above. He began to climb, all silent except for the hollow sound of his footsteps in the stairwell.

"First floor," he whispered at the number on the fire door. Another floor another door another number. "Only two more to go."

It had taken longer than he had expected to reach the top floor where he hoped to find his unsuspecting victim. Now came the greater challenge. Where on this floor would Peter Sagan be at this precise moment?

Now on the first balcony he took a quick look along the line of lighted windows, the first two showing no sign of life. He swung on to the second balcony then a third that he had already knew were void of life.

It was then he heard the music, an occasional laugh, a clink of glasses. His next balcony, brought him close to the open balcony door, and the sounds which had helped guide him there. Taking a deep breath he darted a look inside, drawing back at the sight of Peter Sagan and his wife and another two men standing laughing and joking. Slowly he drew out his revolver, fitted the silencer, and with one quick step was in the room, his weapon levelled at the head of Peter Sagan the man he had come to kill.

Pacing up and down in his study, Jack Kane, beside himself with anger shouted at the top of his voice at the room's only other occupant. "Christ look what he's done, that bastard Sagan!"

Kane threw the small piece of paper across the intervening space between them.

"Sagan's killed Dan! The stupid big fool tried to take him down in his own condo! Must have followed what he had heard from you about how to get in there." Kane threw his hands and eyes to the ceiling." Dan! Dan! You fool what made you do it?"

Quietly Russo sat himself down in his favourite chair by the right of Kane's desk, waiting patiently for him to end his tirade. Eventually hearing that man say, "What do I do now, Russo? It was your job not Dan's to taken down the big man."

Russo ran a finger up and down a little on the arm of the brown leather chair, knowing he'd have to be careful in what he had to say.

"Now that he has, Sagan will come after you. You have your war Jack, but not in the way you wanted. If I had a miniscule of a brain I'd get my ass out of here. Once Peter Sagan connects me with you my usefulness to you is over. There is no way that Faye Dewer will not come to hear of it, and when she does, besides thinking what a shit I've been by using her to get to her uncle, she will have nothing more to do with me. End of story."

Stopping his pacing Kane returned to his desk to throw himself down in his chair. "So what do you reckon I do now?"

"Besides suicide?" Russo chuckled.

Unappreciative of Russo's humour, Kane glared across his desk at him. "Very funny, Jake. On one side I have Sagan, on the other Guardin the big man himself, both after my ass. So what should I do now?"

Russo grinned, unable to resist the quip, "Buy some haemorrhoid cream?"

Kane threw the paper knife savagely down on his desk. "I am serious Russo. If I don't pay Guardin in time I will need more of that cream than you can buy in a drug store!"

"As I see it Jack, give me a few of the boys to take back your casinos that way you will have enough to pay Guardin what you owe, and it will keep me out of sight from both Sagan and his niece."

Kane snapped his fingers, once more in charge of himself, "Good thinking Jake. Take Victor, he's a good man and as many men as you need.

"Not many, I should not want to leave you unguarded." Jake rose.

"Thanks Jake, I owe you," Kane said softly.

"Oh you do Jack, you do. Just make sure that you are around to make the payment."

Chapter 5

It was his seventh day on the run. He had lasted a week.
He could not go on living like this. Already he smelled as
bad as his clothes. Reiter sat hunched on the park bench
though his eyes never stopped from looking around him
like a small creature ever watchful for the sudden
appearance of some large predator, probably in the shape
of a police officer.

Today he'd plucked up enough courage to buy soap and
razor together with some apples and pears from a small
store, watchful of any sign of recognition from the small
sober man behind the counter and once outside looking
through the window ready to be on his way should the man
reach for his cell phone.

His money would not last for ever. Nor would the clothes
he wore. To buy new ones would bite into the remainder of
what he had in the bank. For a moment Arnold
contemplated returning to his apartment. He had all he
needed there, a change of clothes besides his hidden little
nest egg, then he could leave, go interstate, start a new life
where no one knew him. He'd have to be careful, his
apartment was sure to be watched. Perhaps he could fool
them by trying during the daytime. They would not expect
that, they would think that should he return it would
probably be at night under cover of darkness. It was a risk.
But how to know who were watching? He'd have to be
wary of every parked car in his street. Or were they
already hiding in his home waiting? If so he hoped they'd
taken out the garbage, and cleaned out the fridge. Perhaps

the smell would alert him if they had not when he tried, and for the first time Arnold Reiter found himself smiling at the thought.

It took the fugitive the best part of the following day to convince himself that he must try and get back into his own home. He smelled, and badly, if the police did not know where he was all they had to do was follow the public who held their noses and the trail was sure to lead to him.

It was close on three in the afternoon when Arnold Reiter waited at the corner of his street. All appeared normal, well as normal as he could tell as he was usually at work at this time. He counted only three parked cars. Should he casually saunter by, take a discreet look as he passed, and if he saw anyone who vaguely looked like a cop, run for his life? But how to know? They were not likely to have 'undercover policeman' stitched on their lapel, any more than have unmarked police car painted on the side.

Reassuring himself or deciding that all was safe, in other words anything to smother his cowardice Arnold Reiter began his slow careful walk towards his home. Number one car passed; no reaction, car number two; no sudden opening of a door, followed by a warning shout. Car three; empty.
Breathing a deep sigh of relief Arnold quickened his knocking knees across the street. The entrance to his apartment was void of anyone. Should he take a chance and dash inside? Or was this what they wanted him to do while watching his every movement from their hiding place, wait until he was cornered inside?

Arnold walked to the end of his apartment block steeling himself against the expected shout, warning him to halt. At the corner he looked up at the apartment block behind this own at rows of square windows reminiscent of TV sets in a shop window, each showing a different programme. One, an old lady stroking her cat as she looked down on the almost empty street, waiting for something to happen to brighten up her day. Another window, another channel, a male figure clad in his under shirt shouting at his wife. So on and so on.

Arnold shrank into the shadow of the corner, his intention of climbing the back fire escape thwarted by those at their respective windows, who, upon seeing him on the fire escape would consider him more interesting than afternoon TV. He returned to the main street corner, it seemingly hopeless at ever getting into his apartment by the front door, when at that precise moment a car came towards him, and without a second thought walked towards it as the car drew up, blocking anyone's view of the entrance who may be watching from across the street. He was in! Arnold Reiter bounded up the stairs to his floor not trusting the elevator to be empty. Another minute and he was home darting glances all around, waiting for someone to appear from his small kitchen or closet. There was none.

Arnold stared at his bed, a so inviting bed. Could he lie down? Just for a minute or two. No, he had to gather together what he had come for. He ran to the kitchen switched on the coffee pot while tearing off his stinking clothes. A quick wash; he did not think it wise to have a shower as the ancient vibrating plumbing would be heard in every apartment He could always tell who was at home by the sound. Next the set of drawers for a clean shirt, jeans, jerkin, fresh underwear and socks. A sudden noise, Arnold halted. God! They had allowed him into his home! Where better to trap him? He had been a fool. The footsteps faded, he heaved a sigh of relief, found where he had hidden his emergency savings, and returned to the kitchen, pouring himself a coffee. The cookie jar revealed one solitary inhabitant, a chocolate bar. He plucked it out of its prison biting into its stale softness, and gulped down his coffee.

What else did he need? Arnold stood impatiently in the centre of the room flashing his eyes around at anything that may be of help to him. Help him to what and where? Despondently he sank down on the edge of the bed. He had been a fool. Why had he run? After all was said and done, he was innocent, he had not killed Mary Dewer, but he could name a dozen who could have, Mary Dewer had never been the sweet innocent thing that everyone thought her to be.
It was what the police would make of the photos that had decided him to run. Arnold rose and walked to the now almost empty closet, his photo collection of Mary Dewer all gone. He turned. It was time to leave.

Arnold Reiter reached the foyer without incident, no one was around to challenge or greet him, the latter in not the way he would cared to have been greeted, especially from those who had trusted him simply as a good neighbour. There was no going back to his old way of life, his running away had seen to that.

A car speeding past gave him the opportunity to run for the door and into the street, and not turning to see if anyone had seen or was following him Arnold quickened his stride.

A yell. Had he been spotted? Arnold Reiter controlled his urge to run. Perhaps the yell was not at him.

Again it came, Arnold swung round expecting to see the armed figure walking cautiously towards him gun raised. Instead he saw a car, its occupant beckoning him from the open window.

The Ford was old and shabby, not a police car as he had expected, the driver shouting to him to get in, and before he knew what he was doing he was sitting in the passenger seat beside a figure who easily put his shabby vehicle to shame. He was about his own age, dark complexion, a beard that had once began as designer stubble and somewhere along the line had lost its design.

Arnold Reiter swallowed. What had he let himself into?

"Not very observant are you?" the voice croaked beside him.

Arnold gulped his surprise. "You think you know me? And what do you mean by my not being observant?"

"You've got guts, I'll give you that man. But the cops almost had you, had I not come along."

"Why should the cops almost have me?"

"Don't play innocent with me man, why else would you be in this car right now? And do not say you mistook me for a buddy."

"OK. Who am I?"

The driver sniffed a laugh. "Whoever you choose to be. Right now I'd say someone who had just tried to rob apartments in broad daylight hoping everyone was at work. Am I right?"

"Guess so."

"Got a place to hide?" Reiter's new friend asked.

"What makes you think I need one?"

"Just a hunch. You can shack up with me until the heat's off, if you like." He turned a little to smile at Reiter, "no charge."

"Thanks."

The driver turned the wheel and accelerated out of a bend onto a quiet side road. "My name's Sean by the way."

"Arnold," Reiter answered, anything other and he'd most likely forget who he was supposed to be. If only he thought sadly. If only.

Sean pulled up at rundown part of town. "We'll walk the rest of the way from here," he said opening his door.

Reiter swept a not too optimistic view of his surroundings. "Is it safe to leave your car here?"

"I guess not, but as it's not my car I don't give a shit."

Reiter closed the car door. "You mean you stole it?"

"I prefer to call it borrowed."

They started to walk and Arnold wondered whether it was not too late to bid this unsavoury character farewell. Still if this guy offered him shelter even for one night in a comfortable bed where he could close his eyes without having to watch out for the usual midnight prowler he'd be happy. Or so he hoped.

Reiter's new friend guided him to the rear of a brownstone, in what to him appeared in urgent need of repairs.

Sean led him up stairs to the top floor each decorated by the same blind graffiti artist.

"Well here we are. It's not the Waldorf, but at least it's dry."

So is the Sahara, Arnold thought dismally.

"I'll make us something."

Arnold gave an imperceivable shudder hoping that whatever this man was going to cook was not black as he had a feeling he'd never see it on the plate.

It was close on 12am, Anold Reiter sat back on the tattered couch. Whatever it was he had eaten he was going to do again. He belched at the acid in his throat, not feeling at all well. On the other hand his host appeared to be unaffected, no doubt his constitution having gotten used to it, or alternatively having an iron clad stomach.

Sean handed him a Bourbon and a beer, and he took it gratefully letting the cool liquid trickle down his throat. He laid his head back and closed his eyes. Peace for a time. Another beer another Bourbon, more peace. He blinked across the room to where his host sat at a small table sniffing the white powder.

Sean gave a final sniff and glanced up at him. "You wish to participate man?"

Arnold shook his head, a head that now weighed a ton. Had he drank more than he'd realised? He started to count the empty beer cans but gave up after four, finding it too much for his fuddled brain to handle.

He must have fallen asleep for the first thing he knew was the half naked girl on the bed in the corner, his host on top of her while she nonchalantly smoked and studied a ceiling with more cracks than he'd heard from Bob Hope.

Eventually spent, Sean rolled to the side.

Miss America flicked ash on the bare floor and stared at Reiter as if aware of him for the first time.

"Who the hell is this?" she sat herself up blinking at him through a haze of cigarette smoke.

"He's our ticket out of her Lucy. Did I not say I'd make it big time someday." Sean stumbled out of bed gripping a bedsheet to help steady him as his ass hit the floor.

"Big Time! You could not give me big time if you owned Big Ben in London, you loser." His lady friend shrieked, throwing a nearby travel clock at him. Perhaps that is how they got the name, Arnold tittered, though the booze made it sound funnier. He attempted to rise then thinking better of it slumped back down on the couch. He brought up wind and studied his feet, feet so very far away.

It was then he saw the coffee stained newspaper, a photo of him on the front page a headline stating a reward of 20k for his capture as the suspected murderer of Mary Dewer. So this is why he was here.

Reiter got to his feet at the same time as his host Sean. Sean pointed a finger at him. "Where the fuck do you think you're going?"

Reiter staggered away from his erstwhile host towards the door, Miss America launching herself at him and missing landing on the floor amidst a tangle of bedsheets and obscenities. Sean caught him by the shoulder and swung him round, he countered with a punch to his assailant's jaw, and reached the door while at his back Sean screeched to the woman to call the cops.

Having him by the coat all Reiter could do was swing a punch and hope for the best, wincing at the pain shooting through his hand when the blow landed somewhere on Sean's face. Then he was free staggering and falling down the stairs until he was outside gulping in fresh air or what stood for fresh air at this time of the morning in this great city. Somewhere the distinct sound of a police siren. Miss America had made her call.

Arnold Reiter knew he had been drugged, by what and by how much he had no way of knowing. He staggered on round the corner of the building vomit trickling down his front. All he wanted was to get as far away as possible from Sean the druggie and his bitch Miss America, avoid the cops and lie down somewhere peaceful, fall asleep and hope that when he woke up this had all been a bad dream.

Somehow he had reached the docks area. He had been here before but had purposely avoided contact with anyone. Tonight this was different, he was too weak and tired to do anything but lie down at the closest brazier.

A big man clad in an assortment of ill fitting clothes handed him a half bottle of Scotch when he slid down against a brick wall. Although aware of what had happened to him earlier he thought it best not to refuse. Arnold took a sip, shuddered, thanked the man and drew up his knees to his chin. Muttering something his benefactor shuffled away, and Arnold closed his eyes shutting out the flicker of the flames from the makeshift brazier.

When Arnold Reiter opened his eyes again it was to look up at the three black clad monsters staring down at him in the half morning light. He made a weak little movement with his hand to acknowledge their presence, at the same time apprehensive of their next move.

"You got a couple of dollars for a coffee buddy?" The most sinister of them asked, towering menacingly over him.

Reiter reached into his pocket, careful that it was not the one with his last bank withdrawal and his credit cards, extracting a ten dollar bill and handing it up to the man. "That all you got?" the big man snatched it from him. "I don't think so mister."

He took a step back and the other two grabbed Reiter by his coat lapels and wrenched him to his feet.

Arnold's feet buckled under him, and as one of his robbers stretched out his hand to explore his pockets Arnold lashed out before he was aware of what he was doing, yelling in agony as the pain in his already throbbing hand seared through to his knuckles and half way up his arm.

The big man reeled back and his companion hit Reiter in the stomach bringing up most of his evening's liquid refreshment. Again the man hit him, the third helping by holding him by his free hand. Arnold hit the ground, somewhere in the recesses of his tired numbed brain he was aware that someone was raking through his pockets, but he did not care, if only they would stop kicking him. He vainly tried to rise and was punched in the face for his effort. It was no use, he might as well die here as any other place, but not so close to the brazier for sweat ran down his face, then again it could be blood. Then the lights went out in Arnold Reiter's head.

It was 6am when Sam Andrews drew up outside his partners house.

"What the hell time is this to be calling a dutiful cop?" Joe Sims moaned through a yawn, climbing into the cruiser. "Thought you'd like to know, Arnold Reiter's in St Christopher's." Sam pulled away. "Seems someone beat him up."

"For the reward money no doubt," Joe said caustically.

Twenty minutes later both cops strode down the hospital corridor to the room where Arnold Reiter lay unconscious, acknowledging the uniformed guard sitting outside with a nod.

"You wont get anything out of him for a while gentlemen, I'm afraid." the green clad doctor informed them, standing by the bed.

"When do you think we will doc?" Joe asked, his eyes on the patient.

"Difficult to say. X-rays show severe concussion, fractured skull, two broken ribs. Must have taken quite a beating. Could be in a coma for quite some time."

Sam Andrews turned for the door. "Keep us informed doctor. Let us know when we can…"

"Ask him a few questions?" the doctor suggested with a caustic smile.

His hand on the door Sam swung back. "Something like that, something like that."

In the corridor the uniformed policeman stood up at the reappearance of the detectives.

"Officer, with the exception of hospital staff, make sure no one enters that room. I'll get you backup, as I suspect the press will shortly be here when the word gets out. That also goes for any others who may express an interest in that guy lying in there. Tell your duty relief the same when he gets here."

"Everyone sir?" the officer not much older than a teenager asked apprehensively.

Understanding what the young man meant, Sam's answer was decisive, "No one, and that also includes Mister Peter Sagan. Any trouble let me know. Okay?"

The young guard's face lit up with relief. "Yes sir, sure will sir."

Walking back up the corridor Joe chortled,"you sure made his day, partner. "I can just see Sagan's face when refused by someone as young as that kid back there, that he can't see Reiter."

"Yip." Sam agreed. "The Big Shot thinks he can do what he pleases. Sagan has no right to think he can interfere with police business, lord it over us just because he and the Commissioner snort at the same trough."

Sims halted, an amazed look on his face the corridor echoing to his laughter, "Where the hell did you pick that one up?"

Andrews too had drawn to a halt, to answer deadpan, "I believe I read it on the back of a chip packet. Good is it not?" turning to commence his walk up the corridor.

Russo sat mulling over his decision on how to handle the 'casinos crisis' unaware of the flight attendant asking if he would like anything to drink, apologising for his lack of manners he replied that he did not.

Nine men, he had chosen nine men to do the job. Two sat somewhere on board, the remainder on other flights. Russo stared out of the window. Christ. How had he talked himself into this one? Each passing day had found him ever deeper in the pit he had dug for himself. Now he was trapped into helping Kane for no other reason than to ensure that the man paid him what he was due.

Seven weeks now. Seven weeks since he had done what he had come to do, hit old man Ferris and get the hell out. Instead he was still here taking on Sagan, and if things should go haywire Paul Guardin, the boss man himself.

Russo took his eyes away from the window, going over his plan, *'for it was his plan'* for the hundredth time. First, each man was to be referred to by the number already allocated to him. No names no pack drill. Every man had his own room they were not to meet until the start of the job. Five, including himself allocated one of the two hotels.

In the past he'd worked alone and except for the one hiring him no one had actually seen him. Now it seemed there were more each day including those working with him on this job. It could only be a matter of time before Nathan Ferris, Sagan, and worst of all Faye Dewer found out who, and what he was.

Russo let his thoughts drift back to how for him it had all started. He could make the excuse the cause had been a drunken father who had constantly beat up his mother, this of course could not be further from the truth. His father had been an honest working man, right up to his early and untimely death, which had put an end to his own happy carefree schoolboy days.

At sixteen the only work he had found was cleaning up bars after hours emptying garbage or such like and running errands for the district's big hard man, in this case Irish Paddy. This was as far as he had wanted it to go, for once in the clutches of these same men he was theirs for life. In the beginning his refusals had led to his ostracism with no one brave enough to employ him in the meanest of jobs. When Irish Paddy said no work, he meant no work, which left him with no alternative other than to steal. Not from Paddy, that would have been suicide, but from local shopkeepers, and when occasion presented itself an apple, chocolate bar or when really going big time, a loaf of bread.

Of course his mother's in- laws could have helped but didn't. He himself had never gone hungry, as there was always a way of nicking something edible. Not so for his mother. One night it became too much for him, through the window he'd seen what his mother was eating for supper, it made him almost sick. There and then he made for his uncle's house in a better class district, presenting himself at his door in his faded torn denims and, he now laughed, 'matching shirt'.

His uncle's greeting was far from cordial having fallen out with his mother years past over probably something trivial. "So what brings you here to my door at this hour, Jake Russo?"
"My mother's starving Uncle Jim, could you spare a dollar or two please? I will pay you back when I can." His pleading was for his mother's sake not his own.
Jim Niven jerked a thumb, "You best come in."

Jake smelled the food before the door was closed behind him. Uncle Jim slid into his chair where he'd been interrupted from his meal. Jake eyed the food stacked on the plate enough to have fed his mother for a week. He would have drivelled over it had his mouth not been so dry.

"So why is your mother starving? Too lazy to work, is that it?" Uncle Jim cut a piece of steak and lifted it to his mouth.

"You know that's not true, Uncle," Jake replied angrily. "It's my fault she has no work. I angered Irish Paddy. I wouldn't do what he asked me to do."

Jim looked up from his plate, a hint of admiration on his face.

Jake went on. "So, he took it out on my mother, putting the word out neither of us were to be employed on his turf. Of course no one did, they were all too scared."

Uncle Jim nodded. "Understood." He pointed his knife at the coffee pot. "Find a cup and help yourself."

Jim pushed a plate of bread across the table to his nephew, pointing to the cheese board.

Jake needed no second invitation.

"Why did Mary, not come and ask me herself? Too much pride, I expect."

"Something like yourself uncle. My dad said you two were alike. No, my mother does not know I am here." Jake tried a smile not knowing what his uncle's reaction might be. To his surprise the man's face lit up.

"I suppose so."

His meal finished the man sat back. "If neither of you have work, what about rent, food that sort of thing?"

Not wanting his uncle to know how he found his own meagre subsistence, he countered, "We are weeks…. months behind in rent. I expect we will be evicted soon."

"Then what will you do?"

"Probably move away, out of Irish Paddy's turf."

"Would your mother consent to work for me? As a housekeeper, I mean. Of course I couldn't pay her much."Jim poured himself another coffee. "You'd have to find your own work."

Jake's face lit up. "I could ask her Uncle Jim."

"Do that son, then let me know what she says. Or better still tell my sister to pay me a call."

Leaving Jake to wonder why his uncle and his mother had fallen out in the first place all those long years ago.

Chapter 6

Jake touched the attendant's arm as she hurried up the aisle, smiling up at her. "I think I will have that drink now when you have the time, please."
She smiled back. "Very good sir. What can I get you?"
"Scotch, no ice."
He looked at his watch. Fifty minutes to landing.

His mother had taken up his uncle's offer, after a little persuading from him that was. He had made himself scarce avoiding whatever embarrassment their reunion was likely to bring. A month later he was bidding them goodbye. Some people believe that your life...your destiny is already ordained, others like Jake himself believed that you make your own. Whatever the case, Jake Russo's life changed from the day he stepped off the bus, and battered suitcase in hand strode down the main street of his new town, wonder in his eyes at all before him. All, that was except for the man in the dark blue suit stepping out of the Ford raising his gun at the same time that Jake's suitcase sprung open spilling out its contents onto the sidewalk momentarily distracting the gunman from his target. Bending to pick up his belongings Jake, on seeing the gun, instinctively hurled the case at him as the intended victim's shot took the gunman in the chest.
"Well done kid!" A medium built well dressed man calmly walked towards him. "You saved my life."

The man had been in the act of coming down the hotel steps when the gunman appeared. Now there seemed to be people all around, either focusing their attention on the dead man or Jake and the man he had saved.

"Come on let's get out of here before the cops show." The man quickly ushered Jake to a waiting car, bundling him into the back seat.

"What about him?" A bewildered youngster asked attempting to look out of the rear window at the crowd gathered around the fallen man as they sped away.

"Gus will attend to that." The man sat back. "What's your name kid?" he asked in a tone suggesting that nothing out of the ordinary had happened.

"Jake…. Jake Russo," Jake answered swirling around to face the man, not yet fully comprehending what had just taken place.

"Well, Jake Russo, let me see what I can do for you. Where were you headed when this happened back there?" he jerked a thumb over his shoulder.

Jake swallowed. "I am looking for work, sir, just arrived in town. My case! Where's my case?" suddenly realising he was without it. "Stop the car, all I have is in that case."

"Dave will pick up your case when he tells the cops what has happened. Or thanks to you what did not happen."

He searched inside his coat bringing out a cigar. "I take it, Jake Russo that as you have only just arrived in town you have neither a place to live or a job. Something, fortunately I can remedy."

Still in a state of shock and unable to think of a suitable reply, Jake just sat there.

It was not a room but rather a suite that his benefactor showed him in to. Left alone to look around in bewilderment Jake hurried to look out of a window at traffic a few storeys below. Then to a bathroom complete with shower and amenities that he had only dreamed of. A colour TV, white phone, cocktail cabinet, the range of drinks he had only seen back home in Frank's bar.

Jake sprawled himself down on the light brown settee scarcely able to take in what he was seeing.
Clearly this man who called himself Louis Canello could be nothing other than a gangster, and a wealthy one at that. One whose life he had the good fortune to save, albeit by accident but nevertheless saved.

Mr Canello called him for dinner, or one of his men had, and following eventually found himself in a large dining room where a dozen or so men of all descriptions and ages sat, each one better dressed than his neighbour, leaving him to feel like some young tramp invited in to sing for his supper. If so, it went unnoticed by his host.

Sitting at the table head, smiling, Canello beckoned him to a vacant seat close by. Timidly Jake made his way towards the empty chair, aware of all the eyes of the room upon him, each one wondering in his own way who the hell he was and why the boss was treating him in the way he would an honoured guest.

"Gentlemen, I should like you to meet the kid who if it had not been for him I would not be sitting here this evening. And if not," Canello chuckled, "you gentlemen would most likely be debating over a good wine who was to take my place, and each secretly plotting how to dispose of one another should that decision not be in your favour."

For a moment silence followed what the man at the head of the table had said, some shuffling uneasily in their seat others playing with a knife or fork, until the silence was broken by the sudden burst of laughter from the big man himself. "Look at you all!" He stood up. "I have hit the nail on the head,

The tension now broken all began to enjoy the joke, some shouting out their denial, others crying shame on their leader for such a terrible suggestion.

Now completely overwhelmed by what he was seeing and hearing, Jake shrank back in his chair, only once more to become the centre of attention.

"Gentlemen!" Still on his feet, Canello called for silence, "I wish you to be upstanding and drink to the health of this young kid, who earlier today was instrumental in saving my life."

His eyes sweeping the standing men, Jake swallowed, thinking this guy was over the top with his praise of how he had fearlessly thrown himself at the would be assassin, also of the anti climax should he really relate how it had actually happened that the lid of his case had fallen open and bending down had diverted the gunman's attention while attempting to retrieve his meagre belongings, his entire belongings he might add.

The toast over, Jake cringed at the thought of having to reply. What could he say to such an austere gathering whose eyes through the vale of cigar smoke were taking in every small detail of him, sizing him up, assessing him in their own minds what he was, or was likely to be, making him feel more out of place than ever in his shabby clothes. Thankfully, and to his relief, instead, the big man, continued, now in a more serious vein. "The gunman was from the Veulutta mob. I have already set my revenge in motion." The announcement followed by uproarious applause and table thumping.

"So drink up gentlemen and enjoy your meal."

Though only having just turned nineteen Jake was street wise enough to know he had landed in with 'the mob' headed by the man he was credited on saving. Having lived most of his life on the edge of the law, this although a new experience was not an earth shattering revelation so as long as he was fed, given a place to lay his head and the offer of work, which he was sure would follow, he was in no way about to refuse this kind, and dare he say also unbelievable opportunity to make something of himself. But above all he was never again likely to go hungry.

Jake was correct in his assumption of Canello's gratitude towards him. The following day he was taken to the best gents outfitter in town where he acquired not one but three suits chosen by the big man himself, a fact not gone unnoticed by Jake that it was he Canello who was boss. Laden down with shirts, ties, socks and every other accessory necessary to his wardrobe Jake climbed the stair to his suite, given no time before being summoned downstairs by the boss man himself.

"Kid" Canello greeted him cheerfully. It was the name he was always to be addressed by, which in hindsight something he was always to be grateful for, even those who he worked beside never knew him by anything else, hence he had kept his own name a safe secret from enquiring minds.

"You like the suits I chose for you?" It was said in a way that left Jake in no doubt as to was boss.

"Yes Mr Canello, thank you sir." What else could he say, except the truth that they were not his style? But only a fool, which he was not, would admit to this.

"Sit down Kid, Sit down," Canello continued in the same happy vein. "Tomorrow you will begin work for me. I wish you to go with Harry and Len. Learn how we do things around here. Learn all you can." It never having crossed Canello's mind that Jake would refuse to work for him.

Apprehensive yet excited at what lay in store for him Jake walked with both men to the small convenience store, where behind the counter a small fragile looking man stared at them in what he could only describe as abject fear.

"Abe," Harry greeted the owner.

The little man splayed his hands in a gesture of submission. "It has been a bad week, Mister Harry, I can only pay you $50," he pleaded. "Tell Mister Canello I will make it up to him next week."

Harry shook his head. "No can do, Abe. You know the boss does not like his clients to be in arrears, it makes him think they don't value his protection."

Shaking, Abe opened his cash register, extracting a small wad of notes. "This is all I have. You must give me a little more time. I have my bills to pay. Should I fail to pay them I will have no stock, and no stock means no money Mister Harry. Surely you can understand my position?"

Baseball bat in hand Len took a step forward. "Your position will be horizontal Abe if you don't cough up the dough."

The little man gestured again, this time in desperation. "Please, it is all I have."

"Pity." Harry snatched the roll of bills from the old man's hand.

Beside him Len swung the bat knocking over a stack of goods on the counter, swinging it again, and breaking the glass front of the drinks case.

Not knowing what to do, Jake stood there horrified by what he was witnessing. The shop owner was no different from the ones back home who too had to eke out a living as best they could despite having to endure constant threats and beatings from animals like Len and Harry. And to make it worse, he Jake Russo was now party to all of this.

Abe rounded the counter bent on protecting his goods, Len pushing him away amid a scream from the sudden appearance of an old lady who Jake took to be his wife, who tearfully but fearlessly threw a can of beans at Len's head, shouting and screaming at this ransacker in a language he did not understand.

Laughing at her attempt, Len pushed her away. "Go sit on your ass, lady before I decide to do something nasty. OK?"

"I think she got the message, Len," Harry intervened.

"Please, do not harm my wife, she is not a well person."

As if now only aware of Jake's presence, Abe gestured helplessly to him, as if the boy was his last hope at saving his store.

Sick to his stomach, Jake looked away from those pleading
eyes, to Len who obviously enjoying his work took a final
swing at a glass stand beside the cooler.

"That will do for today." Len looked around at this scene
of destruction. "$50 more next week Abe or this will be
nothing to what we will do if you try to con us again. Do
you hear?"

Finally home Jake could scarcely wait to get out of the car,
away from two laughing hyenas who thought it hilarious at
what they had done to two old people who most likely had
battled all of their lives to build up a business which
however small was to them all they possessed.

Later that day the Boss himself summoned him to his
apartment.

"Well kid did you learn anything about the business from
those two you were with?" Canello looked up at Jake from
where he sat glass in hand on his veranda.

Momentarily Jake was about to tell this rich guy what he
really thought of this morning's work, until thinking that
should he do so it meant him blowing everything he had so
far achieved.

He gulped and managed a nod, consoling himself with the
thought that if he refused, old Abe and his like would only
suffer if not by the hands of Harry or Len but some others
just as evil.

"I learned a lot, Mister Canello." There. That was a safe
answer.

Canello took a sip of his drink. "Good. That's what I
wanted to hear, as you will take over from Harry and Len,"
Louis Canello went on at Jake's look of astonishment,

"You will be in charge. Those two will do as you say. It's up to you. I'll pay you 5% on all the takings."

"But Mr Canello I know nothing of that side of the business," Jake stammered, "I will only make an ass of it! You'll get mad at me when I do!" Not bad Russo, this might get you out of a tricky if not undesirable situation he thought.

His boss was unperturbed. "No problem Kid. Harry will show you the ropes until such times as he thinks you capable of taking over."

Canello's look at Jake was not unkindly. "I think I am correct in thinking you are of the streets yourself, Jake Russo, so not so ignorant as to how things are done?"

Jake blushed. "Yes sir."

Canello raised his hand. "Good. Now that we understand one another, go and clean up and I will meet you downstairs for dinner."

That night Jake Russo did not sleep at all well, thoughts of what he might, no probably would have to do filled his brain. How could he smash up places such as old Abe's, and so many like him?

There was that voice again urging him not to be a fool. If not him, there were plenty more who would willingly do Louis Canello's dirty work. But how to look them in the face? That was the question.

Fortunately the next food stores that he attended were a little up market, but with similar consequences.

Speeding away from their last 'client' Jake whistled in amazement. "Mister Canello must make a fortune."

Both Jake's companions let out a loud guffaw. "This is only a side show, Kid. The real money lies in," thinking better of it Len stopped, "elsewhere." Leaving Jake in no doubt as to what 'elsewhere' might be.

To Jake Russo's horror each day became easier to him. As yet he had not again had to visit old Abe or his kind, but no doubt someday he must. Instead, much to his relief his buddies drove him to desert land some way out of town. It was hot. Jake climbed out of the boiling car.
"Take off your coat, kid, and follow me." Harry walked away from the car, Len a step or two behind, and for one fearful moment Jake Russo thought he had misread his situation, for this was the type of location he'd seen in the movies where the baddies had taken their victims for execution. To reinforce his theory, Harry swung round, pistol in hand.
"You ever used a gun before, kid?" Harry's voice held a hint of amusement.
Jake shook his head.
"Then now is the time to learn." Len patted him reassuringly on the shoulder.
Harry pointed at the pistol in his hand. "This is a Glock 21, it carries 15 shots plus one in the chamber." He handed Jake the gun, and turned around. "Gently squeeze the trigger and let the gun do the rest. Aim for those beer cans on that rock. You do know the difference between beer cans and us, I hope?"
Behind him Jake heard Len laugh, but was too scared himself to join in.
It was an afternoon he was not likely to forget.

Inevitably the day arrived when he must visit old Abe and his neighbours. Accompanied by his two mentors Jake

Russo stepped out of the car that had drawn up outside old Abe's.

"Well, Kid you're the boss now. See how you do, Mr Canello will be interested to know how his prodigy has turned out." Len smirked.

The way the big man had said it left Jake more anxious than ever. Not only about the Boss, but also because of Len himself whom he did not fully trust, or Harry, for that matter, as he was sure there could be nothing other than resentment towards him at his taking over, and who could blame them, no doubt having faithfully served Canello until his coming along.

Abe focused on Jake as they entered the shop, and by what the youngster could only describe as a more than worried look stepped behind his counter, as this in itself acted as a barrier, or what the old man still considered to be a barrier against all evil, an evil which today appeared in the shape of The Kid and the two morons with him.

"Good day Abe. Got the goods?" Jake started, hoping no one heard the tension in his voice.

"Good day, Kid. And to you too gentlemen," Abe acknowledge the other two with a nod.

"Abe," Len returned the greeting, leaning on a fridge top at the front of the shop, and smiling across at his partner, both curious as to how Canello's prodigy would deal with his new found authority.

The old man swallowed. "Please, Kid could I have a word with you?" he glanced across at the Harry and Len, "in private."

Abe stood aside, and in anticipation waved Jake to come into the back shop.

For a moment Jake hesitated unsure what to say or do. He dared not look at his companions who most likely would derive nothing other than pleasure at his uncertainty.

"Sure, Abe, sure," Jake forced himself to sound cheerful. Though he did not dare look to where both men stood now astonished by his decision, their seeing this as his first mistake, the cardinal rule being that they, and no one else made demands or requests.

Ten minutes later Jake followed his two henchmen back to their parked car. In the back seat Harry looked across at Jake. "Well, what did the old shit want?"

"Tried giving you the same old hard up story, I bet. Knows you're green.'" Len guffawed swerving to avoid an oncoming vehicle.

Jake handed Harry the old man's money.

"Shit, Kid, the boss will kill you!"Harry peeled off the notes. "He will not be happy."

"Care to bet on it, wise guy?" Jake challenged, and sat back in his seat.

"This is what you bring me, Kid? Pocket money." Harry was right Louis Canello was not happy with his young prodigy. "$50 dollars from each store!"

Sitting beside Len in the corner of the room, Harry had difficulty in suppressing a smile. It was as he had said, his boss was far from happy. Now he might think again about replacing Len and him with a faggot like the Kid.

"You did bad Kid. You let me down. You let everyone of those schmucks take you for a ride. They must have called one another to say what a wimp you are, and they could easily make it $40 next week."

Angrily Canello threw himself down behind his desk, glaring across the room at a smirking Harry.

"You find it amusing, Harry Veld? If so why in hell did you not stop this... this.." Canello stammered at a loss for words.

It was not often that Harry felt good at having one over on his boss, now he was going to make this man see the mistake he had made by appointing a street kid to do the job he and his sidekick had managed for the past three years.

"Do you want us to pay them a visit, Boss, get back what is owing to you?"

The suggestion only further angered Canello, it being unthinkable that anyone should think that he Louis Canello was ever capable of making mistakes. "No." He swung to Jake standing mid floor.

"What made you do it, Kid? You know my cut is $100. So don't kid yourself that they cannot come up with the goods, being lenient can only show weakness, and weakness is the last thing you ever want to show. So what made you do it? You must have had a reason."

"Perhaps he felt sorry for those poor storekeepers,"Len laughed throwing his partner a look of amusement.

"Maybe he'll be known as the Wimpy Kid from now on?" Now feeling humiliated, something he had never before known Canello asked. "Well Kid?"

Jake cleared his throat and began."It's as I see it sir, you ask.... demand $100 every week, but seldom does everyone come up with the entire amount, so when those who do not, or cannot pay, you have Harry and Len teach them a lesson by smashing up their goods, which in turns means what little money they have must go on buying more stock, which in turn means Harry and Len have to smash up the store again the following week."

Canello waved impatiently at Jake. "So? This is not my fault, they should have paid up in the first place. I run a business, not a charity." He was angry and growing more angry by the second, not only by the loss of revenue but also by the impression left by this kid here. He had let his gratitude cloud his better judgement, this kid was not cut out for this kind of business.

Amused, the two onlookers waited Jake Russo's answer, which the youngster did with more confidence than anyone present there expected.

"Your takings are around $2250 to $2400 each week, though it should bring in $4000 if all pay, which they don't, leaving Harry and Len to smash up those who don't come up with the $100.

So, as I see it, each paying $50 gives you a reliable weekly sum of $2000 without any hassle."

"So you want the Boss to drop up to $400 to keep the peace. Keep poor little Abe and his sort happy and in business." Len's shrill voice filled the room.

His patience at an end Canello waved his hand in dismissal. "Get out of here kid. Pack your bags and leave. Len will drive you to the bus depot."

Unperturbed Jake stood his ground. "So, that's it, you won't hear me out Mr Canello?"

Canello glared at the boy. "I have heard all I want to hear. You have cost me money and worse of all my reputation. It will take Harry and Len to make up for your mistakes. Now go before I lose my temper."

Canello turned a little away and Jake took a step towards him. "Old Abe took me into his back shop today Mr

Canello, he told me something very interesting, something which as his new boss I thought was good for this week's reduction."

Now curious, Canello halted by his desk. "Make it good kid or you will still be on that bus."

Jake swallowed. It had taken all his nerve to withstand the wrath of his benefactor, now it was shit or bust time.

"Abe told me, that the reason he and most of the others," Jake hesitated, "under your protection cannot pay you the full amount is because…"

"They're too mean," Harry interjected laughing, already seeing his one time rival on the bus.

"The reason," Jake halted to glare at his antagonist "is because they are having to pay someone else."

Jake halted at the sound of sharp intake of breath from all three. Now having caught their full attention and now more confident Jake went on, this time directly facing Canello. "Have you heard of a Mister Bellito?" Canello nodded, apprehensive of what was to come. "Well he has invaded your turf, which is why Abe and the others are unable to pay you the full amount. As the old man said, they cannot serve two masters."

For a moment Louis Canello's face changed from anger to relief. "See!" he shouted at the two others in the room, "Did I not judge this one correctly? New on the street and already he is trusted."

Canello pointed an accusing finger at both men, "Abe never would have confided this to you two, nor would anyone else." Canello beamed at his new found prodigy. "Now we have to take care of a certain Mr Bellito and teach him what it means to do business on my turf."

Canello sat down and Jake asked tongue in cheek, "Does that mean Mr Canello I don't have to look out bus fare?" At this all three men laughed though two were far from happy.

They were back out at their desert location, Harry pointed to the steering wheel." That's the thing that guides the car. Turn it left and so does the car."

"We hope," Len sighed from the back seat.

"Now grip the wheel Kid. Got it?"

"I know where, and what the damn thing is for Harry," Jake threw at his tutor impatiently. "I have seen you drive. OK? So let's get started before you have to show me where the headlamps are."

Uttering a few well chosen words under his breath, Harry indicated one of the pedals. "that one, Lewis Hamilton, is what is known as the gas pedal. We do not use that one in conjunction with the other one widely referred to as the brake. Understand?"

Jake nodded. "Now that's settled can we get started?"

Determined not to lose his temper with his boss's favourite prodigy, Harry let out a burst of resignation. "First, look into your rear mirror to ensure it's OK to pull out and there's no oncoming traffic."

"Oncoming traffic! Out here in the desert?" Jake shrieked.

"Could be you are about to be overtaken by a batch of meerkats making a commercial!" Len guffawed falling back into his seat.

"Give me a break!" Harry threw his hands in the air.

"That's this one,"Jake said tongue in cheek pressing the lever with his foot.

"Don't you start or I will fail you before you have switched on the ignition."

"Which is here,"Jake tapped the key.

"Got it in one, smart ass. Now give it a turn. Good, now that you have successfully started the engine...."

Two hours later, Harry behind the wheel, confessed, however reluctantly, "You did swell Kid, I thought you'd be one of those smart ass kids who could not wait to hit the ton. And you drove well in the town too. Now tell me for the book, when do you know you are in a built up area?"

His eyes on the road, Jake answered deadpan, "because I'd be knocking down more people."

Harry matched the look. "Correct. Also I have to say you drove pretty well through the streets on your first lesson."

"Yip," Len agreed from the back. "Only next time Kid let's not drive all the way home on the sidewalk. OK?"

Jake swallowed hard. "You expect to do it here?"

"You started it wise guy," Harry smirked, drumming his fingers on the steering wheel while they waited outside of the hardware store.

His throat dry Jake swallowed again, harder this time.

Ironically it was the same hardware store that the young guy had challenged him when calling to collect his 'insurance money' or to be more precise the weekly protection money.

The guy was close to his own age, doing nothing other than he himself would have done in his place.

Jake's adversary held up the shovel threateningly. "Piss off if you don't want to speak through an extra mouth, bastard."

Jake drew back a little from the boy's metal weapon he could not retreat further without Harry or Len seeing him from where the car was parked. "Mr Canello is not going to like this, buddy." There was a hint of desperation in Jake's voice as he made the threat.

"Maybe he would like this instead?" the boy shook the shovel, close to Jake's face."Ma and me work hard every day for what we earn, maybe your boss should do the same and not steal from the likes of us folks."

If he took another step backwards Jake thought the two morons in the car would see what was happening and he was sure to lose face. Maybe burst in and do his job for him which for them would go down nicely when they told their boss.

"OK that's enough." Jake drew out the Glock.

"So that makes you a big man, eh?" his adversary smiled, unaffected by the sight of the gun.

"Sure does buddy. I shoot you, end of story… for you that is but not for your ma, she will still have to come up with the goods. Whereas you do the business on me and...well you know what will happen."

The youngster lowered his shovel. "Ok. You win. But someday..."

"Yea yea,"Jake mocked, with more conviction than he felt. "Someday, is not right now, so pay up and shut up."

Now today he was parked outside this same shop waiting for Bellito's men to arrive and shake down this same young guy who he himself had threatened not so long ago. His eyes on the two men who had alighted from the black sedan that had drawn up three cars away from where they were parked Harry said in a voice that told Jake he was no stranger to this type of situation, "Here they come, guys. Let's give them a Canello welcome. OK."

"You're on, Kid, so lets see what all that practice with the Glock has done," Len said quietly from the back seat.
Jake's eyes opened wide. "Me?" Jake said incredulously.
"Sure. Did the boss not say as it was you who wised him to Bellito homing in on his turf that you should show him what you can do."
"You being his favourite prodigy an' all." Len tittered amused by Jake's reaction. "You know how to shoot that thing? Or was it all only against defenceless beer cans?"
His eyes on the two men walking towards them Harry put his hand on the door handle, "We move together. You take down the guy on the right Kid, I'll take the other guy. Len you are back up. Go!
In an instant Harry was out the car, and firing. His mind a blur Jake followed suit from his side letting off a shot at the unsuspecting man who had drawn his own weapon before going down.
Shouting, his smoking gun still in his hand Harry swung to Jake. "Let's get out of here."

Jake and Len threw themselves into the already accelerating car, passing the bodies of their late adversaries lying in the street, amid stunned passers-by.

Harry gunned the car down the busy street, Jake still in a state of disbelief at what he had done. Followed by a feeling of exhilaration at having proved himself equal to the two men beside him.
He had shot a man!
"I got him, Harry! Len I got him!" Jake exploded, unable to describe the power the Glock had given him.
"Don't think so, Kid," Len said at Jake's ear. "It was my shot that took him down, yours went wild."

"It was mine!" Jake yelled, the adrenalin now at its height, it being inconceivable that only a few minutes before he had almost been sick at the thought of shooting at someone, now all he could feel was elation, an elation that Len was trying to deny him by implying he had missed his target.

"OK, wise guy, you can take the hit; impress that boss of yours." Len did not feel like arguing. He sat back and looked out of the side window at the buildings speeding past. "But you owe me one."

In the front seat, the adrenaline was still pumping through Jake's body, the realisation that he had taken someone's life secondary only to the feeling of elation that with the Glock in his hand he was equal to experienced killers like Harry and Len or anyone else who cared to challenge him, but most of all he had enjoyed what he had done.

Chapter 7

It was well over a year since Jake had last seen his mother and Uncle. Canello had given him time away to be with his only relatives but only with the promise that he be back for New Year. Reluctant yet happy Jake had agreed.
Jake had flown, and renting a car, had driven to his old neighbourhood.
Jake peered through the windshield at the heaped snow banked up at the side of the street: His street.

Only a few had ventured out into the gale force wind, none whom he recognised. He felt sad, angry at no one there to see how well he had prospered. No wagging housewives sweeping snow from their stoops calling to one another that it was Jake Russo who had driven past in the flash car.

Everything was just as he had left it. The same squalor, the same rundown brownstones except this time the weather had hunted kids such as himself at one time off the street. The continual bleakness broken only now and again by the odd snowman outside of a more prosperous household. He was almost home, or to be precise his uncle's home, or to be even more precise Irish Paddy's.

Jake's heart quickened. Although he still had his key and his kin not knowing that he was coming home, to greet them unexpectedly in the kitchen was likely to earn him a bang on the head with a frying pan from Uncle Jim if taken by surprise. So instead he rang the bell and waited, his arms full of presents he had struggled up the steps with from the car, with only a few curtains pulled aside by the usual Nosey Parkers' from across the street to see how well he had prospered.

The door opened, Uncle Jim peered into the snow for who was stupid enough to be out in such foul weather.
"Hello, Uncle, it's me Jake."
Still peering Jim took a short step closer, suddenly recognising his nephew he let out a loud shout of happiness. "Mary! Mary! It's your son Jake, come home for Christmas!"
Jim stretched out to help Jake with his burden as Mary came to the doorstep.
"Jake! Jake! Why did you not tell us you were coming home?" Mary engulfed Jake and his presents in a wide embrace.
"I wanted to surprise you both."
"You certainly did that, you bad boy," Mary scolded her prodigal son, dragging him into the house by the first thing she could get hold of.

Jake looked around the living room, the main room of the house, unprepared for its coldness after the customary comfort of internal heating and kinder climate that he had recently left behind.

"What have you been up to son since you left? We seldom hear from you," his mother asked eagerly, placing a cup of coffee in front of him.
"Whatever it is, it must pay well, sister, look at that car outside, and the suit he's wearing. Must have robbed a bank," his uncle surmised, the admiration on his face plain to see.
"Not quite, Uncle. As I said in my last letter…"

"Your *only* letter," his mother reminded him.

"I am working for a businessman who is very good to me since, as I said before I happened to save his life." Jake took a sip of his coffee. "Pure luck of course that I happened to be in the right place at the right time."

"And what do you do son for this business man whose life you have saved?"

It was a question that Jake had mulled over on his journey here. He could not very well say *I threaten people to pay up or be beaten up.* Instead he said, "I work in insurance." Jake swallowed, well it was close enough, when he thought about it.

Jake looked around him. "How does Irish Paddy treat you? Good I hope."

"No worse than most around here, Jake. I do a little part time work in a store and your mother works the same hours cleaning."

Jake's face turned an angry red. "So the money I send is not enough, you both still have to go out and work."

"Don't be angry son, we could never manage without what you send us, but things get more expensive all the time," his mother pleaded, and Jake saw how old she had become since his leaving.

"Such as?"

Brother and sister looked at one another, and Jake knew they had something to hide, something they did not want him to know.

"It's Irish Paddy. What has he been up to?" Jake's voice rose at the thought of these two, his only family, still at the mercy of this man.

"Oh it's not so bad Jake, nothing you should worry over. He just has to raise the rent now and again," his uncle assured him. Then hurriedly as if to gloss over the affair. "He does it with everyone, Jake, he says it's the rising cost of repairs."

"Forget Irish Paddy. What's in the parcels son?" his mother asked excitedly.

Jake responded to his mother's attempt to change the subject. "Don't be nosey woman, you will have to wait until tomorrow." Smiling he banged the table and stood up. "Now first things first. First we go to Hendry's, where you Uncle will buy yourself a suit, shirt, socks etc. and you mother a dress and all the mysterious things that go with it."

"Why, Jake what do we want with fancy clothes?" his mother asked in astonishment. "You have not come home just to spend your hard earned money on us two old timers."

"Speak for yourself,"Jim teased.

"Well said Uncle. No, you will need them when we dine out tomorrow at Haines. It is Christmas after all."

"Haines!" both echoed.

"You will not get a table there tomorrow, all the big noises will already have them booked," Mary assured her son. "Besides I will feel out of place amongst all those well dressed upper class folk," Mary protested already seeing herself as the centre of attraction in that upmarket establishment. "Already done, Mother. I booked them weeks ago just as soon as the boss agreed to let me come home." Jake winked at his mother, "And you'll look swell in the new dress you'll pick at Hendry's"

For a moment the lady was overcome by her son's generosity, her son, her pride and joy who she knew was destined for better things than working his butt off around here for hideous people like Irish Paddy.

Jake swung to his uncle, "and you'll cut a dashing figure in that suit you're sure to pick, Uncle."
"I guess so, son." Uncle Jim did not know what else to say.

Jake returned from his car parked outside of Hendry's busy main entrance. Pushing politely through the happy festive shoppers he spied his mother and uncle laden with their respective purchases.
"Got all you need?" Jake asked relieving his mother of a large square box.
"More than enough, son," his uncle answered struggling with his own burden.
Jake took it from the old man. "Come on you two, let's find a cafe," Jake led them through the heaving mass of the shopping mall, beating another desperate couple to an empty table.
"Now, let's see what we have here," Jake lifted the menu.
"You two must be starving after your executive stress," he chuckled.
Mary felt relieved at the suggestion. Jake's unexpected arrival had left her unprepared for a third mouth to feed. Eating here would solve the question, for her and Jim would need nothing more till supper time.
Mary was wrong. Arriving home, Jake ushered them inside while he returned to the car.
"Uncle Jim could you give me a hand please?" Jake shouted from the open doorway. "It's freezing out here."
Jim put down the coffee pot where he had been helping Mary in the kitchen. "Let's hope it's not a damned Christmas tree," he joked hurrying to the open front door.

Jim helped his nephew with the three narrow hip high cardboard boxes with a look of perplexity.

"You and mother won't be cold now," Jake told him cheerfully.

A few minutes later, the open boxes stood in the centre of the dining room to reveal three electric heaters.

Not yet having come to terms with her son's latest gifts Mary stood back to give these strange new objects the benefit of her scrutiny.

"Very nice son, but I guess we will never use them, since we cannot afford to switch them on."

"We could always sit a table lamp on one," Jim suggested deadpan.

"OK you two. I will make sure I send you a little something so you don't have to set fire to dollar bills to keep warm," Jake chuckled, though he knew that they were serious. "So what's for supper?"

Christmas day was almost over. Uncle Jim threw himself down in his favourite armchair, loosening his new waistcoat. "That was a swell meal, Jake. I hope to God you can afford it?" he belched.

"Easy when you have a credit card, uncle." Jake made them all a coffee, surprised at finding his mother had reverted to wearing her old dress as she entered the kitchen.

"Dress not fit aright, mother?" he asked, a little disappointed.

Mary handed Jake a cup of coffee she had stirred, "Give this to his lordship in there, Jake, he is too fat to move," she pointed the cup at the reclining figure in the armchair. "Or should I say too greedy." She lifted her own cup following Jake into the dining room. "Two helpings of layer cake. After…." she halted to emphasise, "cheese cake the size of Mount Everest. It's a wonder, brother that you could fit in the car, or Jake and me would have to roll you home."

All three sat laughing at the image, until Jake said. "I hope you enjoyed Haines, personally I thought they skimped a mite no doubt because it was Christmas."

"Skimped! I thought the meal was fantastic son. It will do me till Easter." Jim belched again.

"Do I take that as a hint Uncle?" Jake's smile broadened. It was a long time since he had felt so happy, and would dearly have loved to have hugged them both, but now was not the time, first, he had a few matters to clear up.

The casino was a hubbub of a noisy pushing mass of bodies, each impatient to reach a particular gambling table, all in their own minds certain of winning. Here and there a scantily dressed young female with flashing light antlers, drink tray held aloft, swerved in and out of poker playing clients. One threw a quick quip to one of the many Father Christmases, one of whom climbed the stairway to the office of Irish Paddy.

Without knocking, this Santa opened the door and entered the big Irishman's inner sanctum.

"Don't you have the good manners to knock before you enter a room?" Paddy did not look up at the intruder nor halt in his counting of the various bundle of banknotes stacked on his desk.

At the lack of response to his question, Paddy looked up. "Well Santa, what the hell do you want? Can't you see I'm busy?"

"Too busy to wish an old friend a Merry Christmas?" Jake replied taking off his white beard and pushing back his red hood.

"Jake Russo all grown up! Well well well. What brings you back to this Godforsaken neck of the woods?"

"Besides my kin? *You* Paddy."

"Me? Why me? I thought when you left you had found bigger fish to fry. Or do you have to wear that suit all year?" Paddy laughed heartedly at his own joke.

"Not quite. I thought I'd wish you a Merry Christmas as you will not be around for me to wish you a happy New Year."

Paddy's face lost it's smile at the sight of the Glock in Jake's hand. "What the hell are you up to Russo? What have I ever done to you, except teach you the hard facts of life. And if I am not mistaken I have succeeded."

"Oh you succeeded, Paddy. Succeeded in starving my mother because you put the word out that no one was to employ her. Succeeded in forcing her to eat cat food." Jakes voice rose. "this I saw with my own eyes."

"Get out of here Russo, your mother never had to do that."

"As I said Paddy, I saw it with my own eyes, it's not something a fifteen year old is ever likely to forget. She would have died if her brother, my Uncle Jim had not taken her under his care. But you know all that even now when you raise the rent." Jake added sarcastically.

"I have to. All my other tenants will tell you. It is the constant cost of repairs. These brownstones were not built yesterday. So why the gun? What do you want me to do about it? Lower the rent?"

"No, Paddy I don't want you to do that." Jake reached into the sack he was carrying as part of his Santa outfit extracting a can of cat food. "I brought you a present, Paddy. I hope it is to your taste."

Irish Paddy jerked back in his chair. "You don't expect me to... to?"

"My mother had to, so if you think it was good enough for her, then why not yourself?"

"Get the hell...." Paddy was fast but not fast enough, Jake Russo shot took him in the chest.

All the anger and hatred for the man slowly relieved itself as he watched Irish Paddy slowly die. He could have ended it with another shot but somehow, he could not explain why, it gave him a sadistic pleasure in watching this hated man's eyes change from fear to anger finally to resignation that he was about to leave this earth.

Jake Russo waited, the final words of hatred for him on his victim's lips, as he slumped on to his desk clutching a roll of banknotes, either in pain or a reluctance to leave them behind.

Callously Jake pushed aside the dead man's head where it lay on a pile of banknotes, gathering up the notes and stuffing them into his sack, followed by a few more stacks from the further end of the desk.

It was enough. It was time to leave.

Canello appeared to be happy at Jake's return, though Jake himself felt sorry at not spending the New Year with his folks for one never can tell what is before them. He thought again of his parting with his Mother and Uncle, how he had hugged them, as if afraid that he'd not see them again.

He thought it best to leave however, after dealing with Irish Paddy. Not that he was afraid that suspicion could fall on him. No, Paddy had too many enemies for him to be classed as number one suspect, even though his unexpected arrival had not gone unnoticed by his street. What most disturbed him was his feeling of relief to be once again free from all of the squalor of his old neighbourhood. Jake blushed. The same neighbourhood where his mother and uncle would spend the remainder of their lives. Sure, he had lightened their burden a little by leaving them the money Irish Paddy had had on his desk, which he remembered the big man seemed reluctant to leave behind.

He had seen the pride in his mother's eyes at his seeming prosperity, though having the foresight not to ask how he had come by it. Jake nodded as if to console himself that the money he had obtained 'stolen rather' from old Abe and his fellow shopkeepers was at least going to someone similar to themselves, even in some ways he himself was no better than Canello or Irish Paddy.

It was early evening, the Boss had asked him up to the big room he used for his meeting with his various 'managers', tonight Jake understood was to be a social occasion.
"Ah, Kid," Canello greeted him from the head of the long table. "Go with Harry, he will show you what has to be done."
"This is the kid that saved your butt?" one clearly senior to the others asked through a haze of cigar smoke, as no one else would have had the audacity to address Canello in such a way.

Canello took the question in his stride. "You are sorry that he did, Felix?" he laughed and the rest of the company joined in.

"Good looking boy," the same man asked, "Keeping him for yourself, eh Canello."

"Jealous are you Felix?" Canello answered lightly, though the smile failed to reach his eyes.

"No, I never did fancy you, Louis!" the man guffawed, this time the laughter reached the ceiling.

"What was that all about, Harry?" Jake asked angrily on his way down the backstairs. He jerked to a halt on a step as if the thought had only just occurred to him. "By *Christ*... that old shit thinks I am a faggot." He swung on his heel, "I'll show him who is the faggot!"

Harry quickly caught him by the sleeve, "Leave it kid, that old man you're sore about owns most of the next town, besides it's not wise to annoy him, for that same old man could have you wearing concrete shoes within an hour if he had a mind to."

Still fuming at the besmirching of his character, Jake followed his buddy to the foot of the stairs, halting in front of a single black metal door.

"Christ, Kid I forgot to text Judy. She will kill me if I don't." Harry turned to retrace his steps. "Wait here Kid give me a minute, won't you."

Jake waited in the dimly lit stairwell, looking at Harry standing with cell phone in hand, busily texting his lover, amused, he looked away at the black metal door, his curiosity aroused by what could be inside.

"Sure glad I got that done, man." Harry turned the key in the lock, and switched on an interior light. "The Boss surely trusts us with the key with what is most precious to him." He pushed the metal door open, adding as it swung inwards, "And that includes money."

Bewildered and even more curious Jake followed Harry into the cellar's inner sanctum.
Harry nodded at a head high shelf filled with boxes. "Up there, Kid. Bring down that box numbered eleven. The Boss likes number eleven."
Once down, Harry opened it. "Good. It's there. Now number three." Again Jake lifted down the box, his instincts telling him this could be nothing other than cassettes for a porn show, which was what those rich farts up there were waiting for.
Jake could not have been more mistaken.

This time the large smoke filled room held a large TV screen.
"Well, gentlemen what should you first wish to see?" Canello settled himself down in the best seat in the house, amused by the various loud requests, finally he held up his hand for silence. "Let's begin with the feature, and move on to the main attraction."

Again Jake was certain that he was about to be part of an evening of blue movies, instead a close up of a half naked man tied to beam in what could only be described as a dimly lit cellar filled the screen amid a roar of cheering as the camera focused on the white shirted figure of Canello whip in hand, appeared.

Jake felt sick as the first blows struck the doomed man's midrift. Again and again Canello laid on until the floor dripped with flesh and blood. Finally exhausted Canello bowed to the camera, lifted a drink to his lips to begin all over again.

Harry nudged Jake, "Come on buddy it's our turn."
Horrified that he was expected to take part in anything so grotesque Jake drew back.
Harry grabbed him by his shirt sleeve. "Come on, we have to serve the drinks before the next show."
Relieved that this was all that was required of him, Jake was only too willing to follow his buddy.

Much of the remainder of the evening was the same with Louis Canello the star.
Happy to absent himself with excuses to find more drinks Jake attempted to use his time downstairs, however this he knew must come to an end with Felix shouting across the room to him and holding up his empty glass.
"If he tries anything, I will shoot the old bastard dead," Jake cursed to his friend.
"Best let him have his fun Kid, that way you'll live longer, believe me." Harry seriously advised the angry young man.
Determined to show this old son-of- a -bitch he was no faggot Jake crossed to where he sat. "Anything I can get you Mr Viconti, sir."
"Sure can young fella." Felix held up his empty glass. "Scotch, no ice."
"Yes sir," Jake quickly drew away, empty glass in hand.

Jake returned to the jeers and howls of delight at what Canello's guests were watching on the screen.
This time the victim hung by his wrists while Canello hit him with a baseball bat. First quite gently on the ankles,

then harder on both kneecaps, rising to his chest then finally his face, the sound of breaking bones clearly audible.

Sickened, Jake made a silent exit, no longer willing to watch his sadistic employer at work.

Canello's woman found Jake and Harry busily refilling drinks behind the little bar in the ante-room from where they carried the drinks to Canello's admiring audience.

"Are you not the clever one, Kid" she hiccuped at Jake.

"Just doing my job, Miss Belle," Jake answered without halting in his work.

Belle moved closer to him. "Miss Belle? How about just plain Belle?" she tittered drawing closer.

Out of the corner of his eye Jake saw Harry watching them, his expression clearly warning his buddy to beat it out of here before the big movie star himself made an unwelcome appearance.

"I could not do that, you being the boss's woman and all. Besides you'd never be plain Belle."

"Wrong, Jake," Harry muttered. "Now watch her come on."

Harry was right. Another belch from the lady and feigning unsteadiness Jake found her in his arms.

Jake smelled her nearness, her breasts pressed against his chest, her lips drawing closer to his.

"Best hurry with those drinks Kid," Harry intervened with a shout. "The natives out there are growing restless."

Something like Belle, Jake thought, reluctantly releasing the magnificent figure from his hold.

Harry handed him a drinks tray and winking at Belle Jake quickly made his exit leaving Harry to deal with the situation.

Later, the bizarre show over, Jake helped Harry to replace the videos, wishing there was some way he could have them destroyed, though this he admitted would cost him his life if discovered.

"Why the show, Harry?" Jake asked closing the black metal door.

Harry turned the key. "Oh that up there," he jerked his head. "Those were the people who got in Mr Canello's way, or double crossed him."

"A little behind the times is he not? I mean why videos and not DVD's?"

"Too much of a risk changing them." Harry explained. "It gives someone the opportunity to copy them, and if so the boss is dead, or blackmailed down to his shorts. So he keeps them as a video show instead."

"Purely for amusement purposes,"Jake snorted contempt.

"Not solely, Kid, they are also intended to be educational, just in case someone in there should have a notion to take down our boss. And should he fail?"

Jake The Kid nodded. "Point taken."

Jake had never seen his boss so angry, to say he was afraid was an understatement. It was next morning after the film show, he and Harry were summoned to the main room in Louis Canello's apartment.

"Which one of you did it?" Canello stormed, pointing his favourite weapon at them.

When both mystified by the question remained silent, Canello angrily jerked the bat at them in turn.

"Do not play innocent with me!" he hurled, "you both know damned well what I mean! Three videos are missing, two from last night. Only you two had access to the room, so which one of you took them? Or have you planned it together? Eh?"

Jake swallowed, his shaking matching the bat in Canello's hand. "I never knew that room existed until last night, and that goes for your bloody film show as well Mr Canello." Beside him Harry choked back disbelief at the way the youngster had spoken to his Boss.

Canello stared wide eyed at Jake's audacity. Recovering he fumed at him, "No but you could have planned it with Harry here who did know about the show well in advance, as it was he who helped put it all together."

"No, Mr Canello! I could never double cross you. Have I not been loyal to you since you gave me my first chance to work for you over three years ago. Whereas…" Harry halted.

Canello stopped him, "The Kid has been here only a few months. Is this what you are trying to tell me Harry? Tell me the Kid here, set this all up by himself?"

Forlornly Harry dropped his eyes to the floor. "I guess so, Boss."

Canello's face twisted in disgust. "OK I will find out who is behind it." He pointed an angry finger at the suspects,"And you know what that will mean. Now you, Harry, will remain here tonight in a room upstairs. You Russo," Jake's heart sank at the man's use of his surname, "will remain in your own suite until tomorrow morning when you and your buddy will tell me where you put the videos.

Bruno," Canello addressed one of the three others in the room, "Relieve these gentlemen of their weapons and cell phones." Canello swung a little away before turning back as if suddenly remembering. "Don't think you can threaten me with blackmail. Those videos are only worth a fortune when you are alive, nothing to you when dead, or when featuring in my next film show. OK?"

Jake sat hunched on his settee. Only he knew who had the videos, and that was Harry, no one else. But how had he done it? Harry was next to him when he'd opened the black door.
The man had been with him all the time. Except, Jake sat up, he had left him to text his girl, but even so?

There was no disputing the fact that the videos were worth a fortune in the right hands, or should that be the wrong hands? It was there for all to see, on the screen, Louis Canello savagely beating to death his victims with a baseball bat.

Jake rose. How did Harry expect to get away with it? Undoubtedly the text message had something to do with it. It was close on an hour later before the answer or what Jake hoped to be the answer came to him, and now that it had, there was nothing left to him than to get hold of the proof, unfortunately that proof lay in Harry's cell phone, that same cellphone now in the possession of his boss Louis Canello.
It was dark. Now was the time Jake thought at attempting to prove his innocence. Slowly and silently Jake drew back the sliding glass door leading on to his veranda and tip toed to the balcony rail.

"Shit," Jake swore softly looking down at the green manicured lawn five floors below.

It was not the distance to the ground that frightened him but that he should fall from the floor above, for his greatest fear was that he'd be caught in the suite above, for in that suite and hopefully fast asleep lay Canello, a man whose life he now regretted having saved. Even though by doing so he would not now be living in luxury and helping his mother and uncle financially. "Shit," he said quietly, "what do I mean living in luxury? Living in abject fear more likely, such as now, or having every chance of crashing to the ground upon reaching Canello's suite and thrown out of the window by that same angry man.

Hoisting himself onto the balcony rail and clutching the corner eaves with the fear of the consequences if caught, Jake catapulted on to the veranda rail above, landing with a crash onto the concrete floor, where he lay, certain that he'd been heard, and only now aware of the pain in his back. However the veranda door did not fly open and neither did an angry boss armed with his favourite weapon appear. Thanking his guardian angel for this small mercy, Jake gingerly rose to his feet.
Now for the next step. Was the sliding door unlocked? To his surprise it was. Quietly Jake entered the lion's den, shuffled round the sleeping figure, two sleeping figures, one of whom he recognised as Belle, Canello's constant female companion, and was certain that the snoring did not come from the boss himself.

Jake looked swiftly around, and stepped silently to the bedside table. A further snore made him jump. His heart pumping, he sifted through the table's contents; keyring, wrist watch, wallet, bill folder, then he saw what he was searching for, his cell phone, lying beside Harry's. Unable to believe his good luck, Jake quietly put them both in his pocket and to add to his good fortune on his way to the door spied his Glock in it's holster hanging from the arm of a chair.

Jake took the backstairs to the ground floor, gasping for breath he edged open the door. Across the foyer the relaxed security guard sat behind his counter reading the evening paper. Jake closed the door, there was no way he could cross that open space without the guard seeing or hearing him. What he needed was some sort of a distraction, but how and where could he find one?
Again Jake gently opened the door. A pot plant stood a few feet away, if only he could reach it and throw it down the corridor.

The sound of a car passing in the street gave him an idea. He'd wait for another one, hopefully in not too long a time. Minutes passed, hours to Jake, then came the distant sound of a car approaching.
Taking a chance, crouching, Jake reached the plant, lifting it off its stand at the same time as the car passed outside. One deep breath and he had thrown the plant down the corridor and was back behind the door at the same time as he heard the crash.

Lifting his head at this sudden mysterious sound, the guard dropped his paper, and muttering at this interruption to his education crossed the foyer to investigate. Jake gave him just enough time to pass before he was heading for the door, praying that it was unlocked. It was not.

Now he was out in the open with nowhere to hide, the loud mutterings of the guard returning in his ears. There was nothing for it, before the unfortunate man was aware of what was happening, Jake ran at him full tilt knocking him to the floor and quickly freeing what he thought was the right key from the unconscious guards belt. "It was either you or me," he apologised "Might still be me if I don't get out of here and quick."

Seconds later Jake the Kid was crossing the intervening space between manicured lawn and the street, running for a cab to take him across town to where Harry's girlfriend lived. She, he decided was his only chance of proving his innocence.

The house was in darkness when Jake arrived, the cab paid he banged on the door, followed by impatient pushes on the doorbell. There was no time to lose. Except? Jake took a step back, had Canello's men already paid Harry's girlfriend a visit? Or was the girl he knew as Ruby now in his evil boss's custody? Suddenly a light went on and a nervous female voice asking who was knocking at the door at this time of night.

Satisfied that it was Jake who had answered, Ruby opened the door, Jake almost knocking her over in his haste to be inside.

"What's the damn rush, Kid? Do you know what time it is? And why are you here?" Ruby looked past him as if expecting to see her beau.

"Listen Ruby, I know you helped Harry steal the videos, when the Boss finds out he will have his men over here in double quick time."

"What the hell are you talking about, Kid? What videos?" Angrily, Ruby pulled her house coat tighter.

"Don't play stupid with me, Ruby." Jake crossed to the window and took a quick nervous peek out through the drawn curtain. "Canello may decide to grill Harry and me before he has you brought to him. You do not want that Ruby, I have seen what the mad bastard can do with a baseball bat and it is not at all pretty. Hopefully he believes I am still in my room."

Now a little less nervous, Ruby gave Jake a faint smile. "Maybe his guess is that you are guilty after all and are already on your way out of town?" She gave him a crooked smile, "With the videos."

Jake was losing it. "You bloody well know I never stole those damned things."

"Maybe not, but your running away might prove that you have."

Jake pulled Harry's cell phone out of his pocket and held it up to Ruby. "I had time in the cab to read a text from Harry to you, in it he mentions the name Verdo. I don't suppose that's whose doing the copying right now?"

Ruby shook a little at this knowledge, regaining her composure she hurled back, "Who the hell is this Verdo guy? What's he got to do with you stealing the videos?"

"Nice bluff, Ruby but you're wasting time, Canello's men can be here at any minute. Or do you want me to wait and show them Harry's cell phone?"

"OK! OK!," Ruby surrendered, "It was all Harry's get rich quick scheme. He said that he knew a way of getting hold of videos showing Canello beating to death those who had got in his way, or double crossed him." She looked at him soberly. "Harry said they'd be worth a fortune in the right hands, so we concocted this plan. Harry found out the date of his boss's next horror show, with Canello as usual giving him the key of the vault to bring up the videos, which in turn gave Harry the golden opportunity of taking a wax impression."

"So that was what the bastard was doing on the landing, he wasn't texting you but making a…."

"An impression," Ruby finished the sentence for him.

"Oh he made an impression all right, you can bet your sweet bibby on that," Jake swore. "Then what?"

"We had already lined up Verdo to make copies...for security purposes, you will understand, then all we had to do was sit back and watch Canello, the big man himself sweat his butt off awaiting our call and the amount of the first payment."

"You didn't expect to get away with that? Once Canello knew who was shaking him down he'd be onto you in a flash." Jake shook his head in disbelief.

"Not if he did not know who was behind it all. Of course Harry would still go on working for Canello as if nothing had happened. Then when we thought we'd made a big enough hit we'd move on. Maybe try it out again in some other place. Keep us in luxury for life, so to speak."

Dejectedly and despite the urgency of the situation, Jake threw himself down on the settee. "It won't work Ruby. Either Canello beats the shit out of Harry, or he does the same to you."

"And you, Kid what will happen to you? Canello might think you are no longer his wonder boy, now that you have run away?"

Jake halted her, "You are forgetting Harry's cell phone, Ruby. Canello will break every bone in his body to find this Verdo and stop him from making copies."

Ruby sat down opposite Jake, "So what do we do now boy wonder? Return them with I'm sorry Mr Canello we should not have taken them in the first place, but they are all there and we didn't copy any of them, honest?"

"It's all we can do, get those videos back from Verdo, and return them to Canello."

"You mean hand them back to Mister Big and have him kick the shit out of us?"

"Not me Ruby, you are forgetting Harry's cell phone."

Beaten, Ruby gave a sigh of resignation. "I guess so." She rose, "Best we get started and hope Verdo is at home and not out on the booze again."

The journey to the mysterious Verdo was only a few minutes away. The man himself answered the door.

"Ruby! What the hell?" the man's eyes travelled to Jake. "Who the fuck is this with you?"

Instantly Jake took a dislike to this sturdy looking thirty year old who reminded him that he himself was a slightly built boy just out of his teens, something most folk were not aware of, as a result of his responsibility to his boss.

"We've come for the videos and perhaps by this time DVDs' as well," Jake threw at him, "And we don't have time to argue, Verdo."

The man in the doorway let out a gasp of indignation.
"Watch it sonny, or I might have to separate you from your
school lunch."
"Nicely put wise guy, but maybe you can hurry your sad
ass along before Canello's men get here to rearrange a few
muscles."
"Less of the wisecracks you two, can we get on with why
we are here in the first place?" Ruby pushed angrily
through the open door.
Reluctantly Verdo followed. Jake on his heels.

"The Kid tells me Canello has Harry." Ruby stared into the
man's eyes.
Verdo let out a low whistle. "So there's a change in the
weather?"
Ruby gestured impatiently, "Let's get it over with."

Jake was totally unprepared for what happened next.
Before he was aware of it Ruby was pointing a gun at him.
"Bad luck, Kid, we sure as hell do not have any intention
of returning Canello's videos to him."
Verdo took a step forward and hit Jake full on the mouth,
throwing him against the wall and knocking over a lighted
table lamp on his way to the floor.
Still in a state of shock, Jake struggled to his feet. "So
what's the game? What about Harry? How is this going to
help him?"
Ruby's answer chilled Jake to the bone. "Fuck Harry, Kid.
He knew the risks. Did he not Fern?" she winked at Verdo.
"Now all we have to do is let the stupid bastard squirm
while we get ourselves out of here."
Verdo nodded in agreement. "What about him?" he
gestured at Jake.

Ruby shrugged."You can have that pleasure. Or would you like *me* to finish him off?"

"So you both double crossed Harry?" Jake shook his head, his voice scathing. "You're leaving him to be beaten up by Canello."
"Something like that, pal," Verdo smirked. "But first we have you to deal with." He flicked his fingers at Ruby. "The gun. Give me the gun, I want to see how Canello's favourite boy takes it in the guts."

Now was his only chance. While in the act of handing Verdo the gun, Jake launched himself at the woman swinging her round to shield himself from an angry Verdo at the same time wrenching the gun from her. Too late Verdo was on him while he fumbled for the trigger, Verdo letting out a cry of triumph as he tore the weapon from Jake's grasp. This time it was Verdo who failed, Jake pulling out his own gun from it's holster and blowing a hole in the man's belly.

"Amateur, you should have frisked me first." Jake seethed amid the screams of horror from Ruby at what he had done. He stared down at the writhing figure on the floor. "Now how are *you* taking it in the guts, buddy?"

Jake grabbed the hysterical woman. Show me where this shit copied the videos."
Ruby winced at the fierceness of Jake's grip on her arm. "There." she pointed. "In the back room."
Roughly Jake pushed her towards the door the sobbing woman had indicated.

The room was small. Jake scanned the work bench recognising a few of Canello's videos.

"Where does your lover keep the copies?" Jake released her none too gently.

Ruby shouted angrily. "You should have asked him before you blew a hole in his guts, you stupid kid."

Jake pointed his gun at Ruby's mid-rift, "Maybe you would like one to match?"

"Bastard."

"Never mind the niceties Ruby, just give me the info before Canello's men get here."

"Behind the curtain, you'll find them all on a shelf."

"All of them?"

"Maybe not all of them."Ruby indicated the workbench, "that could be some of them he's working on now, or, should I say, was."

Jake had no idea what to look for, only that he had to retrieve his boss's original videos and hopefully the copies as well.

"You're looking for videos, and DVD copies," Ruby smirked.

Surprised that Ruby should volunteer such information, especially after having just killed her lover and the rough way he had treated her, he threw her a look of gratitude. Ruby understood the look. "Don't think I'm doing you a kindness, Kid, I am just as anxious to get the hell out of here as you are. You can tell Mr Canello his performances are all there," she pointed at the shelves, "or on that bench."

Hastily Jake gathered together the original videos as well as scooping up everything in sight on the bench in the hope that he was now in possession of everything that could incriminate his boss.

Jake took a last look around the tiny workshop."Come on, let's get out of here."

Ruby was first to leave the room, Jake a few steps behind when the pistol shot rang out missing his head by inches, the moaning figure on the floor struggling to get off a second shot from Ruby's discarded pistol. Drawing his own weapon Jake threw himself to the side firing from the hip as he went down, Ruby's screams filling the room. Jake fired again. This time the body on the floor grew still.

Letting out a gasp of relief at the shot having missed him, Jake stooped to lift his sack of videos and DVDs' straightening to stare into the gun this time held by an angry tearful Ruby.

"I'll take that sack, Kid." she menaced him with a shake of her pistol, "and drop your own. Things might work out OK for me after all. Now it's all mine, and won't Canello pay for it as that gentleman is about to find out. Now hand over the sack, Kid."

"OK if that's how you…" While Ruby waited for Jake to finish the sentence Jake swung the sack, diverting the pistol away from him at the same time as he fired his own weapon. Moaning Ruby collapsed to the floor.

Jake sat in Ruby's car one hundred yards or so down the street from the burning house, the sound of hastily approaching fire engines ringing in his ears. He sat back, remorseless at what he had done, already anticipating Canello's gratitude when handing back the white sack of original videos.

Less than an hour later, Jake drew up outside Canello's condo, crossed the lawn and waited while the security guard, fortunately not the one he had previously attacked, came to unlock the glass door, Jake wondering as he did so why his boss did not have a security system installed, and not have everyone having to carry a key, but then again technology was not one of Canello's strong points.

In the elevator, Jake suddenly found himself strangely agitated, why he did not know, he had no reason to be. Had he not retrieved his boss's videos? If it was not that these were his only proof of his innocence he gladly would have let them burn in the house together with Ruby and Verdo. Jake stepped out of the elevator and almost directly into the arms of Len.

"Christ, Kid I thought you'd be miles away by this time. The boss is almost frantic. Everyone is keeping well out of his way. I have never seen him looking so angry. Why did you and Harry do it? You must have known you'd never get away with it." Len walked beside Jake a little away from the elevator. "He already has Harry down in the basement. He's also sent out for his girl Ruby, and you if you can be found. He's had all the bus, rail depots and airports covered."
"What about rented cars?" Jake smirked. "Surely he has not forgotten rented cars, seeing as he has my car keys."

"It's not funny, Kid, unless you have a few tricks up your sleeve, and I hope to God blackmail is not one of them, for even though you may have those damned fucking videos safely stashed away, in the end you'll be more than happy to let him have them, long before he has finished using that bat on you."

Jake had halted at the mention of Harry being in the basement. "Is the boss down there with Harry, Len?"
The man nodded. "Canello believes you and Harry are in it together. He also thinks this slut Ruby is part of it all, that's why he is having her brought in. And since he believes you have left your partner Harry to face the music by himself, he might just have already started on him," Len hesitated, "As a warm up."

Jake tried to hide his emotion when entering the cellar at the sight of Harry bound against the stone pillar, his bare chest running blood.

Canello eased up on his work, not yet aware of Jake's presence. Suddenly he turned at the sound.
"Well! Well! Well! What have we here? Come to see the show Kid?" Canello pointed his favourite weapon at Jake, ordering of the nearest man, "Frisk him. I no longer trust the son of a bitch."

Though he was aware of his face burning at the insult, spreading his arms gripping the white sack in one hand Jake allowed himself to be relieved of his weapon, his hatred for the man overpowering his fear.
"This is yours I believe Boss." Jake threw the white plastic sack at Canello's feet. "They are all there, including up to date DVD copies."
With one hand leaning on his baseball bat, Canello's face broke into a wide grin, one devoid of all warmth. "You think that by returning those," he pointed with his free

hand at the sack on the floor, it will save you this?"
Canello raised his bat to point at a moaning Harry.
"Guess so, sir, after you hear the full story."
"Which is, Kid?"
"Harry made a wax impression of the door key, then stole
the videos which he passed to his girl Ruby, who in turn
had a man called Verdo copy them into DVDs'. As I knew
where Ruby lived I had her take me to see this Verdo.
Cutting it short boss, after a little persuading I had him
hand over those," Jake pointed to the sack, "Unfortunately
after further discussions shall we say, the house caught fire
and with it both Verdo and Ruby. Although I believe the
fire department will log this as arson they'll find there's
nothing left to incriminate either you or me."

It was though a weight had lifted from Canello's shoulders
at knowing all the evidence either of the copied videos or
those who would have blackmailed him all the way to 'the
chair' were gone, and if the Kid was to be believed he had
once again saved his ass.

"You still say you had nothing to do with stealing the
videos, Kid?"
"If I had Mr Canello, do you think I'd blow the chance of
holding a few…" Jake hesitated, "dollars in my hand to
come back here to end up like Harry there."
Jake searched his coat pocket extracting Harry's cell
phone. "The proof of my not being involved is here in
Harry's phone. How he texted Ruby instructing her to get
to Verdo and have copies made."
Jake handed the cell phone to one of his guards to give to
Canello.

"OK, OK I believe you kid, though," he gave a wry smile, "I still would like to know how you made your escape." Jake's face lost it's tension. "Nothing doing Boss, nothing doing," he grinned.

Jake, the Kid, was surprised to find that he had slept most of the night without interruption and feeling better rose, showered, and made his way to the dining hall where most of Canello's men ate breakfast.

"When you're finished Kid, the Boss man wants to see us both in his study." Len informed him sitting down opposite. He drew the sugar bowl to him. "I think it's about Harry. What do you think will happen to him?" "Whatever it is, it's of his own making, he knew what the odds were before he started." Jake pushed his empty plate away. "Come on," he rose, "lets get it over with."

"Kid, Len," Canello solemnly greeted them, "It's time to deal with that shit Harry." He threw himself down in the chair behind his desk. "Kid, you and Len will take your buddy out to a place I do not wish to know. You, Kid will personally make it your business to deal with him. Is that clear?" Canello reached for his cigar box. "Make sure he is not found. OK?"
Jake's eyes opened wide in disbelief. "You want me to do the hit, Boss? I don't think I could do that. Not to Harry."
"Why Kid? What does the asshole mean to you? Unless of course you have been lying to me all along and were in it with him."
"You know I wasn't Boss, but Harry was my... was our buddy." Jake protested.

"A buddy who would blackmail me all the way to the Big House and even the chair itself."

Canello lit his cigar and blew smoke into the air. "You are his boss, as I am yours. It is your responsibility to see he receives what he deserves."

Canello sat back in his chair, blowing more smoke into the air. "Of course as boss you could delegate this responsibility to someone else, such as Len here."

Beside him Jake heard Len gulp in air, terrified by what this man was asking.

"No, Mr Canello, as you say I was Harry's boss and it's my responsibility to see he pays the price for what he has done."

Len drove the car with Jake by his side. Harry was with three of Canello's men, in the car following.

Jake stared unseeing out of the side window, heading for the same spot where ironically Harry had taught him to shoot.

"Are you going to go through with it, Kid? Ice, Harry?" Len asked as he changed gear and drifted in behind a truck.

"Guess so, unless you have a better idea."

Len jerked his head,"We could deal with those three behind us."

"Then what? Run with a rear view mirror up our ass for the rest of our lives? I don't think so, Len. And when, and I do mean when, Canello catches up with us he will have a field day swinging that fucking bat of his, with only a slim chance that he has a heart attack before he is through with us."

Len accelerated, but not too quickly, and Jake realised the man was giving him time to think of a way out.

"Look, Len, Harry knew what could happen to him, and for that matter Ruby, should things go pear shaped, which it did. He never gave either of us a second thought should his plan succeed, so no way am I going to risk my ass by helping him escape. End of story."

Angrily Len hit the steering wheel with the palm of his hands."Louis Canello surely picked the right guy for the job when he chose you over us, Kid." Len's perception being the last words they had between them until they reached their destination.

Jake stood by the bushes where, ironically Harry that first day had let him use the Glock, the same weapon he now carried. Escorted by two men while crossing the dusty ground Harry's eyes never left those of the boy he knew as the Kid. His chance at making it big time had failed, this was his reward, his last minutes on earth.

Beside the Kid, Len stood silent his mind awash with thoughts of how to save his buddy, or even that the Kid himself might not go through with it. But how could he not? To disobey Canello was to invite certain death, or at the very least a beating by that same sadistic boss.

Jake swallowed, his eyes as were Harry's on each others faces. Harry was closer now, closer for him to see the blood stains on his open white shirt, and the red weals on his bare chest where Canello had beaten him.

Harry's hands were tied behind his back. Jake swallowed again. At least the man would never know of Ruby's betrayal, of her plan to desert him for Verdo, she, as well as her lover, deserved to die the way they had. Now all this man had left was to kneel down while he shot him in the head from behind. That final moment while wondering what it would feel like when the shot came, then oblivion.

Harry held his head up high, his final act of defiance waiting for that final instruction to kneel. It never came, in a flash the Glock spat out one solitary shot and Harry felt silently to the ground.
Holstering the gun Jake walked past the body, at least he had spared the man the indignity of dying on his knees, and without turning shouted angrily to those nearest, "Bury him, bury him deep, and with decency, or you will keep him company if you don't."

The guy Jake knew as Mac slid into a seat opposite while he was in the act of finishing his breakfast in the usual dining room.
"You don't believe in playing it safe, man," he offered Jake a broad grin.
Jake put down his knife and fork neatly together on his empty plate. "Meaning?" he glared at the man.
Sill grinning Mac shrugged. "Playing around with the Boss's woman. You must think you're untouchable since you saved the Boss's ass."
"So? What's your point?"
"Not point Kid. Advice. Your messing with what belongs to the Boss might be misconstrued as baby snatching. You being just out of school so to speak."
Jake glared angrily at him. "Watch your mouth, slime ball, talk like that could earn you an early grave, and I know just the place."

"Sorry, buddy. No offence intended. However she sure as hell has the hots for you. Is being so young the attraction?"

A sudden feeling of uneasiness surged through Jake. Should this moron know of his and Belle's relationship it stood to reason it would be no time at all before Canello himself became aware of it. Perhaps he had gone too far. He had known for some time that he was playing with fire, the trouble was the fire was in his belly as well as a few more intimate places. He had never known a woman, a real woman before. Perhaps she was just teasing him. Jake bit back a bout of fear, was Belle setting him up for Canello? Did that man already know of their affair? Was this a way in justifying having him hit? It made sense, no one could blame the Boss, doing what he had to do, even though he had saved that man's ass on more than one occasion should that same man be hitting on his partner.

"You think I'm too young for her Mac? So far she has had no complaints. She's just teaching me a few things, giving me hands on experience so to speak." Jake forced a grin. "Depends where you put your hands good buddy." Mac rose. "All I can say is be sure you don't leave any fingerprints." Laughing, Mac left while a few tables away Len had heard every detail of the conversation.

When Louis Canello broke into his bedroom Jake had never seen him so angry.
"This time you have overdone it Kid. No one steals my woman and gets away with it."
Screaming, Belle hauled up the bed sheet to hide her nakedness and stumbled out of bed backing into a corner of the room.

Taken by surprise it was useless to mutter the well known adage of 'it's not what it looks like', for it was, Jake had no excuse either in his mind or lips to deny why Canello was glaring at him in the way he was.

Flourishing his bat menacingly, Canello advanced to the foot of the bed. "The trouble with you Kid is your head is now so swollen at saving my butt that you think you can do and take what you like. Maybe so, but not my woman, the buck stops well before there."

Canello took a tighter grip of his bat. "Now I am about to swell that head of yours even more. And I won't stop there! Nor will I stop until your own mother doesn't recognise you!"

Jake edged himself up the bed a little until the pillows were at his back. "I do not think so Mr Canello, something tells me you have used that bloody thing for the last time." Canello's eyes opened wide as if unable to believe that someone whom he had raised from off the street should have the audacity to speak to him, Louis Canello, in such a manner.

Towering over the naked figure in the bed, with the bat in full descent Canello's face twitched from anger to one of disbelief as the Glock in Jake's hand blew a hole in his chest, Belle's screams halting abruptly to one of sobbing as she sank to the floor.

Without troubling to hide his nakedness, Jake threw his legs over the edge of the bed, as sounds of hurriedly approaching chattering people led by Len arrived to look down in dismay at the motionless figure of their late leader lying on the floor.

Silently thanking Harry his late mentor for advising him always to sleep with the Glock under his pillow, Jake, aka the Kid muttered, "Now is the time to move on, and damned quick too."

Chapter 8

The bus drew away, Jake looked around him his first glances telling him that the town was not huge but sufficiently large for him to lose himself in. He took a few steps down the sidewalk finding the heat not overly oppressive deciding to find a coffee shop and make a few enquires regarding accommodation.

A few blocks further and he spied what he was after, a few minutes later and he was enjoying a cheeseburger at the counter.

The place was not busy. Jake waited until the young waitress passed again.

"Excuse me, please. I am new in town and was wondering if you knew a not too an expensive hotel?"

A twitch of her lip informed Jake that this girl was deep in thought or maybe the question was just too much for her.

"Not this side of town." She refilled his cup. "Best you go down town, cross the river, mister. You are sure to find something there."

"Thanks." Jake drew his cup to him. "Is it far?"

"Take a bus, an eight or a ten will drop you off where you want to go. Ask the driver."

Jake was almost at the bust stop when he noticed the hotel, it did not look so expensive perhaps he should find out.

The desk clerk greeted him politely and much to Jake's surprise and delight found that the rates were well within his means, at least for a little while.

His room was sparse, but then again what did he expect for a few bucks?

Showered Jake threw himself down on his bed. It was three weeks since he had taken Canello down. Three weeks from where he had gone from living in his own suite to this. Jake stared at the fading wallpaper. Where did he go from here? His money would not last for ever.

Jake rose and stood by the window looking down into the unfamiliar busy street. He'd have to find a job. Maybe shelf filling, Jake chuckled. Well at least it was honest and keep him hidden until the heat was off, for he was sure some of the syndicates men would be looking for him. No one could take down their leader and get away with it, especially not someone as young as the Kid. It was bad for morale.

Evening came and with it a sense of loss and the usual bustle around Canello, this and having no one to talk to: Even Len would do.
Jake rose from where he'd lain on top of the bed, finding his room depressive. Time to take a look at his new town, and find an inexpensive place to eat.

Jake found one. Only having just finished his meal when aware of two men standing by his table.
"Boss sent us to take you back to his place."
Jake cursed at having left the Glock in his room not wanting to be stopped by cops asking questions as to his reason for being in town, something that some town cops did with unfamiliar faces.
Silently Jake allowed himself to be led to a waiting car, angry at having been found so quickly.

The car ride took him to what he understood to be the upper class district of the town, halting not in front of a

mansion or similar building but a small but well kept block
of apartments to find his car door opened for him and
politely requested to follow his two new acquaintances.

Jake walked through the front door into a large semi circle
foyer, and quietly escorted to one of two elevators.
The elevator rose and Jake eyed the panel above the doors,
his attempt at conversation failing as the doors slid open
and he stood looking directly into a well furnished room.

At the sound of the doors sliding open a large man of
around fifty rose from the sofa, switching off the TV set as
he stood to greet them.
"Who the hell is this Thomas?" the big man roared angrily
at the sight of Jake.
"Simon, Pa, the one we had to meet in the Royale."
The big man took a few angry steps across the room. "This
is not Simon, you jerk."
"No sir, my name is Jake Crawford," Jake offered in a
voice intended to sound bemused.
Clearly these bonzos had picked up the wrong guy, and if
so he had to play the innocent young man.

"Did neither of you think to ask this young gentleman his
name?" The big man asked, his voice softer, attempting to
offer Jake an apologetic smile.
"He was sitting at the table where you told us he'd be,
Boss." Thomas's accomplice explained in the same
frightened tone Jake had heard so many times from one of
Canello's men when found to have got things wrong.
"I am truly sorry about this, eh...Mr Crawford, my son was
supposed to escort a Mr Simon back here as we had some

business to discuss." The big man apologised again, this time his smile a little broader.

Jake nodded, clearly the boss man was embarrassed if not inwardly seething at this inconvenience. He would not like to be in their shoes when he got them alone.

The big man drew back a little. "Now that we have probably ruined your evening would you care to join me in a drink before you leave? Just to show there are no bad feelings."

Unhesitatingly, remembering the character he was playing Jake answered, "Thank you but no, sir, I don't drink." adding a little quieter, "Perhaps when I am a bit older."

"Well said." the Boss beamed, turning to Thomas. "Did you hear that son? Maybe you should take a lesson from Mr Crawford here?"

And by the look on 'son's' face Jake thought he had not made a friend there.

"Well perhaps another time?" The Boss put a hand on Jake's shoulder guiding him towards the elevator.

"When he's older," Jake heard Thomas chuckle.

It was as Jake drew near the elevator that he saw the photograph on the wall, swiftly his eyes swept to the opposite wall well away from the offending photo, for there in a gilded frame was a portrait of this man here with no other than Louis Canello. beside him.

No one appeared to notice his slight hesitation, especially Thomas and his buddy. His glance had been no more than that a curious visitor would have given.

"Once again my apologies for this little misunderstanding" the boss man said from behind him.

"My son will drive you wherever you wish to go."
Jake turned a little. "No need sir, but back to the restaurant would be good."
"She will have gone by now," Thomas chuckled.
"If it was a she," the other said with a burst of laughter.
"Enough you two!" the boss rebuked them angrily.
Still playing the part of the innocent young man Jake's blush was not contrived, though inwardly seething and wishing more than ever he'd be packing his Glock.

The entire journey back to the restaurant Jake sat in the back of the car silently enduring the young men's attempt at humour and innuendos. At last the journey over, Jake stepped out of the car and somehow appeared to meekly walk away, the laughter loud at his back.
Jake kept walking, *"Next time I meet you two, you will find a different Jake Crawford," he promised himself.*

Now this next step was what to do. With the Boss man knowing Canello, there was the possibility that the word was out to look for him. Fortunately the boss had not in least suspected him of being the 'Kid'.

By the time Jake had reached his hotel he had finalised his plan. Tomorrow he'd withdraw money from the ATM and be on his way. Once he knew his next destination he'd have the remainder of his savings transferred there, something he had intended for this fair city.

Inwardly Jake was seething at having discovered that the bank where the bulk of his savings was lodged while working for Canello was closed for the holiday weekend, now there was nothing left other than to wait until it reopened on Monday then be on his way.

Jake entered the department store. He'd withdrawn enough from the ATM to pay for his hotel and buy a T-shirt jeans and a few toiletries, with a little left over to last him until Monday and be on his way out of town.

Having bought himself a small case, Jake approached the good looking girl at the clothes department. "Excuse me miss, where can I obtain a pair of jeans?"
The assistant smiled at Jake's politeness. "To your right there sir. Is there anything that I can do for you?"
Jake hesitated. "T-shirts?"
"Yes, I believe I can help you there. If you care to follow me."
Anywhere, Jake thought, and at the double.
The girl halted at a rail of hanging shirts." Has sir any particular colour in mind?"
"Sir thought about something in blue," Jake beamed, his present dilemma momentarily forgotten.
Having chosen two shirts Jake looked on while his obliging young assistant wrapped up his purchases, wishing he had more to spend and delay the inevitable departure from this lovely young creature.
"Cash or card, sir," the girl asked.
Jake swallowed, his mind still on the girls looks."Oh cash."
"I have not seen you in the store before. Are you from out of town?"
Jake handed over the banknotes. "Yes just passing through."
The girl handed Jake his receipt. "Pity."
Jake's eyes opened wide. Was this an invitation to stay? "Pity?"

"Yes I thought perhaps you'd be looking for work. We need someone down in the storeroom. Only temporary of course but it could lead to something better."

Jake's brain was giving him reasons for accepting the offer, while another part was warning him to be on his way before some big shot whom he believed by the brief glance at the name on the foyer door last night was called Monaro found out that Jake Crawford was indeed the Kid and could still well be in town. Or was Monaro completely ignorant to this fact?
The words were out of Jake's mouth before he was aware of it. "Well I could do with a few extra bucks until my money is transferred here."

The girl smiled knowingly thinking this guy has not two cents to rub together. "Swell, if you care to wait here, I can speak with Mr Dobson. He's our store manager. What's your name by the way?"
"Jake Crawford."
"I am Jill, she gave Jake the same smile that had instantly won him over."

Jake eyes followed his new friend as she left. Was he being a fool thinking he could come on to this girl when she probably had men falling at her feet. And if he listened to reason were women or at least one woman not the reason for his present circumstances? Jake exhaled. Well he was only young *once,* and in his business there was every chance he'd never be old *once,* so better to make the best of it while he could.

Jake returned from his interview with 'Mr Dobson' a pompous asshole if ever he saw one, and should circumstances have differed would have found a Glock up one of his nostrils.

"Well how did it go, Jake?"

"I start tomorrow. You must be hard up for staff."

"We are."

"Thanks for the compliment," Jake pretended to be insulted.

Jill laughed. "Oh I did not mean it that way."

"OK. You're forgiven."

"I got you these in anticipation that you got the job."Jill pointed to the tie and two white shirts on the counter. "You are entitled to staff discount, now that you are one of us." She appeared amused by Jakes click of his teeth.

"Yea, old stuck- up Dobson down there said I had to look presentable whilst on the floor." Jake pretended to be pushing a trolley, "Even when..."

Jill held a hand over her mouth. "Don't make me laugh, Jake, or it will be me looking for work."

Jake, reluctant to leave waited until Jill had attended to a customer. He could ask her out, with the sad line that he was all alone in this new big city, except circumstances might lead him having to leave sooner than he expected and if so he'd need all the money he had at present in the ATM.

Behind the counter Jill walked to where Jake stood. I don't suppose you have a place to stay as yet?"

"Nope. But the girl in the coffee bar told me there are places downtown."

"Yea. Try Mrs Greer at number 17 Elm Street. There's sure to be a vacancy there. If you leave now you can catch a number eight bus, ask..."

"I know,"Jake grinned,"ask the driver where to drop me off."

The driver did drop Jake off at the appointed stop and he quickly found number17 Elm Street.

It was a neat two storey house, with an equally neat front lawn. Jake rang the doorbell and stood back. All this was far from his so recent lifestyle that for a moment he thought he'd awaken from a dream.

However his dream was short lived when he found himself asking the friendly lady who answered the door if in fact she had a vacancy as the nice girl in the apartment store had hinted that there might be.

"You must be Jake. Jill said you might call," She smiled broadly at him. "I have one room upstairs that might suit you, Would you care to see it first?"

Already anticipating that he would, Jake followed the lady. "My name is Sarah," she opened the bedroom door wide. "This is it."

Jake stepped into the neat clean tidy room picking out a TV, shower, small dressing table and single bed besides two cosy looking chairs. He turned to face his host. "This is swell. I'll take it."

"Jill said you may be short of cash right now since you are newly arrived in town, so we will come to some arrangement later in the week, should you find this OK."

Normally Jake would have found himself insulted by the insinuation that he was short of cash, but in this instance he understood the lady's intention.

"Swell, lady, I hope to pay you as soon as I can, hopefully before my first pay check."

Sarah nodded. "Jill said you were starting work in her store tomorrow. Let's hope you like it."

She stepped to the door. "We dine at 7, that should give you an hour to change." she hesitated. "Of course you might like to dine out?"

"No, I think that would suit me very well."

"Good...Jake, see you downstairs at 7."

Jake wiped the steam off the bathroom mirror drawing a hand over his shaven jaw, now glad at having picked up a packet of disposable razors, at the same time surprised by the sound of a car drawing up.

To show good manners Jake waited a couple of minutes after 7 before going down for dinner.

The small intimate dining room that he entered smelled of the same brand of furniture polish that his mother used, bringing back long forgotten memories of his childhood.

"Take a seat Jake. Chicken soup all right for you?" the lady of the house greeted him cheerily.

"Yes ma'am that would be swell."

"Good, then I will leave you for a moment," and as she left Jake eased himself into a chair, a familiar voice taking him by surprise.

"So you found us?"

Jake's head flew up. "You! You,"

Grinning at the look of surprise on Jake's face, Jill sat down opposite him.

"Why did you not offer me a ride? I could have waited until the store closed. Saved me from asking...."

She halted him, happy that he was here. "From asking the bus driver where to drop you off."

Suddenly serious Jill continued. "I thought it might embarrass you if I was there should mother's place not be to your liking."

Jake looked around him, "What's not to like, more so knowing you'll be here."

"You think my being here will make a difference?" she asked mischievously.

"Sure does," Jake replied seriously. "With you here I can bum a ride into work."

"You will be required to wear a dust coat when you deliver goods to the various departments, Crawford. When you have done so, load that trolley and take it to hardware," Dobson snapped at him.

Jake eyed the goods. "Sure. Somehow I did not think it would be to ladies wear."

Nearby a storeman laughed adding to Dobson's severity. "*Now,* Crawford. And less of the wisecracks. Or you will find yourself out on the street."

"I know," Jake tittered, "before I can say panties."

"You have lost a friend there, buddy," the amused storeman crossed to shake Jake's hand, after Dobson had left. "They call me Jim."

"Jake."

"Pleased to meet you Jake. Say, hows I help you load this lot before Napoleon comes back."

"Is that what you call him?" Jake addressed the back of his new friend bending to load the trolley.

"I thought Little Caesar would be nearer his style."

Jim straightened. "Best he does not hear, Jake. No sense of humour has our little fearless leader."

Jake was singing the tune 'Who will Buy My Sweet red roses?' clowning his way past Jill's counter pushing his trolley.

Jill eyed him with mock despair. "Hardware is not on this floor, Jake."

"I know but you are."

"Honestly Jake you will hold the record for shortest serving member of staff if Mr Dobson catches you on this floor."

"He won't." A bucket fell off the trolley quickly followed by a saucepan. Jake heaved a sigh. "Then again he just might."

Jill burst out laughing already having given up on this new friend of hers, Jake retrieving his goods and hastily making for the elevator.

"Do you always live dangerously, Jake Crawford?" Jill asked whilst driving back home.

Jake could have laughed at that. *If only you knew,* he thought, deliberately turning his head to look out of the car's side window.

Intentionally ignoring the question, instead he answered. "Swell that you gave me a ride into the store in the morning considering that I begin work a half hour before the store opens."

"No problem, it gives me more time to set up my counter before the doors open."

"And customers like me coming rushing in to make your day." Jake mused.

"Something like that. But you are by no means the worst."

"Touche," Jake answered and sat back in his seat.

"Nice parkland,"Jake commented his eyes sweeping the trees to his right.

"We like it, Mom and I, "Jill explained. "Dad brought me here from when I was tiny."

Jake waited.

"He died two years ago." Jake thought it best not ask how. Jill went on. "We miss him so much. Mom has been wonderful, she converted the spare room...your room so that we could rent it out."

"And has it worked?" Jake asked. "The renting out part I mean."

"Not really. You are the first this month. But it helps pay expenses."

Jake's heart was pounding, the very thought of being with this girl excited him more than he could ever say.

Impulsively he swung her round holding her close.

Jill gently pushed him away. "No Jake, don't spoil it."

Embarrassed at her having made him feel like a schoolboy again, he drew back. "Sorry that was quite ungentlemanly of me."

She saw the hurt in his eyes. "No. It is my fault Jake. I do like you. Only," she halted. "I have a boyfriend, his name is Alan. He is a technical engineer and is often out of town." Then hurriedly, anxious to appease. "He will be back Monday."

Why he felt so disappointed Jake did not know, when after all there was no reason that a girl as lovely as Jill should not have a boyfriend. And if she had not, how could *he* ever fill that role?

He who was nothing other than a murderer, a killer who would never be anything else, forever hunted by the law. Whatever he might like to think of himself he was a gangster, and gangsters never could live their lives as honest citizens: Honest citizens such as Jill and her mother. His fate had been decided a long time ago, even before he had met Louis Canello, and all the way back to Irish Paddy. The wall between him and honest good living folk may be unseen but it was there, a wall high as it was wide, never to be scaled by such characters as himself.

Jake left his thoughts to look up at the sky. "I best get you home. It will be dark soon and you don't want to catch a cold and give it to Alan."

Jill gave a little smile at the boy's attempt to lighten the situation. "No I suspect not. Nor do I want to sneeze all over you on the way to work."

"No, your driving is not at all to be sneezed at Jill."

"Ha ha," Jill mocked. "Perhaps you would care to walk to work?"

"No the bus would be OK, the driver would let me know when to drop me off."

Next day Jake was late returning from the bank at lunchtime, a fact that did not go unnoticed by the ever imperious Mr Dobson.

"You are late, Crawford."

"Well spotted, Mr Dobson," Jake replied cheekily.

"Do not be impertinent young man or I will show you the door."Dobson retorted.

Jake decided not to reply that he very well knew what a door looked liked having used them on several occasions. His restraint all the more admirable by the fact that his money having been transferred to the local bank, there now was no reason for his remaining here to listen to a puffed up buffoon whose reign stretched no further than the door of his storeroom. *If you only knew, Dobson what I am, you'd be shaking in your shoes.* And now that Jill was beyond his reach, and for that matter always had been there was no further reason for him staying.

Jake stared out of his bedroom window. He had enjoyed being here, even if only for a short time.
Of course knowing Jill had made all the difference.
Jake was about to turn away when the car drew up outside the house and a jauntily dressed man holding a bouquet of flowers got out and swaggered towards the door his expression saying *I am the son of Tony Monaro so don't mess with me.*
"Thomas Monaro!" Jake swore at the egotistical figure.
"How come you are here?" For a moment he could not believe what he was thinking, surely Thomas Monaro was not Jill's beau? No he could not be, not someone like Monaro who was like himself nothing better than a gangster. Jill would never allow herself to be mixed up with someone like Monaro. Then he remembered Jill's boyfriend was called Alan. Then why the hell was Thomas Monaro here?

Jake could not see Monaro at the door from his bedroom.
Should he go down and confront the man?
Scolding himself for being so stupid Jake drew back. At this stage it was best that the crook was not aware of his presence.
At first the sounds were muffled then as they grew louder Jill's angry voice reached him where he now stood at the top of the stairs.
"No thank you Mr Monaro, as I have told you before I have a fiancee, so will you please leave me alone!"
"You do know who you are speaking to?" Thomas Monaro's voice was seethingly cold.

"Of course, I do you have told me often enough. So please take yourself and your flowers and leave." The firm request, followed by the sound of a door banged shut.

"You really did tell him, Jill." Jake trotted down the stairs. Sill angry, Jill glared up at him. "He will not take no for an answer, Jake. He thinks because his Pa is a big shot he can have what he likes," she choked, "but never me Jake. Not in a million years."
"Has he bothered you before?"
Jill nodded. "He tried to come on to me the first time he came into the store. Then again a couple of weeks ago. I did not know he knew where I lived. Must have followed me in his car."
"Or had some one else do it for him."

Now Jake was worried. Did this man know he also lived here? And if so who did he know him as, Jake Crawford or The Kid?
"Better watch out for him, Jill, his kind are used to having their own way, and take unkindly to being rejected.
"Well this guy better get used to it, for this is as far as it gets." Jill replied angrily.

Lying in his bed that night, Jake cursed what had happened between Thomas Monaro and Jill, now he'd have to change his plan to leave, for as sure as God made little green apples the guy would not leave it there. His reputation would not allow it, nor could his pride. But what to do that was the question. Jake yawned and turned on his side. He best wait for the dandy to make his next move.

Jake turned hearing Jill's cheery voice call up the stairs to him, "Jake, come down and meet Alan."

He did not want to meet this man who had Jill for his own. Had things been different, no make that if *he* had been different then he'd have fought for this lovely girl, but as it was?

"Jake, I should like you to meet Alan my fiancee," Jill's eyes bright with pride and happiness.

Jake forced a smile and held out his hand. "Glad to know you Alan."

The young man shook the proffered hand. "Likewise, I'm sure. Jill has told me a lot about you."

"Lots?" Jake's smile was genuine. "In so short a time."

"All good pal, I can assure you."

"Good judge of character has your gal, Alan."

"Right you two, cut the mutual admiration society." Jill pretended to be serious. "Should you still go for that walk, Alan Millar, we best get started before it gets dark."

From his bedroom window Jake watched the couple walk hand in hand into the parkland, so angry and envious of the man that he wanted to run down and wrench him away from the girl he had fallen in love with.

He turned away from the window no longer able to watch the happy scene below.

Would it always be like this? A window to look through at happy people, but never a part of them or their world. Should he in time find love it had to be one from his own world, someone like himself, but never one as happy and innocent as Jill Greer.

At first Jake was not aware of the sound of the near hysterical screams until he turned down the volume of his

TV. The sound came from downstairs Jake jumped up and ran to the door and down the stairs into the hallway, where Jill, beside herself in her mother's arms was screaming that Alan had been attacked and lay badly beaten in the parkland.

Jake tore Jill away from her mother, forcing her to face him.

"Who did it, Jill?" he shouted at the hysterical girl, shaking her by the shoulders, already knowing the answer.

Sobbing, Jill stared at him with uncomprehending eyes. He shook her again. "Come on Jill. Did you see who did this to Alan?"

This time the girl nodded through her sobs, "One of Monaro's men. Thomas stood by and watched.

He just stood there laughing, Jake, all the while Alan was being beaten. I tried to stop him but he just kept pushing me away. I will have to call the police."

Jake gripped her shoulders tighter. "No, Jill phone for an ambulance, guide them to where Alan is, but no cops. Not just yet, not with the Monaros' involved."

"But Jake…"

"No Jill not yet leave it to me. Now do as I say."

"I will phone for an ambulance, Jake" Sarah held her daughter. "Go to Alan Jill. Tell me where exactly Alan is and I will tell the ambulance men where they should go."

"Good, Mrs Greer." Jake turned quickly for the stairs. "But remember both of you, if you value your lives, no cops. Get it? Now Jill can I borrow tour car?"

Jake sped the little car to where he hoped Thomas Monaro and his buddy would be, and that was his father's apartment. He was wrong no car sat outside the apartment. Jake cursed, he could not have been too far behind. True he had taken a wrong turn or two having only been here once.

Patiently Jake sat back in his seat, strangely calm at once again being on his side of the fence: dealing with the type of people he knew and understood.
He glanced at his watch in what was left of the daylight. Where were those two? Raving it up somewhere, enjoying having beaten up a decent young man.

Jake understood the logic of Monaro junior. Now that he had finally realised that he could never make it with Jill, he'd make sure that no one else would. This, Jake feared was a warning to Alan which if he ignored would be his last.

Jake had sat in the little car for over an hour before the black sedan drew up. In an instant he was out and running the few yards to where the black car was parked, catching the driver with only one foot on the sidewalk, hitting him with the Glock with the full force of his hatred.
Again Jake brought the gun down on the unsuspecting driver's head, then his jaw, then again the face before turning the weapon in the direction of his passenger, at the same time relieving his victim of his weapon."Do not even think about it Monaro. slide your piece out gently, or daddy will not have an heir to leave his crooked business to."
Hatred in his eyes, Thomas stared, silently mouthing, "You."
"Yea, little Jake the faggot Crawford." Jake seethed. "Now open your door and take me to your leader." Jake smiled.

"Him?" Jake wagged the Glock at the moaning near unconscious man, "we can safely leave here."

At the entrance to the apartment Thomas punched in the code to open the door. "Pa is not going to like this, Crawford, he will have you wearing cement shoes before the night is over."

Jake drove the Glock into Thomas's back. "I think you are right, buddy but it's you and your sidekick he will not be happy with, not me."

The elevator clomped to a halt and Jake pushed the man into the room.

Monaro senior looked up from his evening newspaper. "What the hell?"

Jake stepped from behind his prisoner. "I brought your son back Mr Monaro, it is not safe to have him out at this hour."

Throwing down his newspaper Monaro rose. "Well, well, if it is not the timid Mr Crawford."

"Not so timid," Jake waved his gun. "And the name is The Kid, the late Louis Canello's kid to be precise."

Gino Monaro's expression clearly showed that he did not believe this young man, then again this young man was standing here in his house with a gun expertly held on him and his son.

"You took down Louis Canello? Why?"

Jake shrugged. "Lets say I did not fancy the idea of being crippled by a maniac wielding a baseball bat."

To Jake's relief and surprise Gino Monaro threw his head back laughing. "I can see your point...Kid. That's why he and I went our separate ways."

Now it was Jake's turn to be surprised. "But the photograph?"

Gino grinned. "Oh, you saw that one." He pointed to the wall. "Taken a long while ago. We no longer do business together."

Morano moved a little towards his drinks cabinet, Jake following the movement with the Glock.

"I should not do anything stupid Mr Monaro, there is no need." In full control of the situation Jake relaxed a little. "It is your son I have the beef with."

Gino made a face. "Why my son? What has he done to offend you, Kid?"

"There is a gal he wants, a decent gal I might add, whose panties he should like to get into, only that, no love involved. Your son, probably like yourself will not take no for an answer, it hurts the Monaro pride. He could walk away, find someone more...co operative, shall we say. The problem is Mr Monaro she wants nothing to do with your son as she already has a finance." Jake halted. "You get my drift?"

Monaro senior nodded. "Then he should walk away."

"Could do, had not your moron of a son not have his sidekick rearrange the boyfriend's face, and probably some other bits and pieces."

For once Gino Monaro looked perturbed. "Christ Thomas what were you thinking of?" he exploded.

His son bowed his head studying the floor, a floor he no doubt wished at that moment would open up and let him disappear.

"Should this young woman call the cops and identify you or Sol we are all up the shit creek."

Jake held up his free hand. "It may not come to that Mr Monaro. I think I have convinced her and her mother not to call the cops at this time. However," Jake halted for affect. "There might well be some compensation to the injured party?"

Gino nodded rapidly. "Will be done."

"And no further visits from Thomas here?"

Again Gino nodded.

"Good, Mr Monaro that concludes our business."

Holstering the Glock Jake turned for the elevator.

"You never know, Mr Monaro you and I might do business some day." Then to a nervous Thomas. "I'll not stay for that drink you are only too willing to offer me, Thomas." Adding at the elevator door. "Perhaps when I am a little older. OK?"

At first Jill could not understand what all the commotion was about around the elevator. Curiosity having got the better of her she quickly rounded her counter to join the laughing crowd gathered there.

"What's going on?" she asked, using a shoulder to help her better see what all the fuss was about around the open elevator door.

Then she saw it. The trolley with the figure of a man strapped to it, a lipstick painted face, the body attired in a woman's dress howling with indignation and that face was no other than a humiliated Mr Dobson shouting that was Jake Crawford who had done this to him.

Smothering a laugh Jill slowly walked back to her counter. Dobson was right it could be no one other than Jake, the letter and the two thousand dollars she had found in his room having confirmed this.

As it was still ten minutes to opening time, she took out Jake's letter from her purse, reading the few words that he had written.

It began;

Dear Jill, I think it better that I leave, even to pacify a certain Mr Dobson? It was swell being with you and your mother and having me in both your lives even for so short a time. There is no need to worry, a certain Thomas Monaro will no longer worry you. And I advise you to accept the sum he offers in compensation as regards what he had done to Alan, who when we visited him in hospital is well on his way to recovery, and who despite his injuries even now looks more handsome than me.

You have made a good choice there. I have also left a few dollars which as well as my keep, will also help for all the trouble I might have caused.

Life is strange, so who is to say that we might not meet again, maybe when you are Mrs Millar, mother to several little Millars. Who can tell?

God bless you all I will always love you. Alan is a lucky man.

PS. I left early by bus, (the driver again was most helpful) before the storeroom was open to say my farewells to dear Mr Dobson.

Yours ever,

Jake Crawford.

Jill stifled a little sob."And God bless you Jake Crawford or whoever you really are, certainly not timid Jake Crawford.

Chapter 9

"Please fasten your seat belts. We will be landing shortly."
The captain's voice brought Jake Russo back to the
present. Louis Canello was now only one man in his past.
His taking the man the way he did when only twenty two
had earned him a fearful reputation. Some never quite
knowing whether he was a bright young man to do such a
thing to someone as prominent a figure as Canello or on
the other hand just quite stupid. Whatever their verdict he
had prospered on that one incident.

To have taken over from Canello was of course plainly out
of the question. Those old men at his former boss's film
show would have seen to that, his demise being their only
solution.
Immediately following the Canello killing he had left the
State, with no one at the time knowing where.

Those he had left behind had somehow shown it to have
been an accident, none in that business wishing it to be
anything otherwise in the face of the Law. Again only a
few, if any at all, knew him by anything other than the Kid.

Jake stared out of the window. If he was to be honest with
himself that is how it had really started, how he had made
his living even up to the death of his mother and his Uncle
Jim, both only a few months apart. Now he was alone, then
again, he conceded he really always had been.

Buckling his safety belt Jake sat back in his seat, telling
himself he must concentrate, although he had gone over
his plan a hundred times.

He had chosen nine men to return Jack Kane's casinos to him, three of whom sat in this very plane the others in two other separate flights, each due to arrive from early to late evening when their presence should not be so easily noticed in the hubbub of either establishment.

It was two hours later before Jake brought his team together in a small back room a few streets away from the nearest casino. Gathered around the pool table, Jake began. "You Victor will take Josh and Will to the Mayfield, wait for the call on my cell phone from the Lakeland to say all has gone to plan. You on no account will make a move until you hear from me. OK?" His question was followed by a chorus of understanding. "Good. Then get yourselves all into position. I'll head up to the Lakeland and pay Mister Jeff Blake, Kane's previous manager, a visit and his explanation for double crossing his boss."

A few laughed at his joke. Jake he went on. "There has to be no gun play, we don't want to alarm paying guests." He halted to emphasise his point, "*Our* paying guests, or they soon will be. Should you find it necessary to call out to one another use the code name I have given you all. Any questions?" When no one spoke, Jake continued, "you are all sure that you know your job? If not, now is the time to speak up." Again when no one spoke, Jake ended. "Then let's do it."

Jake entered the Lakeland casino to the clatter of poker machines, the murmur of excited players at the various tables, amid squeals of delight above the rattling sound of dropping coins from some lucky players.

Above the crystal chandeliers and bright lights sat a line of sober faced individuals staring into their computer screens monitoring every move of those below, searching for the slightest sign of fraud, from either Croupier or player.

Absently Jake put a few coins into a nearby poker machine his eyes on the long glass panel above. A sudden scream of delight gave him the perfect opportunity to make his way to the door leading to the back stairs, one of his men close behind, another two heading for the elevator where they would again meet on the third floor.

Jake halted on the stairwell landing of the third floor, nodding reassurance at the man who had followed him before opening the door into the empty corridor now strangely quiet after the din downstairs. The elevator door opened to emit two more of his men.

Although Jake had already studied the plan many times, he thought it best to follow one of the men who had previously worked here, and therefore knew the outlay of the casino better than he, who led him to a door at the end of the corridor.

Without a word passing between them, Jake threw open the door bursting into the room.
Two men leapt to their feet at this rude interruption, one reaching inside his coat before a wave from Jake's Glock quickly dissuaded him.
"What the hell?" The other one stammered.
"I take it you're the boss here?" Jake asked. Beside him his guide confirmed that he was.

"I have come at Jack Kane's request to have you relieved as manager and have his property rightfully restored." Jake had said it almost flippantly.

The little man's eyes darted angrily. "These premises belong to Mr Peter Sagan. Legally I might add."

"You might, Mr Blake," Jake smirked, "but it won't do you a mite good. So let's cut out the shit and come with me."

"Where?"

"To the Mayfield to inform your staff that their premises are now under new management."

Jake swung to his men. "You two remain here. You know what to do. The rest of our boys are already in place. Make sure you find the ones who dumped Jack Kane to work for Sagan, deal with them quietly. The others have the choice to remain here in their present position, or look for alternative employment."

"What you are implying is impossible, Mr…."

"Never mind the name, just spit out what you're aiming at." Jake was already irritated by Kane's previous manager.

Unperturbed, Blake went on. "I have managed both of Jack Kane's casinos for the best part of five years. Five years in which Mr Kane has well prospered by my expertise. So how in the hell does he expect to replace me with someone who knows nothing of this business? Or even close."

"I think Jack has already figured that one out. Someone he can trust, not someone who betrays him when a better illegal offer comes along."

"Illegal!" Blake fumed. "Sagan himself showed me the papers of transfer. Even if they were false what could I do with a gun at my head?"

"Sadly, this is what you are about to find out, Mr ex-manager." Jake answered softly.

The expression on Blake's face turned from one of anger to one of fear. While the now whimpering man beside him, having accepted this also as his own fate slumped down in his chair.
"You cannot just kill me, not after what I have done for Mr Kane. Just let me go. I promise he will never see me again."
"You got that last bit right, mister," Jake smirked.

Jake had ever despised anyone who pleaded for his life, especially those who were evil enough to have killed or wronged someone, especially a friend.
That this man here had betrayed his friend's trust was enough for him. Blake had betrayed Jack Kane once, and could easily do so again should the occasion arise. As to the man beside him, he had never worked for Kane, therefore could be sent on his way when the time came, but for now he was happy to watch him squirm.

Their business over at the Lakeland, in company with Jake and another, the little casino manager was escorted to his second casino, where most of the same business was more or less re-enacted, leaving Jake's men with only the betrayers to deal with.
Jack Kane had regained his casinos.

Sipping Southern Comfort on the return flight, Jake mulled over the time it had taken to conduct Jack Kane's business for him. He had been in Kane's city now for close on three months and was no closer to the hit Kane had promised to pay for, the hit on Peter Sagan. Every day brought him closer to discovery by either someone like Sagan himself or Faye Dewer, the latter, a worry in itself.

Sure he had the hots for her, but every encounter made it that little bit more awkward, sometime and he guessed not so far off she was sure to ask a little more about his life, and when she did what was he to tell her other than lies? At least Kane had got his casinos back, perhaps this would keep him happy until he thought up a plan to deal with Peter Sagan.

Alex Ferris pushed the eldest boy into the room, his other two smaller companions receiving a similar fate.
"Caught them stealing again Pa, though we warned them what would happen if they did."
Standing with his back to the empty fireplace Nat Ferris studied the young culprits.
"You!" he pointed his unlit cigar at the tallest of the trio. "What's your name?"
"Rudoski sir, Harry Rudoski" the boy answered lamely, his eyes on the carpeted floor.
"And these other two delinquents?"
"My brothers, sir."
"Not much of a role model are you, Harry Rudoski?"
Without looking up the boy's answer was scarcely audible. "No sir."
"Any more like you at home?" Alex Ferris asked, amused by the boys fear and discomfiture.
"So what do think we should do with them Pa? This is the fourth time they've picked on old Wallis. Perhaps they don't know the old man works for us."
"What was it you stole this time boys?" At their silence, Nat asked again, this time more sharply, "I won't ask again

boys. You are already in deep shit with me, do not make it worse for yourselves."

"A silver plate and cup," Harry murmured.

"Why those?"

"We need to eat, mister," the second brother answered angrily taking a step towards his tormentor, with all the defiance he could muster.

"You cannot eat silver you stupid little shit." Alex mocked giving the rebellious little boy a clip on the ear and sending him back into line.

"No sir," Harry conceded, "but it sure as hell can fill your belly for a while."

Although amused by the logic, Nat refrained from smiling. "Good thinking, but your mistake was One: getting yourselves caught, and Two, stealing from me. Now you must pay the penalty by paying the price."

Nat gestured to the third man in the room. "Him."

"Yes Mr Ferris."

Following his boss's orders the man Jeb hauled the youngest boy to him, Harry flying to his brother's rescue before a well aimed punch from Alex Ferris knocked him to the floor.

Struggling to his feet Harry yelped at the man,"Leave him you fucking big moron!"

"Now Harry, language, language," Nat taunted him, "Your brother will now pay the price for your poor leadership."

His eyes wide with fear Harry followed what was happening to Joel his nine year old brother.

"Don't whip him mister, it's me who is to blame."

"Whip him, Harry? We don't mean to whip him. We only want to teach him… you all a lesson, that however great or small your intended heist might be, no one, and I repeat no one, steals from Nat Ferris."

His warning over, Nat nodded to Alex and Jeb who were holding down the screaming struggling little boy one hand held outright on the table palm upwards.
What happened next had Alex Ferris almost wrenching up as Jeb sliced off the tiny finger, throwing it laughing to the distraught Harry, with, "Here kid, a souvenir from your brother."

"We cannot say who did this to you Joel." Harry had his arm around the whimpering injured little boy's shoulder. "Doc Gus will know what do. Don't cry," he encouraged him as all three brothers ran up the busy side street.

At length they reached 4th Street running up the steps to a house where they knew the man known as Doc Gus lived. The man himself opened the door to the thunderous banging of three overwrought children, one of whom had his hand wrapped in a none too clean handkerchief. Without speaking Doc Gus stood aside while they rushed past him into his front room.
Harry turned on his heel. "Can you fix him doc, I'll pay you later, I promise." The boy's words were rushed.

Calmly the old man unwrapped the dirty handkerchief, holding the tiny hand in his own, knowing better than to ask as to the cause. "This is going to sting little fella, but it's got to be done, if you don't want it infected."
"Do it, please Doc." Harry pleaded holding his little brother and swearing under his breath to pay back the

monster Nat Ferris for what he had done to his nine year
brother, however long it should take.

The uniformed police officer put his head round the office
door, "There's a guy at the desk wants to talk with
someone regarding the Mary Dewer case, says he has
some info that might help."
"We'll see to it, sergeant. Take him up to the interviewing
room, we'll speak with him there." Sam Andrews, rose.
"Hope it's the break we have been looking for," his partner
too rose, slipping into his coat.

The man the officers hoped would give them a new lead in
the now three month old case was about thirty, clean
shaven, with short black curly hair. Andrew's guessed him
to be around six feet.
"Now Mr...?" Andrews looked at the sheet in his hand.
"Roberts, Jon."
"Roberts," Andrews smiled an apology, sitting down
opposite him.
"I am Detective Lieutenant Sam Andrews, and this is my
partner Detective Sergeant Joe Sims."
Introductions over Andrews began, "I believe you have
some information that might assist us in the Mary Dewer
case. Is this correct?"
Roberts cleared his throat. "Not quite officer." He halted at
Andrews change of expression. "Well not exactly. I
mean…. information about Arnie."
"Arnie?" Sims asked furrowing his brows.
Roberts nodded. "Yea you know, Arnie Reiter, the one
they say killed that girl a few weeks back. The one in
hospital."

Andrews threw a quick glance at his partner, maybe at last they had their breakthrough.

"So what can you tell us about Mr Reiter, Jon?"

"Well, the night they say she was murdered."

"Can you tell me the exact day that was?" Sims asked in a tone belying his excitement.

"I know it was a Sunday, it was May sixteenth as it was my sister's birthday and she had arranged that she and her boyfriend would call and take me out for a meal. That was why I was able to give Arnie a loan of my car as I would not be needing it that evening. He said he would bring it back in the morning.

"You see he knew I used it to drive to work. And I remember thinking what a pity it was that he did not work close to where I worked, then I could have offered him a lift…"

"Quite, quite, Mr Roberts…Jon," Andrews halted him impatiently. "Let's go over this once again before we take your statement. What you are saying is that your friend Reiter had your car the night of Mary Dewer's murder?"

Roberts nodded vigorously. "That's why I'm here. I don't want involved. After all it is my car that he used."

Andrews sat back abruptly in his chair. If he was not mistaken here at last was their breakthrough. All along the difficulty was on how Reiter could have buried the body in the mountains without the use of a car. All other avenues such as car thefts, car hire, etc. having failed. And should Roberts sister and her escort corroborate his story he too also appeared to have an alibi for that night.

Andrews stood up signalling the interview was at an end. "Thank you Mr Roberts. Can I ask you to come with me

downstairs where in the company of my senior officer you will be invited to make a formal statement?"
Roberts almost jumped to his feet at the opportunity, and no doubt the possibility of becoming famous, even rich, as the man who helped catch the murderer of Peter Sagan's niece.
"Of course. And if I in any way can be of further assistance, do not hesitate to ask."

At last it was all coming together, Andrews and Sims were now on their way to the hospital where they had just learned that Arnold Reiter had regained consciousness. Sims steered the car into a parking bay outside the main entrance. Andrews got out and closed his door.
"This time I bet the old adage of 'I should like to ask you a few words' will apply, and in double quick time."
A puzzled expression on his face, Sims looked across the top of the car at his senior. "I don't get it Sam?"
Andrews walked round the car, explaining "that's what all we cops begin with, 'may I ask you a few words', is it not? Well, here there will only be a few, for I bet my bottom dollar that's as far as we get before some caring angel nurse says, I think that's enough for now, officer. I think he should rest now."
Andrews was wrong, the attendant nurse allowing him longer than he expected to ask his 'few questions.'

The unhealthy sight of Arnold Reiter swathed in bandages did nothing to deter Andrews from coldly asking.
"We know you borrowed Jon Roberts car the night of Mary Dewer's murder. Roberts has just confessed this to us. So now that you had the means, all we need is the motive, and that motive we believe is rejection. Mary

Dewer's rejection. This to you was enough reason to want her dead.

Perhaps you called on her the night she was murdered, and brought with you the photo we found on her dresser as a reminder of your college days and hopefully this time have more success with her than you had in college. Is that not so Mr Reiter? And when she again rejected you it was too much. Now that you realised you could never have Mary Dewer for yourself you murdered her, took her to the mountains in Jon Roberts borrowed car where you dumped her."

"No." Reiter's voice was little more than a croak. "I could never do that to Mary Dewer."

Andrews glared down at the injured man in the bed. "Then can you explain why that particular photo was on the dressing table? Did you put it there?"

Reiter nodded weakly, "Yes."

Sims drew closer to the bed. "So you admit you were in her apartment the night she was murdered."

Again a weak denial from the patient.

Of the two detectives, Sims showed the greater impatience. "So how did that photo get there?"

"I put it there after the apartment was sealed off. I put it there in sympathy for what had happened to her."

"So if that was all you did, why run away?"

"I knew intruding into a crime scene was an offence. I got scared. Next thing I knew was my picture was all over the papers. It did not take long for me to realise you'd find all the photos of Mary in my apartment and come to the conclusion that I was obsessed by her."

"So what took you to the dockside? You could not have chosen a more dangerous place."

Reiter's shrug was scarcely perceivable amongst the bedclothes. He did not feel like telling this dispassionate officer of the law what had happened to him, or of Sean and the dumb broad he'd named Miss America.

Sims took a step away from the bedside, angered by the injured man's confession, the man he was convinced murdered Mary Dewer.

In the corridor Andrews halted to speak to the uniformed policeman guarding Arnold Reiter, ironically the same young guard whom he had previously warned regarding the imminent appearance of Peter Sagan. This time Andrews warning was more severe. On no account was Sagan to be allowed to speak with the suspect.

Jake Russo had mixed feeling at meeting Faye Dewer again. Not that he did not enjoy her company, it was that after all this time she was sure to ask more about his past believing him to be a computer salesman. To lie would only lead to more lies and so on. Each day brought him that much closer to discovery if not by her but by others he had been forced to work with, or worse still, those others he had come in contact with.

Jake rang the doorbell and found himself unexpectedly excited at the prospect of seeing the woman again.

"Jake! How nice to see you." Faye stepped aside to let him enter the apartment.

Jake turned mid floor to face her. "I thought we might take a spin, or go somewhere together."

"That would be nice Jake," she crossed the floor to kiss him. "It's such a lovely day. How about the lake? You could take me to the lake," she suggested happily. "It's so long since I've been there."

"OK, you've got it." Jake released himself from her hold. "Just as long as you don't ask me to row one of those crazy boats. I don't swim easy."

Faye drew away laughing." But you can swim a little I take it?"

"Only to the bottom, I'm still teaching myself the return journey."

Enjoying the exchange, Faye walked to the door of the bedroom. "Then what are we waiting for?"

"You, I guess on deciding what you're going to wear."

The sun shone down on the blue water of the tiny lake. Faye lay beside him her eyes closed against the glare of the sun. Jake pushed back his hair a little wiping his brow with a handkerchief, deciding it was hot. Now more than ever he felt trapped. Trapped by the thought that he had not yet fulfilled his contract to Jack Kane by killing the uncle of the woman who lay beside him her eyes closed enjoying the afternoon sun.

Every other contract he had undertaken had him on his way immediately after its completion, normally that same day or close as dammit to it, here it was now over three months, every day bringing him ever closer to discovery. His using Faye Dewer to help him kill Peter Sagan would bring all this to an end. There could be no other way.

"What do you really do for a living Jake Russo?" the figure beside him asked without opening her eyes to look up at him.

At last it had come, the question he had most dreaded. To answer that he was a computer representative would not wash, a few minutes on the internet would swiftly invalidate his claim.

"You don't want to know honey. Best you enjoy your day."

"Are you FBI or something Jake?" Faye raised herself on to an elbow staring into his face as he sat there with his knees up to his chin.

Jake chuckled, slightly relieved by the suggestion. "Worse, Faye. I work for the IRS."

Faye sat up straight, alarm in her voice, asking, "You're after my Uncle? Is that it, Mister Jake Russo? While all this time I thought we had something going you were only interested in my Uncle." Faye was on her feet now, angry, and Jake as many a man before him had discovered to their cost, deadly.

"Hold on, there! Why should I be interested in Peter Sagan, pillar of the community, when I have other bigger and more deadly fish to catch?"

Had he convinced this angry young woman who stood glaring down at him, with the joy of the day all but forgotten?

Faye, doubt in her face, made a gesture that she might believe him. "Swear to it Jake Russo that you're not here to investigate my Uncle."

Jake smiled his relief, "Easy, I am not here to investigate your Uncle's affairs. Now what do you want to do while the sun still shines?"

Faye smiled mischievously, pointing at one of the passing row boats, "A sail on the lake would be nice."

Relieved that the questioning was over, at least for now, but not relishing having to row one of these damned contraptions Jake surrendered "OK. Let's do it."

"You do not appear to be enjoying yourself Jake," Faye cheerily observed lying back in the comparative comfort of the bow of the small craft.

Sweat running down his face his wet shirt clinging to his back, Jake gave a far from an endearing smile, thinking this was not really what he had in mind.

"Look out Jake, they be a small craft approaching from yer starboard quarter!" Faye cried out in her best pirate imitation.

Jake swung his head round, Faye was right to have warned him. Not the best of sailors or probably the worst, Jake dipped his oar in a frantic attempt to steer clear of the small boat, whose captain was in the act of doing something similar amid the high screams from a little girl hugging her mother for dear life, who was in turn hanging on to anything in sight.

All pitiful maritime manoeuvrers from both captains having failed, inevitably both crafts collided with a bump.

Jake leaned over the side of his craft to retrieve a floating oar. "Sorry about that skipper. My fault ,you had the right of passage." He did not know what it meant but it sounded OK.

"Hope you have off shore insurance buddy?" came the cheerful question from Jake's opposite number.

"Yea, when I heard about the Titanic, I rushed to get one," Jake shouted back, hauling his rogue oar aboard.

"What say we head for the nearest port, share the salvage money together?"

"Sounds good to me,"Jake agreed.

Faye struggled awkwardly to her knees, giving the woman and little girl a smile and a friendly wave. "Men," she declared in disgust.

"Men," the little girl echoed.

Jake was in the act of hauling his little craft ashore when their three new acquaintances joined him.

"Charlie Simpson." The man held out his hand. "And this is Jenny my good woman, and Alice, my little devil." He squeezed the 'little devil's' shoulder.

For a moment, stunned, Jake could only stare at the figure before him, then quickly recovering held out his own hand, "Jake Russo. Pleased to meet you all."

It could not be, this one chance in a million of meeting the man who he had only seen from a distance. The man who had killed Mary Dewer.

"What say we all have a coffee," Charlie suggested cheerfully.

"Swell. I could just do with one after my seafaring experience," Faye Laughed.

"As your captain, who gave you permission to go ashore?" Jake asked deadpan.

"If you don't want a mutiny on your hands, I think you should comply, captain, this motley crew could turn ugly, especially the small one," Charlie pointed to his daughter.

Jake pretended to consider the suggestion, "If she does she walks the plank licking an ice cream."

"Can we go for our coffee now you two, Captains Bligh and Useless?" The women turned together.

"Looks like the mutiny is over, Buddy," Charlie gave an artificial sigh of acceptance, followed by, "Guess so," from Jake Russo.

"Swell family,"Faye agreed happily.
Jake nodded. "Pretty girl."
"Which one do you mean?" Faye teased, her eyes
sparkling at him as they drove back home.
"Both. Cannot wait for the little one to grow up."
Faye squeezed Jake's arm. "Until then you will have to put
up with me." She stared out of the side window, thinking
how it had been such a lovely day.

Jake hung up his coat neatly in the wardrobe, poured
himself a shot of Southern Comfort before flopping down
in the room's one and only comfortable chair.
"Christ." he swore, The last thing he ever wanted to do was
come in contact with Charlie Simpson, or for that matter
his family.

Jake Russo cursed the man who in his eyes had everything
going for him. A lovely wife, a good looker in his opinion,
one who had she been his, he never would have found it
necessary to look at another. Jake sipped his drink. And if
this stupid shit had not, he'd not be in this mess now.
He rested his head on the back of the black leather chair,
closing his eyes. There was no way out for the poor bugger
Charlie. No way at all, soon the police were sure to find
him, then it was over for him, and sadly more so for his
lovely wife and kid.

Chapter 10

Charlie Simson had not enjoyed himself so much as he had that day at the lake. It too, was nice to see the flush back in Jenny's cheeks, the sparkle in her eyes, her happy laughter, once more the girl he had known when first they'd met. Charlie stood by his office window, that, he told himself sorrowfully was a long time ago.

"If only…. If only," Angrily Charlie punched the palm of his hand, "If," he said aloud, the most indicative word in the dictionary. If only Irene had not introduced Mary Dewer to him, if only he had not succumbed to her body, her wiles, he'd not be in this mess now, jumping at every ring of his doorbell and expecting to see the police officers standing there. And when they did, it would be all over. For him, Jenny, and little Alice. Almost gladly the office door opened and he was once again able to engross himself in the day's work.

"The Boss is not going to like this, Sam!" Sims flew into the room.

His partner looked up from where he had been studying a case file. "Not like what?"

Sims banged down in his chair behind his desk. "Arnold Reiter! The man threw himself out the window!"

Andrews sat up with a bolt. "Christ! Where was the officer on duty? Don't tell me. He was on his coffee break."

"Made no difference Sam. Reiter opened his room window. Threw himself from nine floors up. Poor bugger."

"You say that now, you hypocritical bastard. All along you have said he was guilty. So don't give me that sorry bit, now."

A little put out by his senior's angry reprimand, Joe Sims quietly asked. "You don't think Reiter did it? Is this what you are trying to tell me, Sam?"

Sam threw the pen down on his desk. "The evidence we had on him was purely circumstantial. It never would have stood up in court."

"Then why kill himself if he knew that he was innocent?"

"The guy was shit scared, he had never been in trouble before. Maybe he had other things to hide. Perhaps Mary Dewer was not his one and only obsession." Sam stood up. "We can theorise all we want, Joe, but right now we have to face the man upstairs."

"And most probably also with a certain Peter Sagan."

The name having Andrews shudder at the thought that the young officer on guard may also be the one he had warned, regarding this same Peter Sagan.

Jenny was setting the table for the evening meal when she heard the female TV broadcaster announce the death of Arnold Reiter who had taken his own life whilst recovering in hospital. She had gone on to say that he had been the chief suspect in the murder of Mary Dewer, niece of entrepreneur Peter Sagan.

Leaning on the kitchen door having heard the end of the news, Charlie did not know whether to feel elated that the death of the unfortunate man would mean the end of police investigations, and hopefully no more awkward questions, or that in some way he should feel responsible for the man's demise. After all was said and done the man was innocent, it was he and he alone who was responsible for Mary Dewer's murder. Charlie stopped to think. Not quite he alone. Whoever had taken Mary out of the trunk would also be aware of Reiter's innocence.

Charlie walked to the sink and turned on the cold water faucet. And whoever this person was, he was sure to contact him at some point, then the blackmail would begin. That the blackmailer had not already contacted him had him on edge, each day awaiting the dreaded call. How much did this person know?

How had he come to borrow *his* car in the first place to inevitably discover Mary's body in the trunk. What kind of person was he? A glimmer of hope shone inside Charlie's head. Perhaps there'd be no blackmail call? The person could be already locked up for some previous crime? Even dead was Charlie's hope.

Then there was the man Reiter himself. Obviously he was innocent, but should the law regard him as guilty and leave it there, then he, Charlie Simpson was a free man again. Free to go on with his life as if nothing had happened. Charlie put down his glass. No, not quite, he could never really be free. But at least Jenny and Alice would never know of his guilt and right now that was all that really mattered.

He could of course send a letter to the authorities exonerating Arnold Reiter without endangering himself. This could be a nice touch in the event of the man having a family somewhere, and ensuring that there was no stigma attached to the family name.

For a moment Charlie mulled over the thought until finding a loophole in his scheme. "Bloody stupid dick, if I do that the cops will probably keep the case open. Better to leave things as they are.

The poor guy's death was now his chance to resume his normal life, he'd not get another one. This way his secret was safe. Or was it? He still had a blackmailer to consider.

On the opposite edge of the city Jake Russo had also heard the news of the death of one Arnold Reiter, his immediate thoughts turning to Charlie Simpson, and what he must be thinking right now.
A little part of him wished the man well, especially after having met him and his family, while another part said that the man was still a murderer, albeit a reluctant one, or so he was inclined to think of Charlie Simpson. He, as did the man himself believe that matters were best left as they were. So thinking Jake Russo left it there. For he above anyone did not have the right to judge.

"Halt here," Nat Ferris ordered his son as they approached the open doors of the large empty warehouse. Nat wound down the window of the car signalling the other two vehicles to do likewise.
"While I go inside have the others turn the cars around. You cannot be too careful, especially with these guys."
"You don't want me to come with you Pa? Chris could do this for you." Alex felt uneasy at the whole affair. His Pa dealing with some new guys he did not know.
Nat got out, waving the rest of the men to him, while Alex turned the car around.

Black leather case in hand Nat Ferris led his men towards a warehouse reminiscent of an old empty airplane hanger slowing his stride as he reached the large open wooden doors.

"Keep your eyes peeled guys," Nat warned walking into the semi darkness, where in the centre of the open space stood a case similar to that which he himself carried. His eyes adjusting to the dim interior, followed by three men Nat walked towards it, halting at the sudden appearance of the men emerging out of the shadows.

"You got the goods?" One asked taking a step closer to Nat.
Nat held up his case. "All in here."
"Then let's do it," Nat's opposite number suggested stretching out his hand.
Nat handed it to him, signalling to his own men to retrieve the other case, when all hell broke loose.
On both sides of the galleries above a deadly fire poured down on Nat Ferris and his unsuspecting men.
"Run men! Back to the cars!" Nat shouted running, almost tripping over one of his own wounded in his haste to reach daylight and the safety beyond. But not before another man went down and he himself was hit.
"Flynn you bastard!" he squeezed out, grasping his chest, and letting off shots at a pair of dark shadows closing in on him.
"Pa!" His son's voice rang in his ears. Then Alex was kneeling down beside him struggling to help him to his feet, the gunfire intensifying before he himself was shot and forced to let go of his parent.

For a second Alex lay there, his brain registering that the shot was fatal, until with all his remaining strength hauled himself to his knees lifting his father into his arms.
"Joe!" Alex grabbed the man as he ran past. "Get him out of here! Take him to Doc Gus!"

The panicking man hesitated, his thoughts that this same man was the very last man who would stop to do anything for him.

Alex understood the man's reaction. "He'll make it worth your while, Joe!" Alex threw at him in desperation.

Without speaking Joe stooped and threw his wounded boss over his shoulder and ran for the door, saved only by his own side's covering fire.

Then what remained of the Ferris Empire made it to their cars.

Alex Ferris lay as though dead amidst the sound of cheering, and the occasional gunshot. They were killing his wounded.

It had been a bad mistake to have trusted these new business people. This they now knew to their cost, but his Pa had been adamant that this deal would make them a fortune. A deal that grandfather Ferris himself would have been proud of. Instead all that they had accomplished was total destruction of what that old man had himself built. All gone in one day's work.

The gunshots were closer now, soon they'd find him and that would be the end.

Alex crawled painfully to his left amongst the shadows. If he could reach what appeared to be some sort of machinery he might be able to lie there out of sight until their ambushers had left.

He was bleeding badly, but he must make an effort not to just lie there and die.

An eternity later Alex reached his goal. Now there was less jubilation amongst the victors. Although he could not see, he heard the sound of cars leaving. Then total darkness as the great doors were banged closed. At last Alex surrendered, even should he reach those same doors he lacked the strength to open them so much as a fraction. Better that he just lie here and pass away peacefully.

Alex's mind went slowly over how he had lived his life. Of a life he had known nothing other than one of crime. He'd never had a choice. His only consolation, that he never was as cruel as either his parent of grandparent.

Without warning, lights flooded the vast empty arena, and a voice behind him saying, "Mister Alex Ferris, at last we meet,"and the face of Carlos of the Boricuas was grinning down at him.
"So it was you who set this up, Carlos?"
"No, Mister Alex, someone else set it up as you say, we only did the shooting."
"Then you have your revenge after all."
Carlos took a cautious step nearer his victim. "Not quite. I still have my brother's death to avenge, regrettably not with the man who was responsible, but his son will do, I am sure."

Alex could only guess what the man had in mind, and did not blame him, his brother had died in no way a human being should have died, and that was at the hands of Nat Ferris, his own father.
"You're wasting your time Carlos, I'll be dead before you make your first move to make me squirm."
"Maybe. We shall see." Carlos lashed out with a kick. And a kick was all it took to give Alex Ferris the time to bring his gun up from beneath his coat and fire up at his

tormentor, before he himself caught the full force of
Carlos's own weapon.

The black car squealed to halt, Joe jumping out to pull the
wounded man out of the back seat.
"I'll have you inside in no time, Boss." he assured the
barely conscious man.

About to cross the dark street to Doc Gus's house Harry
Rudoski held his little brother's hand.
There were two men at the Doc's door, one of whom
appeared to be badly injured; no new thing in this district
where the Doc was always on call to attend to those who
would rather be treated by him than answer awkward
questions in hospital, and inevitably the cops.
Harry held his brother's hand tighter as they crossed the
dimly lit almost deserted street. He looked up, Doc was at
the door now taking a hasty glance in either direction
before hurrying in his patients, the injured one who he was
certain was the one who had ordered the job on little Joel's
finger.
Now on the sidewalk, Harry drew to a halt. Doc had asked
him to bring his brother at this time tonight, so these two
must be an emergency. Hopefully fatal to the injured one if
he was indeed the Big Shot Nat Ferris.

Harry turned his brother round, looking down at the little
boy, the feeling of guilt for what had happened to him
overpowering, as it was his fault that Joel had paid the
price for their being caught, and as a punishment Ferris
had not taken it out on him but Joel in order to teach him,
Harry Rudoski a hard lesson. One he'd be reminded of

every day for the rest of his life each time he looked at that hand missing a finger.

"Joel, wait here kid, first let me talk with the Doc he might not have time to see us tonight. OK?"
Joel nodded that he understood. If Harry said to wait then that's what he'd do.
Harry looked around him. "Wait in those bushes over there, and when you see me leaving the Doc's, run to meet me. OK kid?"
Joel nodded. "Ok Harry but don't be long, I have to pee."
The little boy held himself.
For a moment Harry was annoyed. "OK, pee in the bushes. Don't let anyone see you, especially anyone who knows our ma, then you know what will happen. We're in enough trouble with you losing your finger, so we don't want you losing any more parts."

Harry left Joel to climb the stairs of the stoop to the doc's door. For a moment he stood there listening, the only sound a faint cry followed by a sharp yell. Gently Harry pushed open the door taking a peek inside, drawing back at what he'd seen.

It was indeed Nat Ferris who was the injured man, he sat eyes closed hunched in a chair, a blood filled bowl on a small table by his side.
Harry drew back, who else beside the Doc was there was in the small room beyond. It was this same room that the doc had emerged from with what he'd required to stitch up his brothers hand.

Harry shook. Maybe he'd not have to wait years after all to get his own back on what this moaning man here had done to his brother. Harry's eyes travelled to a chair nearby where a holstered gun hung. Probably that of Nat Ferris himself. Now was his chance. Could he do it? Could he kill this shit with his own gun? But should he fail? He'd lose more than a finger, of this he was sure.

Harry's eyes were drawn back to the injured man who still sat with his eyes closed. In the background muffled voices from the other room. Harry choked. This was his chance. Carefully on tip toe he crossed the small room to where the gun hung, one eye on the moaning man the other on the other room door expecting to be caught by either at any second.

Then he was there silently drawing the gun from its holster, surprised by how unexpectedly heavy it was.

Whether by chance or by a creak in the floor Nat Ferris opened his eyes to stare into the barrel of his own gun and the boy who stood there holding it nervously in both hands.

"You," he croaked, a glimmer of a smile on his face. "Come for you brother's finger?"

Nat Ferris stared at the boy. Maybe he deserved this for all the cruel things he had done in life. Right now he just could not care, though he'd like to see Alex again.

"You best hurry if you want to use that thing kid. They'll be back any second to patch me up."

The gun shaking, Harry's answer was, "Maybe I can save them the trouble." And the boy pulled the trigger.

"We got them boss, all of them!" Detective Mark Sale closely followed by his partner burst into Captain Gordon's office.

The senior officer jerked a look up at the intruders. "Calm yourself, Sale. So I believe what you are trying, no spluttering to tell me is that your snitch came though."

"And how, sir," his partner endorsed Sale from over his shoulder.

"Good I cannot wait to read your reports."

"Can we not at least tell you now sir?" Sale could not contain his excitement.

Pointing to his officers to be seated Gordon gave in. "Let's hear it then."

Sale began. "Our snitch as you put it told us about the deal going down last night between Flynn and Ferris. Although he did not know where he did know the time, so we decided to wait for Flynn at his home."

"Catch him red handed with the goods," Stewart explained.

Gordon threw him a look of derision. "I gathered that officer. Go on Sale. What next?"

"Sure as death itself Flynn and his crew turn up. So we book them for being in possession of narcotics."

Appearing to be unimpressed Gordon sat back in his chair. "Is that it? That's all?"

Sale shook his head disappointed by his boss's reaction. "No, later we did find out where the deal had gone down."

"It was in a disused warehouse down town." Stewart added.

Sale continued, "Must have been some gunfight, boss. We found seven dead bodies." Purposely Sale halted, already savouring Gordon's response to what he was about to tell him. "Alex Ferris was amongst them, besides three Boricuas."

Gordon sat forward a little. "Nat? What about Nat? Was he there?"

"That's the funny bit, boss," Stewart started to explain.

"Funny! Funny! What's funny about seven dead bodies?"

"I mean," Stewart started again, "I mean strange sir. We found Nat Ferris's body a few doors down from Doc Gus's house. He had been shot twice."

"So he did not make it to the old Doc's door." Gordon twitched his lips.

"No sir, that's not it. Forensic say one of the bullets came from Ferris's own gun."

"Decided to end it himself, do you think, guys?"

"Could be, boss."

Gordon sighed and sat back in his chair. "So where do we go from here?"

Sale chose to answer. "If any weapons from Flynn's mob match forensic from the bodies in the warehouse we can place them at the scene of the crime. Maybe even get someone to confess to killing old man Ferris himself."

"Now you are clutching at straws Sale. Flynn may be responsible but how to prove it is another matter."

Gordon sat back. "However you have both done well. I will let the boss know. Meantime get those reports done and have them back to me quick time. OK?"

Chapter 11

Despite the occasional twinge of conscience over Arnold Reiter, Charlie Simpson was now at last beginning to believe that his life had every chance of returning to normal, or close to normal as it was ever likely to be.
It was now close to four months since Mary Dewer's death, a long agonising four months, but with Reiter no longer alive it could very well have been worth it.

His home life was much better, thanks to his tailoring down his drinking. The office too, held less worry for him, time having dimmed at what had happened to their workmate, other gossip having taken its place.

Charlie pulled a sheet of paper towards him, perhaps his nightmare was at an end.
It was not. No longer had the thought left his mind than the phone rang and a voice was asking to speak with a Mister Charles Simpson.
"Charles Simpson," Charlie answered cheerily glancing at the foolscap sheet before him.
"Would that be the same Charlie Simpson who was acquainted with a certain Mary Dewer?"
Charlie almost dropped the phone. It was here, the call he most feared, the call he had always expected.
"Yes, I am Charlie Simpson. May I ask who is calling?"
"You may," his caller chuckled, "But I am not likely to tell you, am I?" The tone from the other end quickly altered.
"Now let's forget the shit and get down to business. I was there the night you killed Mary Dewer, May 16th to be exact. I watched from the bushes in the driveway. I saw you leave her house and return with your car. Then you

went back inside and carried her back out covered by a white bedsheet and tumbled her into the trunk. Am I right so far?" the voice asked in a tone suggesting to Charlie that he was enjoying himself.

Charlie choked, his hand that held the phone trembling. "You say you were there, perhaps you read some of the details in the paper," Charlie tried to bluff.

"What details, old buddy. I was there. I even saw the blood on poor Mary's blouse when the sheet slipped as you carried her to the car. Want any more details?" the voice mocked. "So, as I said, let's get down to business. I'll make it easy on you buddy, that's if you don't try any funny business such as calling the cops."

"Why don't you?" Charlie countered, "If you are so sure that I did it, why not inform the law? When you do they will as sure as hell want to know why you waited so long to get in touch."

"Telling the cops is no use to me, good buddy, there's no margin of profit in that. No, this is strictly business between you and me, this way I can get ahead for the first time in my life. This time shit like you will have to listen to shit like me."

Charlie felt himself tense at the thought of this man whom he was talking with could well be some sort of maniac, someone whose irrational thinking could lead to harming his family if he did not comply with his wishes, such as unable to meet the payments he now would undoubtedly disclose to him.

"I think we could start with $500, Charlie, that's not too steep. I'm not a greedy man."

"500?" Charlie shook.

"Yea Charlie, 500 each week is not beyond a manager's reach. After all it probably cost you more to have your jollies with little Miss Muffet, who, being the niece of a certain Peter Sagan would insist on a certain standard of living from you, if she was to keep your little affair secret."

"$500? Where the hell can I find that sort of money without my wife knowing where it has gone?"

"You managed okay all the time you were with sweet little Miss Dewer. She must have made a packet out of suckers like you."

Charlie stared into his phone in disbelief. "You are not implying that Mary was seeing someone else?"

A chuckling sound reached Charlie from the other end of the phone. "Seeing someone else? You are seriously saying you believe that you were the only person having an affair with that unfeeling bitch. You were not the only one playing her tune." Again there was chuckling, except this time, louder. "She was conducting a fucking philharmonic orchestra of which I was one, buddy."

For a moment Charlie sat stunned by what he was hearing. That anyone could think this of the one he adored. Yea, she could be demanding, even cruel at times, but never in one hundred years had he thought he was not the only one in her life. Was not one of the issues his refusal to divorce Jenny? So why would she do this if she was seeing someone else?

Charlie's thoughts were cut short by his tormentor, continuing. "Here is what I want you to do. Take the mountain road as far as Selma. It's straight for over a mile from there, you can easily see any car approaching from

either direction. Standing back from the road about midway down there's a derelict farmhouse. Stop there and walk to the old rusting mail box into which you will place your first week's contribution. Make sure no one sees you Charlie Simpson. It's in your interest as well as your families. OK. Make your first drop Tuesday next. And Charlie don't try doing anything smart."
Then the phone went dead, and Charlie was left thinking that his nightmares were about to start all over again.

Each day that passed increased Jake Russo's frustration at not having quit the city. It seemed an eternity since he had agreed to take down Peter Sagan and was no closer in doing so. Trapped. That was his feelings right now, or a man on a treadmill. Dating Faye had not brought him the desired effect, the desire and effect were not of the same genre.

A chill breeze in the encroaching darkness had Jake seek the shelter of somewhere warmer. He spied a bar shying away at the sound of twanging guitars, searching for a quieter place more conducive to his mood. He saw one and crossed the street, pushing the door open to a much more agreeable clientele.

Jake ordered a Scotch without ice, using the mirror behind the bar to size up his mostly silent fellow drinkers, eventually his gaze fell on a drinker sitting by himself at a corner table. His eyes on the lone mourner Jake sipped his drink, the man obviously was in some sort of distress the way he sat head down staring at his glass, as if contemplating if he had the strength to lift it to his lips.

When he did, Jake suddenly recognised him as the man who he and Faye had met at the lake. This could not the same man, at least not by his present demeanour. Lifting his drink off the bar, Jake crossed the floor until he stood over the quiet drinker.

"Mr Simpson, I believe?"
Charlie stared up at the speaker through a drunken haze. "Don't quite know myself, buddy," he tittered patting the seat beside him. "Here, take the weight off your bankbook."
Ignoring the invitation Jake slid into the seat opposite, silently waiting while Charlie sipped his beer.
"*You* got troubles, man?" Charlie hiccuped. "Nothing like I have, for sure," he belched.
"Jenny has left me, she took little Alice with her. All my fault of course. I thought I had it all worked out then the bastard got to me on the phone at the office, lucky if no one on the switchboard heard, if they did I am..." he left the rest unsaid.
"That bad," Jake sympathised.
"Worse man. Worse."

Jake did not know whether to pry or not. He had a rough idea who on the phone had upset him to the extent that his lovely wife had left him.
"Want to talk about it?" Jake finally asked, lifting his drink to give the distraught man time to decide.
"You seem a regular guy, at least you were when we met last at the lake. That was a good day," Charlie conceded with a crazy grin. "That was before the blackmailing bastard put the squeeze on."

"For what?" Jake ventured, half expecting to be told to mind his own damned business, instead Charlie went on. "I did a bad thing, and this bastard is blackmailing me."

"Suppose you tell me why." Jake put down his drink. "It sometimes helps to share, or so they say."

"I swear it was an accident. I did not mean to kill her." A tear ran down Charlie's cheek.

Realising he had said too much he lifted his glass unsteadily to his lips.

Patiently Jake waited. A waiter passed and Charlie ordered them both a double Scotch.

"You were saying?" Jake prompted, hoping Charlie might be drunk enough not to know that he had not finished his story.

"She left me… took the kid with her. Says she cannot stand my drinking." Charlie pointed his empty beer glass at Jake, slurring, "I had stopped it too. Did not touch a drop, until this son of a bitch came on the phone."

"What did he want Charlie?"

Charlie sat back in his seat to let the waiter set down the drinks. "Who?"

"This guy on the phone?"

"$500. That's what he wants. Says he saw me from the bushes. Saw the blood on her dress and knew she was dead and that I killed her."

"And did you Charlie" Jake asked softly.

"It was an accident. We had an argument." Charlie waved an unsteady hand, "I cannot remember why? Something to do with me not getting a divorce." Charlie stopped to stare drunkenly into Jake's face, "I love my wife… eh?"

"Jake."

"Jake. Then this bastard on the phone tells me she has been seeing lots of other guys."

"I take it you mean this girl what's her name?" Jake clicked his fingers, as if having forgotten.

"Mary Dewer." Charlie burped, "Yea, including this son of a bitch on the phone. Maybe this is what we fought over. She went down hit her head on the coffee table. There was blood, so I knew I had killed her."

Charlie stared into space reliving that night. "I panicked. Went for my car. Found a bedsheet to cover her with. Put her in the trunk," Charlie gulped his drink. "I went home. Did not know what else to do. Left her in the car until I decided what to do with her."

Suddenly halting, Charlie sat up straight staring across the table at Jake. "When I figured out what to do, the car wasn't there! My car was not in the driveway, Jake! Now I know it was this son of a bitch on the phone who had stolen it, buried poor Mary so he could blackmail me later."

"OK, So what has this guy on the phone asked you to do? I take it, it's money he's after?"

Charlie brought himself back to Jake across the table. "He wants me to meet him…."

Jake reversed his car a little way up the side track a few hundred yards from where he could still see the old mail box by the side of the long empty country road. Now all that was left was for him to wait. A few minutes later a car sped past from the direction he had just taken, neither slowing or halting as it sped past the mail box. A few minutes on, another did likewise. Jake glanced at the car clock. It was already past the allotted time. Was this phone guy on the level? Or was it some weirdo doing it for kicks?

At the sound of a car, Jake sat up. This car was much slower than the other two. It passed where he sat, slowing, then halting on the opposite side of the road from the old metal box swaying gently in the breeze.

Jake started up the car, gunning the engine down the empty road, drawing quickly to a halt in front of the parked car.

Across the empty highway, 'Phone Guy' was already on the way back to his car an artificial smile on his face at Jake's sudden appearance.

Jake waited by his own car, while the man made his way to his.

"No mail today, I'm afraid," the man said in way of explanation as he passed.

"All the way out here? Especially, I should say since that old mailbox has not been used since the days of the Pony Express."

The man's grin quickly disappeared at the sight of the gun in Jake's hand and him saying. "Now cut the shit and come over here." Jake motioned for him to get in the car.

Now scared, the young man slid into the passenger seat beside Jake.

"What's this all about mister?" he asked. "I don't have much money….. I…."

"No you don't but you expected to have should that old mailbox hold what you planned."

"I don't know what you mean," the young man stammered. "Who are you anyway?"

Jake smirked, "Just say an agent for a certain Charlie Simpson, the one you intend on blackmailing for a crime he did not commit."

"As I said, I don't know what you mean. I think you must have got the wrong guy. Who is this Charlie… what's his name?" The young man's questions cut short by the gun thrust into his side.

"Cut the shit. You know who I mean. The one you are framing for the murder you committed."

"The one I…" the man jerked at the increased pressure of the gun in his side.

"Yea," Jake poked the gun a little deeper. "What's you name anyway, punk. No harm in telling me, is there?"

"Adam," the man gave a little nod. "But why do you think I killed Mary Dewer? She meant nothing to me."

Jake looked amused. "Who mentioned Mary Dewer?"

"Shit."

"Exactly."

Angry at the denial, Jake pressed the gun harder. "Adam, if that *is y*our name? Here's what I think happened that night Mary Dewer died." Jake released the gun's pressure, while he began.

"You arrived at the girl's house the reason known only to you, where you saw Charlie Simpson acting suspiciously. Let's say you saw Charlie leave her front door open and run round the corner for his car, giving you the opportunity to go inside where you saw Mary Dewer lying bleeding on the floor from where she had hit her head on a coffee table. Now, Adam, this is only my assumption of course, but you hated Mary Dewer, maybe she had dumped you for Charlie or even some other poor unsuspecting guy, but at least you had the opportunity to make a few dollars, but to do so you needed her dead. So you strangled her."

Adam sat there, his eyes staring through the windshield. "I was in the bushes, I saw Simson carry Mary to his car and dump her inside. He had her covered with a white sheet, it dropped a little that's when I saw the blood."

"You're lying Adam. I took a look there myself yesterday. You could not have possibly seen the blood on Mary Dewer's dress from the bushes. Charlie told me the sheet only fell as he was laying her in the trunk. Of course we could clear all this up by taking a little drive to the cops."

"No!" the shout filled the car. Adam shook his head vigorously. "OK! OK! I did the bitch, she was asking for it, leading me on about us getting married, when all the time she was teasing me, Charlie Simpson and God knows how many more. Living in style even though her tycoon of an Uncle was also plying her with money. Little money grabbing bitch," the man seethed.

Jake withdrew his weapon and sat back. "Here's what you do, Adam." Jake indicated the glove compartment. "In there you will find your sworn statement where you confess to having killed one, Mary Dewer."

"No!" the distraught man screamed. "I'll get the chair..... life at least."

"Not if you do what I tell you." Again Jake pointed to the glove compartment.

On the evening of that same day, Jake Russo pulled into the Charlie Simpson's driveway, getting out of the car as Charlie Simpson, garbage can in hand, opened his front door.

"Jake?" Charlie vaguely remembered the name. He laid down the can and stood aside.

"Come on in, Jenny's not at home I'm afraid, so I am dining alone. You are welcome to join me."

"No time," Jake lied. He handed the man the brown envelope. "It's all in there. The man who intended to blackmail you, Adam Inglis's confession on how he murdered Mary Dewer."

Charlie stood wide eyed unable to digest what he was hearing. "But it was me…."

"No Charlie. It was you telling me how he saw the blood on the girl's dress that had me thinking."

Jake took a step back, "He and I made a deal. He cannot go to the cops or disclose your involvement with her without giving himself away. Same applies to you with him." Jake nodded to Charlie holding the brown envelope. "His confession is in there, all neatly…" Jake corrected himself with a grin, "No that's wrong, not neatly, shakily signed. So now you can go back to living with your beautiful wife and little daughter." Jake turned towards his car. "It's your second, no make that your only chance to put this behind you Charlie Simpson, so see you don't mess it up. OK?"

Charlie took a hurried step down from the door, calling out to the departing man who had given him back his life. "Who are you? I mean, really?"

Jake turned back, a broad smile on his face. "Really? Only a simple Computer salesman."

Then with a wave he was gone.

His feeling of entrapment had grown, in fact it had never left him. His only consolation Jake Russo thought was in knowing Faye. Despite using her he was no closer to taking down her Uncle, Peter Sagan, who he learned was once again leaving town, and sadly with none other than with Faye herself. Perhaps it was time for he himself to leave, the feeling of suffocation having become more overpowering each day.

To do so would of course end his kind of work should word get out that he Jake Russo had failed to complete his contract. If so he may as well begin looking for work packing shelves in a supermarket, any supermarket.

His mind on this Jake drove to the small private airfield where Peter Sagan and his niece were due to take off, once again for pastures unknown.

It was not a situation he cared to be in, for should he succeed in taking down Sagan he'd have to high tail it out of town as the old cowboys were wont to say without a backward glance at the woman he'd be forced to betray.

The field came in sight, and he drove towards it parking outside the main building, where Faye said she would meet him.

Inside he saw her immediately amongst the few gathered there either awaiting their flight or to see someone off.

"We're having a coffee wont you join us?" Faye greeted him cheerfully.

Jake gave her a peck on the cheek. "OK. Lead on."

Faye led him to the tiny bar where Peter Sagan was talking animatedly to someone, a someone clearly overawed by the big man.

Sagan saw him and interrupting his conversation gave him a welcome wave. "Come to see us off," he grinned cheerily, "or should that be my lovely niece?"

"Both, sir," Jake answered polite, holding out his hand in response to Sagan's.

"You will just have time for a coffee and a fond farewell to my niece before we take off. Over there is a quiet spot." Sagan indicated a table by the window. "Go," he urged them, turning quickly to resume his conversation with the same unfortunate man.

Cup in hand Jake walked with the girl to the table.

"Is he not something else?" Faye laughed.

Solemnly his thoughts on how easily Sagan could be taken down but with no chance of himself getting off scot free, Jake answered that he was.

"When will you be back,?" Jake laid his cup down on the table.

Faye sat in a seat across from him, her attention drawn to a little girl showing her doll to her. "Will you miss me, Jake?"

"Sure." Jake took a sip of coffee.

"You don't sound too sad about it," Faye pouted teasingly. His depression at losing her, however briefly, momentarily lifting Jake grinned, "I could sing you a sad farewell song, should that help to hurry you back."

"Don't you dare," Faye warned him.

"Miss Dewer, it's time to leave," a man in a light blue uniform, informed her.

Jake rose taking Faye's hand. "Text me when you get to wherever you're going," he told her on their way to the small departure lounge.

"I will, Jake." She halted briefly. "I wish I was not going, but you know how Uncle is." She started again. "I'll let

you know when I'm due back. You can come and meet me."
"OK, it's a promise."

Outside Jake watched Peter Sagan's little private plane clear the runway, certain that he had seen Faye wave out of one of the windows.
He put up a hand to shade his eyes from the afternoon sun watching the small craft circle before climbing, then a solitary flash as the tiny plane exploded amidst fragments falling to the ground.

Almost immediately there was the clanking sound of a fire engine on its way, together with the competing screams from within the lounge, this same lounge where only a few minutes ago he had said his farewell and his promise to be here for Faye's return.

He needed fresh air, put it all together. Jake walked to the grass verge of the runway. One car sitting a little way from his own took off. At first his thinking was that it was newspapermen rushing off with story of the crash, until he saw the grinning face of Jack Kane sitting beside Victor the driver, and instantly he knew that the plane explosion was no accident. Jake ran for his car, he had to get out of here before the cops arrived to seal off the area. Get away to deal with Jack Kane.

There was no guard on the door when Jake rushed into Jack Kane's room. The two men there, each a champagne glass in hand laughing until they saw the reason for this untimely intrusion.
Laughing still, Jack Kane held up his glass to Jake. "Good Jake, just in time to celebrate my success."

Kane lifted an empty glass from the table. "Will you join me... us," he acknowledged the room's other occupant with a raised glass. "Now with Peter Sagan's demise and Nat Ferris out of the frame, I own all of this damned city." Jake swept Kane's hand away. "Was it necessary to kill the pilot as well as the girl. Neither posed a threat to you Jack."

"Better safe than sorry," the other man smirked.

"Victor's right Jake. I gave you ample time to dispose of Sagan but you let love get in your way. You lost your cool man. Something you have never done before. So I gave Victor here the hit, who also I might add took care of the Nat Ferris job."

"And Dan," Jake seethed. "A man who gave you nothing other than loyalty. You set him up Jack, you let this ape here let Sagan know of Dan's attempt to kill him."

"And it worked," Victor chuckled, taking a sip of his drink, "In two ways. One, I gained Sagan's trust to let me deal with Ferris and enough to get close enough to sabotage his plane."

Kane saw Jake's anger rise at the mention of the plane. "Come on Jake I know it's hard for you to accept, but I owe you for old Ferris and that you also got back my casinos for me."

Kane had said it quietly in an attempt to defuse the situation. He turned to the open safe extracting several bundles of banknotes, throwing them on the table. "This is for you. The Ferris hit, and retrieving my casinos," he halted "and for all the work you put in over Peter Sagan."

"And his niece," Victor cackled.

Though inwardly seething at the crass remark it took all of Jake Russo's willpower not to react. Instead, stepping to the table he gathered together the bundles of banknotes and slid them into the white sack lying there. Without saying a word he turned and had almost reached the door when he heard the click.

Jake Russo spun round, his snap shot hitting the wise cracking Victor in the chest, his second in the head as he crumpled to the floor.

"OK! OK Jake!" Kane stood with his hands up in surrender. "The guy asked for it. Now get he hell out of here before I have to explain this to the guards."

Jake gave a little movement with his gun. "See you sometime Buddy," he turned, spinning round at the same instant that Kane had raised his own gun.

"Jesus... Jake," Kane crumpled forward, his last words uttered in surprise.

"You should know better than to trust anyone in our business. Too late for you now of course Jack Kane." Jake smiled sardonically.

Jake Russo waited patiently for his cab to take him to the airport. At last he was on his way out of this damned city, leaving behind him memories of his girl and the way she had died. Also of Charlie Simpson, and his second chance at life. And what of himself? He had more money than ever.

Perhaps it was time to start something new, such as stacking shelves he laughed. Perhaps not, that was a job where one could also feel trapped and somehow he had had enough of that. At least for now that was.

Chapter 12

Five Years Later...

Tom Haines, better known as Bubba pushed back his
Stetson wiping his forehead with an already soaking
handkerchief. God, he thought it was hot, and it was still
shy of noon.

Bubba stepped on to the sidewalk standing for a moment
to breathe in the slighter cooler air than that of the
suffocating heat of the police car, debating whether to head
down the main street for a cool iced drink or alternatively
poach a coffee from his sister working in the office of Jake
Russo.

Having decided on the latter Bubba walked up the almost
deserted high street crossing the forecourt of the used car
yard, the bunting above hanging listlessly having died
from lack of air however humid, while Jake Russo
patiently watched his approach from his open office door.

Jake Russo had appeared from nowhere to settle in his
town almost five years ago, buying the used car business
and the eight chalet motel on the edge of town.

A little checking up had revealed that Jake Russo, should
this be the same one, was a person of interest in five states,
but happily this was not one of them, without as much as
parking ticket being issued or brought in for questioning,
on some serious crimes that was as far as it had gone.
However since the man had arrived here there had never
been so much as a hint of trouble, and when Russo had
offered his sister Annie work in his office he had made no
attempt to intervene. Now five years on sister Annie was
much more than just Jake Russo's office assistant.

Bubba mopped his brow, whatever Jake Russo had been or done was now in the past, and although Annie had never mentioned it he thought Russo had kept this part of his life to himself.

Annie greeted her brother with, "Come to bum another coffee?" She looked up from her computer, "Coffee's on the stove, as if you did not know."
"And a cheerful good morning to you too, sis," Bubba answered stepping into the small kitchen.
"Hot today again, Bubba," Jake sat himself down behind his own desk. "Not much criminal activity in this heat I should guess."
"Giving out a ticket for parking or speeding to some unlucky soul, I should say," Annie called out across the room.

The policeman came out of the tiny kitchen cup in hand. "Only a single one for speeding on the highway."
"Welcome to Kent, stranger," Annie feigned a sigh. "You really do boost the town's tourism brother."
"Such is the life of a cop," Jake chuckled.
"It is my duty to see to the safety of the community," Bubba answered deadpan. "But forget the praise, am I to be invited for supper tonight or not, sis?"

It was to Annie's house that he referred she and her brother choosing to live separately, she in her late parents home, Bubba to police accommodation, an arrangement that appeared to work fairly well.
"If you have a mind but you are likely to be eating alone, since I am making supper up at Jake's place."
"Ok will do. The usual time?"

"Usual eats, beans and toast should Jake have a mind to do the cooking," Annie laughed.

Bubba swallowed the last of his coffee returning the cup to the kitchen. "Well, it's alright for some, but others have to earn a dollar."

"Must be a chore having to write out a speeding ticket in triplicate would you not say Jake?" Annie teased giving her beau a wink.

Pretending to ignore the intentional taunt, Bubba turned at the door. "OK see you tonight for beans and toast."

"Sure will," both echoed watching him leave.

Jake yawned. The day was likely to slowly drag to a close, no one likely to venture out unnecessarily in this heat. He sat for a time his eyes on Annie busily typing away at her keyboard.

"Why not call it a day, Annie? Give yourself a rest before you start on the beans. Not much doing here today that I cannot handle on my own, and should there be an unexpected rush of clients I will not hesitate to call you. How is that for an offer from a very considerate employer," Jake joked.

Annie looked up from her work. "Sure could use a break in this heat." She waved a hand at the screen. "Nothing here that will not wait till tomorrow."

It was close on an hour after Annie had gone and Jake's thoughts were to call it a day when the door opened, and someone vaguely familiar to Jake Russo stood framed in the doorway.

The figure smiled. "Cannot quite place me, can you Kid?"

Jake Russo rose slowly, stunned by the use of a name he had not heard himself called in years, not since his rapid departure from the night he had shot and killed Louis Canello.

"Len," the smiling figure prompted, "You, Harry and me used to be partners in crime. Don't say you cannot remember?"

The smiling figure drew closer into the room, searching for a chair to sit down, all the while amused by Jake Russo's lack of reaction. "So what have you been up to Kid since the night you took down Louis Canello?"

"That was a long time ago, Len. I have moved on since then."

Len scanned the office taking a glance out at the car forecourt. "Seems so. But this is not all you have been up to since that night."

"Such as?" Jake replied, anger in his voice. Anger that he should have been so easily found and by someone he hoped never to meet again.

Len spread himself out in his chair, taking time to study the handkerchief he had extracted from his pocket. "Sure is hot here, Kid." He drew the handkerchief across his brow. "Such as you working for the late Jack Kane. Or so they tell me."

"Could be they are wrong. You should not listen to those who are as dumb as yourself."

For once the smile left the unwelcome visitor's face.

"So let's cut to the chase, Len, why are you here?"

Len, regained his composure and smiled across the floor at the man he most hated in the world. "Perhaps I heard about the real good deals you give with your cars."

"Could be that I fit you up with one with no brakes."
Len threw his head back laughing at the joke. "No doubt you could, Kid." Len drew serious. "Somehow the Kid no longer suits you, you having grown up and all, Jake Russo." Len stood up. "Is that coffee you have on the stove? Smells real good."
Jake gave an indifferent shrug. "Help yourself."

Coffee cup in hand Len returned from the kitchen. "OK, big man, I will come to the reason that I am here, and it is not to see your ugly face again." Len sat down sipping at his coffee. He made a face. "My compliments to the chef this coffee sure is good." He took another sip. "Lacks a little something."
"Such as arsenic,?" Jake suggested.
"Maybe so, Jake. Now let me get to the point, before I melt in this heat."
"I can wait."
"Guess so Kid but unfortunately I cannot. You remember Felix Viconti? The one you thought called you a faggot the night of the film show?"
Jake nodded remembering that night when Harry stole the videos.
"Well that same old guy took over as a result of you having dispensed with Mr Canello."
"Are we speaking about the same guy? He must be about a hundred and ten by now." Jake asked, surprise in his voice.
"Not quite,"Len chuckled. "But you are right there, Kid, Viconti is by far too old for the job in hand. Too old fashioned in his ways." Len waved a hand. "OK. He can organise, I can give him that much, but he still wants to deal in the protection racket, will not even consider dealing where the money is, and that is.."

"In drugs" Jake interrupted.

"Quite."

"So you want shot of him, or words to that affect."

"Shot being the appropriate word, Kid."

"So who is behind all this? I mean who takes over? Do you call a board meeting to decide?"

Len laughed at the absurdity of the question. "Of course not kid. You know how these things work. Felix would not stand down voluntarily." Len wriggled a hand to emphasis his point. "The old guy needs a little push. That's where you come in Jake Russo, to give the old guy that final push."

Jake Russo choked back his surprise. "Why me? There must be a dozen guys who could do the job."

"Maybe so, Kid but we need someone well outside the organisation, someone with a sound track record, such as yourself. Someone not connected with our organisation."

Jake stared across the room at his protagonist. "You mean you do not want anyone in your organisation to know who has done the hit? Or should that be, do not want anyone to know that it was you who authorised the hit?"

Len's expression was one of reluctant admiration. "There's still no fooling the Kid, is there?"

Jake shook his head in disbelief. "You figure to take over? You believe with the old man gone you can take his place? You who....."

Len halted him abruptly. "Okay when last you saw me I was your sidekick helping you in the protection racket, but that was as you say a long time ago. I have climbed the ladder since then. I have respect. I am now Viconti's right hand man."

"Beware the Ides of March." Jake smirked.

"What the hell has March got to do with anything, and further still who is this Ides you are on about?"

Jake could have laughed at the man's ignorance, contenting himself by saying. "You mean to take over after the hit? Not everyone will agree to your being number one, Len." Jake halted. "Have you ever thought that when you do, someday the same might happen to you?"

Len waved a hand. "They will have to be up early, Kid."

"May be Len, but if they are you will have to be awake all night. Perhaps having to watch your right hand man."

For a moment Len sat silent digesting what this man sitting across from him was implying. Suddenly, clearing his throat he said. "Will you take the hit or not?"

"No, Len. That kind of work is all in the past." He waved a hand, "As you can see I am quite happy here, I have a thriving business, non thriving at present I grant you," he chuckled "But thriving."

Len heaved a sigh. "That was what I was afraid of. Now I will have to do it the hard way."

Jake's silence forced him to continue. He started warily preparing himself for the inevitable reaction to what he was about to say. "You have the hots for a gal called Annie so I believe." Len moved his hand cautiously.

Totally unprepared for what he was hearing, and inwardly seething at the mention of Annie's name, Jake leaned forward. "Whatever you have in mind, I strongly advise you to forget it Lenny my boy."

Len made a buffer of his hands. "First hear me out, Kid. You do the job and I assure you nothing will happen to your gal."

"And if I do not?"

"Accidents can happen, Kid, least when you expect them."

"You do know who you are talking about, Len, the local cop's kid sister."

"She don't look like a kid sister to me, Jake. However, more to the point, do this little thing for me and I promise no harm will come to your beloved Annie." Len halted smiling, "You never know there might be a few dollars in it for you."

"Stick your dollars. Leave Annie out of this and I will do the hit. Ok?"

Grinning, Len stood up. "That's what I want to hear, Kid. Now for the details."

"Annie that supper was simply sumptuous. What do you say, Jake?" Bubba pushed his chair back from the table.

"I would agree if I knew the meaning of the word," Jake responded, folding his napkin and setting it down on the white linen table cloth, "the word's much harder to digest than your cooking Annie," he rose, "Need a hand in there?" he asked of the woman in the kitchen.

"No, thank you Jake. You two have yourselves a beer while I clear up."

"Sure you can manage?" Bubba asked hopefully, thankful that he had not to do his own cleaning up for once.

"And should I have a mind to say no, Tom Haines what would you do?" came the reply.

A little later both men sitting on the porch, Jake cautiously began what had been on his mind since Len's leaving. "I have to leave for a few days or so, Bubba. I cannot say the reason."

"Nothing to do with your out of town visitor would it Jake?"

For a moment Jake was taken off guard, until remembering that it was the duty of this man to know all that went on in this small town.

"Could be, Tom. However there is a favour I would ask of you, it concerns us both, it's about Annie."

From where he stood on the hillside Jake Russo followed the approaching car through his binoculars, a second car, some distance behind almost completely obscured by dust on this brown country road below.

Jake lowered the glasses. Annie was driving that first car in the belief that she was taking it to be sold, out at the old Denis place. Jake swore at the lies he had told the woman, something he had not done before, but he could think of no other way to have her out of the office and on to this deserted road.

He put the glasses back to his eyes, muttering a thanks at the sight of a third car further back.

Annie was almost directly beneath him now, the second car keeping its distance, then the wail of the police siren as Bubba in the third car drew quickly up behind Annie's pursuer, forcing him to stop.

"Let's see you get out of this one, fella," Jake muttered starting back to his own vehicle on the hillside road, and smiling at the sight of Annie's car in the distance.

Jake extracted his cell phone from his pocket punching in Annie's number waiting until she answered.

"Jake?"

"Annie? There has been a change of plan, old Denis has opted out of the sale." Another lie, he had only used the old man's name as an excuse.

"Bloody hell, Jake, what a waste of time and gas. And me here sweating my tootsies off in this heat." Annie's angry voice reached him on the hillside.

"Never mind gal, I'll dry your tootsies when I see you," Jake guffawed into the open hillside.

"So I guess Jake Russo you want me to return to the office? Is that what you are saying?"

"Not quite. My sale went pear shaped as well. Tell you what, call it a day, go home and cook me up something swell. I should be there about seven. OK?"

"You are all heart, boss." Annie sighed now a little calmer. "See you around seven. Keep safe."

From where he pulled up outside the jail house Russo could see Bubba's black and white in the yard. Pushing open the door he stepped into the fairly quiet office. Flo looked up where she sat busy fingered on her computer. "He's been expecting you Jake, go on in," she greeted Jake without hesitating from her work.

"Thanks Flo. Enjoying the heat?" he asked the thirty something woman cheerily.

"The heat I get is not from the weather, Jake," she replied good humouredly.

"Well Jake Russo, I have your boy all locked up, but for how long I cannot say." Tom Haines sipped at a cup of cold water.

"Thanks Bubba." Jake took a seat across from where the police officer sat behind his desk. "I should have all this business done in a week or so."

Bubba jerked a thumb over his shoulder. "No way can I hold him in there that long. I am surprised he has not already hollered he wants his lawyer. His story is that he was not following Annie but as a stranger simply found himself on the wrong road. Sounds feasible if you had not told me different. So would you mind telling me what all this is about?"

Russo shrugged his shoulders.

"Nothing to do with your visitor yesterday, I guess."

"A little. But you know I cannot say anything, you being a cop and all." Jake smiled wickedly.

"Guess not." Bubba pointed a finger at Jake. "I am only doing this because you say it is in Annie's interest."

He drew closer to Russo across his desk. "Should it be anything to do with your past... shall we say... activities I have a right to know, Jake Russo, and should you have a mind to break the law in this state I will lock you up as surely as Annie makes the best apple pie in the county. You hear?"

"I hear."

"So how long will you be gone?"

"As I said, two, maybe three weeks at most."

"Christ Jake I can not hold that guy in there more than a couple of days, neither can I keep an eye on sis until you get back."

Jake heard the anger in his friend's voice. Understanding what Annie meant to the man, Jake replied with more composure that he felt. "No, but you could hold our friend long enough to have Annie out of town to visit the aunt she always talks about. She'd be safe there should only you and I know about it. I'd close the yard, tell everyone I am away on other business and Annie is on vacation. Gus can run the motel as he usually does. Ok?"

"Seems reasonable. But break the law and I will make sure that you will not see my sister again."

Jake could not resist saying, "Seems reasonable."

Tom's face broke into a grin. "Get out of here."

"Why should I go on vacation all of a sudden?" Annie wanted to know setting down the plate of fried chicken before Jake. "Especially to Aunt Clare's. What are you not telling me Jake Russo this taking off on business? What kind of business? If it is another woman, then tell me to my face, tell me it's all over between us."

For a moment Jake was stunned, the absurdity that he was unfaithful or tired of the woman he loved never having entered his mind. He toyed with his fork his appetite for such an enticing meal suddenly gone. But what excuse other than the truth could he give?

Yet again if their friendship was to flourish with marriage at the end did he not owe this lovely girl nothing other than the truth?

"No it's not another woman, Annie. There never could be anyone else." Jake pushed away the plate. "I do not have a shining past Annie, some things I have done were bad, real bad. I am hoping this thing I have to do will end it all for good. But I have to know you are safe until it is all over."

"And when it is, I am to carry on as if nothing has happened? Never to know the real Jake Russo or his past. Do you expect this of me, Jake? Do you think it really fair?"

Annie was angry and close to tears and Jake knew he could not blame her. Perhaps he should call it a day between them, give this lovely woman the chance of meeting someone she would be proud of, live a normal decent life. "All I can ask is that you trust me, Annie, and that I do love you. This business is the end and hopefully a new beginning for me and you. When I return I will tell you all you want to know about me should that be what you want."

Annie had tears in her eyes as she asked, "And when you do come back, Jake? What if it's not what I want to hear?"

"Then decide. I will walk away should that be what you want. But for now all that I care about is your safety."

Annie fought back a sob. "Then I will do as you ask Jake, I'll wait until you come back."

Chapter 13

Jake Russo had driven most of the day to reach here, now he sat looking across the lawn at the condo where Louis Canello had brought him that first day all those long years ago.

The place had altered somewhat during those past years, small bushes had grown almost head high, trees now reached above the suite where he had lived for a time. The same suite Canello had caught him with his woman Belle. That same night he had shot his benefactor dead.

He looked closer to where a gardener worked by a new entrance, and saw that now a press pad was used to gain access instead of the method of having to use a key as he had to.

Jake started up the car deciding there was little to be gained in reminiscing. Now to find a place not too close to the condo, after which he would arrange a meeting with Len and the two men he had hired to assist him in the hit.

It was close on nine before Jake heard the tap on his room door. Rising from where had stretched out on top of the bed he walked cautiously, gun in hand to the door.

There was no warmth in Len's greeting, only a quiet hello Kid as he stepped into the room.

"Cosy." Len gave the room the benefit of his scrutiny and sat down on one of the two chairs.

Jake slid the Glock back into its holster and sat down on the edge of the bed.

"Trip OK?" Len asked without any real interest.

"Yip."

"Good. Now down to business. I can give you two weeks to do the hit. Only contact me if there is trouble. I do not want any of the organisation to know that I am behind Viconti's..." he hesitated searching for the right word, "removal, shall we say."

"And if they do?" Jake asked a hint of amusement in his voice. "Would you still be in the running for head honcho, shall we say?"

"It would make it more difficult of course, but I believe I have the backing of most heads in the organisation who believe that it is time to remove Felix, although they have no idea what exactly I have in mind for the old guy."

"After I do the hit, I want your promise this is the last time you will contact me. Then we are all square capisce."

"Sure Kid but no hit, no expenses."

"Agreed. So who have you got lined up for me?"

Len eased forward in his chair. Two guys, Joe and Jed. A bit young but they will do as you say. I have arranged you meet them in Sally's Bar on the freeway out of town around noon. You remember Sally's? We used to have a drink there sometimes after collection."

Jake nodded, understanding the reference 'collection' to mean after collecting that day's protection money. "Sally still there? If she is I cannot take the chance that she may recognise me."

"You have been away a long time Kid, Sally has been pulling beer in that big bar in the sky for nigh on four years," Len smirked. "So it is safe enough." he rose, "Work out with your guys how you want the job done. As I said do not contact me unless it is entirely necessary. The least I know of the hit, the better." Len grinned in a way that reminded Jake of those days when he Harry and himself had worked together. "So I will leave you to it Kid."

That evening, Jake decided that he should call Annie.
"Hello, is that you Jake?" Jake heard the familiar voice ask.
"Sure is. Who else were you expecting?" He teased.
"Oh hard to say. I have so many callers, especially when my man is out of town."
"I asked for that, did I not gal? Everything all right where you are?"
"Guess so, Auntie is doing well and happy to see me." Then a little more soberly, "When will you be back, Jake. I miss you?"
"Same here Annie, but I really cannot say when, but the sooner the better for both of us."
"I do not know what business you are involved in, Jake Russo, but whatever it is be careful. I want you back in one piece."
"Don't worry, I mean to with all my pieces in good working order."
"You had better or I will set Bubba on you, and you know what he is like with a few beers."
"Or even less,"Jake laughed, already missing this woman he loved. There was a moments silence before Jake said, "I better close now, Annie, I have a few things need doing if I am to soon make it back home."
"OK Jake. Look after yourself and call me whenever you can."
"Sure will. Love you." Jake closed his phone before he said things that might embarrass him when he thought them over later. After all was he not anything other than a real insensitive hit man?

Jake entered Sally's bar a few minutes before the time arranged, pleasantly surprised at who he considered to be his two accomplices already seated at a corner table. He halted at the table, and one looking up said quietly, "I am Joe, this here is Jed. I take it you are Mr Kid?"
Jake smiled at the deduction. "Not really. You can call me the Kid. Perhaps the name is a little past its sell by date but it will do for now."
While both nodded their understanding Jake slid into a seat, asking, "Have you eaten?"
While the waitress was discussing his order with the bartender Jake discreetly studied the two sitting across from him, deciding that both really were young, perhaps too young for the job in hand. Len had said that although they were, both were sufficiently experienced to help carry out the hit on Felix Viconti. He better be right for all their sakes.

Over a few drinks, Jake decided that both men would fit the job, although he had some reservations regarding Joe who he thought may be a little compulsive, hopefully not at the wrong time.

After the men had left, Jake sat revising what they had discussed and the orders given. They would not meet again until Thursday two days from now, by then should they have carried out his orders to the letter, he would know all of Viconti's movements, schedule, and layout of the condo including all new renovations there might have been since his living there. Now he had things to do, providing Len's information was correct that was.

It was around noon next day when Jake Russo got the call. Putting the cell phone to his ear listening to the voice on the other end, saying, "Sorry boss Joe tried to take Viconti down, and has been shot in the arm."
Jake cursed.. "Meet me at the crossroads out of town."Angrily he snapped the phone shut thinking his appraisal of Joe may had been correct, but now was not the time to ask for details.

"I want that son of a bitch, here, and now. He should not be so difficult to find, Andy plugged him one in the arm," A shaken Felix Viconti shouted at Len. "Plus, I want to know who hired him to see me dead."

Cell phone in hand, Len watched his cursing boss leave the room. "Jesus H Christ, Kid you have made a right botch of this one," he muttered to himself, punching in the numbers waiting impatiently for a reply, eventually hearing Russo's voice, "Hello, Kid. What the hell have you done? Viconti has me putting the word out for whoever is responsible, and more importantly who is behind the hit. You know what that means."
"Calm yourself man, just tell me, is Doc Jones still available, and can I expect to find him in the usual place?"

"Yes to both, but you cannot take him there the Doc still has contact with the organisation. He'll let Viconti know right away."
It was the end of the conversation, Len was left staring into a dead phone.

Jake Russo drew up his car close to the car already sitting a little short of the deserted crossroads.

Jake walked swiftly to the parked car pulling open the passenger door ordering of the driver as he sat down, "Drive straight ahead, Jed. Joe here can tell me exactly what happened, on the way. He also may be good enough to explain why he attempted to take the old man down without first letting me know?"

To Joe the sarcasm hurt more that the wound. Clutching his arm, Joe leaned forward awkwardly. "It just happened, boss. I was trailing Viconti as you ordered. I was hiding amongst the trees on the seventh, and his partner had just driven off, when the old man decided to head for the bushes, may be to…"
"Okay. We know what for. Then what?"
Joe stared at the back of Jake's neck from his seat. "It was too good an opportunity to miss, boss, seeing as his nearest bodyguard was busy at the golf bag and all, and Viconti had disappeared out of his sight into the bushes, so I ran out of the trees!" Joe halted banging his fist on the back of Jake's seat. "I swear I had him, boss. Then another bodyguard came from nowhere, firing before I could get a shot off. He hit me in the arm and I ran back into the trees."

Jake held up his hand. "Would this guy, this guard recognise you if he saw you again?"
"Guess so, boss, he was close enough. Only the trees prevented him from getting off a second shot. Sorry boss." Exhausted, Joe sat back in his seat.

Scarcely anything was said for the remainder of the journey until finally the silence was broken by Jake instructing, "turn right at the next junction, then take it slowly, it is some time since I was last here. And before you ask, I was not the patient."

Jake did not recognise Doc Jones or he him, but the doc did recognise 'the mob' when confronted by it. Asking no questions the MD got to work.

Drifting to the window, Jake took a look out at a street he did not recognise. How everything had changed since his early days when if fact he had indeed been The Kid. He turned away from the window and with it the memories of how young he had been then, even younger that these two here.

"I think that should hold you," the doctor was saying to Joe while Jed helped his partner on with his shirt. "I will give you something to kill the pain. You will have to change the dressing twice a day, more, should it become necessary. You don't want it to become infected."
Joe slid himself off the bench. "No doc, and thank you."
"Same here, Doc," Jake handed the doctor a fistful of dollars, "And thanks again."
The doctor eyed the roll of banknotes his eyes gleaming. "A mite too much, fella, half is the usual fee Mr Viconti expects me to be paid."
Jake saw the look of alarm on both faces of his men at the mention of the name. He gave the man his widest smile, "In this case Doc, you deserve it."

Outside the three men had reached the third step, the door had closed behind them when Jake suddenly swung back. "You two go on. I'll meet you back at the car."
Trotting back up the stairs Jake cautiously opened the front door and quietly stepped inside.

From the corridor Jake heard the doctor's voice on the phone. "Can I speak with Mr Viconti please, it is very important."

Jake had scarcely returned to the car before Jed alarm in his voice asked, "What about the Doc back there, he is sure to let the mob know he's patched up Joe. They'll be on to us before we have a chance to do the hit."

"I say we should forget about Viconti and get the hell out of here." Joe sounded scared. "Don't you think so, Boss?"

"All taken care of, Doc back there won't be telling Viconti or anyone else, that's for sure."

Jake heard the sharp intake of breath from both men. "So let's get out of here before I die of starvation." Adding as Jed started up the car. "You see what your little mistake has cost, Joe?"

"I wont make any more Boss, this I promise. I owe you one"

"I know you do. But any more mistakes and you are history, Joe. Capisce?"

"Yes, Boss," came the meek reply from the back, seat.

Jake Russo slid into his coat. He had to get out of a room that was closing in on him. Things were starting to go wrong, and in his experience one unfortunate incident was usually followed by another. Joe had started this and now the Doc had paid for it.

Jake shook his head at the recent memory of the doctor standing phone in hand knowing he would soon be dead for this man standing there could not afford to let him tell Felix Viconti that he had just attended to his intended assassin. Jake patted his breast pocket, priding himself at having taken back the money he had given the MD. Now there was a little less for Viconti's men to go on, but only a little less. The Big Man would soon find out.

Jake Russo drove into the town centre, well away from his hotel and even more from Viconti's condo. One Neon sign advertising food caught his attention. He pulled into a parking space on the main street and walked the short distance to the entrance.
The place was only half full at this time of night and he selected a table some distance away from the front window.

Jake looked cautiously around him sizing up everyone there, most of whom were either busy at their meal or chatting with one another, and suddenly he wanted to be back home with Annie.

The waitress came before he had time to study the menu. She was an older woman than those who usually held such a position, reminding him of Fanny back home who would be of similar age, moaning about her poor feet and how it was too much to ask of her at her age. He had laughed at knowing that it was her husband who owned the place.
"Ready to order, mister?"
Jake looked up at the woman standing there waiting pad and pencil in hand. "Not quite honey, but I could sure use a cup of coffee while I study this here menu."
Jake knew he sounded phoney, but he needed someone to remember him should there be any inquiries from the mob regarding strangers in town, though drawing attention to himself was the last thing he needed right now.
"You new in town mister? You don't sound like anyone from around here."

"Guess so, around an hour ago. Got me a place to rest my head for the night then on my way first thing in the morning."

"Travelling man are you?"

"Yip."

The waitress took a step away then turned back, looking puzzled. "You never been in town before?"

"Sure. I have passed through on my way back up north but never stopped even for so much as a coffee. Now I realise my mistake." Jake gave the waitress the benefit of his widest smile.

The waitress did not succumb to the intended compliment. "I am sure that I have seen you somewhere before."

"Never been there," Jake replied deadpan.

"Never been where?"

"Somewhere."

Giving up on this 'strange' stranger, muttering the waitress turned away.

It was fifteen minutes or so later, Jake looked up from enjoying his meal, where two men were talking with his waitress at the counter, her occasional glance in his direction telling him that he was the subject of their conversation. Now he would know if his ruse had worked. Would she convince them that he had only recently arrived in town and therefore had nothing to do with the attempt on Viconti's life? Jake having no doubt in his mind that these two were nothing other than Viconti's men.

At length the two black suited men with a final long look in Jake's direction, and saying their goodbyes to the waitress made for the door.

Relieved by their leaving, Jake moved his hand slowly away from his Glock. Perhaps they had believed what the woman had told them as he had no doubt that the conversation had been about him.

"You ready to order dessert mister?" His waitress was at his table again, eyeing him with more than her usual curiosity.

"Thanks, but no. I don't believe I have enough room left for blueberry pie. Sorry."

She tore a sheet out of her pad, placing it on the table, saying as Jake lifted the tab, "That does not include the tip, mister."

"No, I guess it doesn't, whatever your name is," Jake reached inside his coat for his wallet.

"Belle, everyone calls me Belle."

It was as if the name struck a chord. Jake stopped what he was doing, the waitress stopped too staring at him.

"You could not be him, not the Kid?" Belle stared at him now wide eyed in disbelief.

Jake choked out, "Belle…. not?"

"Sure is, you son of a bitch," Belle's angry voice filled the almost empty restaurant. She sank down in a chair opposite from where Jake continued to stare at her. "You left me Kid, left me with nothing that night you took down Louis Canello!"

She was almost shouting now, no longer concerned about her job, only that she vent her anger on this man sitting here. "Now what do you see Kid, an old woman with arthritis and Christ knows what else serving tables? Until that night I was on top of the world. Louis gave me everything I ever asked for, then you had to spoil it all by shooting him down in cold blood."

"As I remember it Belle, no ones blood was cold that night, especially Canello with his baseball bat ready to beat me to a pulp." Jake smirked. "And as I remember, your blood was close to boiling before the old bastard rushed into our room."

Belle did not appreciate Jake's attempt at humour. "OK you were... we were a lot younger then."

"I was little more than a teenager, Belle." Jake reminded her.

"OK, but did you have to leave me in the way you did? You must have known with Canello gone no one was willing to hitch up with a moll, for that was what I was to everyone, a gangster's moll."

Jake splayed his hands in way of apology, "I did not know, Belle, but I had to high tail out of there before the mob got wind of what I had done."

Belle nodded in a way that said she understood, though to her his pitiful explanation fell well short of forgiveness. "You owe me big time buddy. You reduced me to this," she threw a hand around. "At my age."

"What would you have me do, Belle, compensate you for having seduced me when I knew nothing better? And I reckon you would have gone on doing so had Canello not found us both together that night. I am not entirely to blame for all that may have happened to you since then."

For a moment Belle sat silently fuming, ignoring a client's call to be served. The Kid was right of course, but this was her only chance to prise a few dollars out of the son of a bitch. Also she had an ace up her sleeve, one which she hoped could scare this cocksure bastard to the core.

"You look swell, Kid. Life has been good to you, so how about a few bucks to keep me from lifting the phone, just to let Viconti know that the Kid's back in town, especially on the day you tried to take him down."

Here was a situation Jake Russo had not foreseen. "What makes you believe I had anything to do with the hit on the old boy, since I am newly arrived in town, eh Belle?"
"Come off it wise guy that phoney accent showed you were up to something, something you wanted to hide, such as being in town a lot longer than you are trying to make out." Belle smirked. "So, I am sure old Viconti would pay handsomely to learn you are still in town, probably with the intention of making another hit."
Now the situation was dire, it only taking Belle to lift the phone and he was as good as dead, unless of course he could fool her.

Belle was still beaming at Jake across the table, her expression saying she had him by his family jewels, when he said quietly, "I do not think that is a very good idea Belle, this telling Felix Viconti that I am in town, not when it was him who hired me to guard him."
Instantly Belle's expression changed. She had almost killed herself by exposing Viconti's plan, and to no other than to the old man himself.
"You mean?"
Jake nodded. "Viconti does not want anyone to know I am here and why. He knows someone is ready to put him down so called me in."

He waited for Belle's reaction to a tale that could be so easily disputed, such as his being the last man that Viconti would want around considering what he had done to the mob's former boss Canello. Instead he was pleasantly surprised when Belle said that she believed him, and how fortunate it was that she had not called the Big man.

Jake rose, throwing down a few dollar notes on the table. "So now that's settled, Belle I will call again tomorrow for dinner. Hold this table for me and there will be a few dollars more for your years of inconvenience. OK?"
Belle looked up at him. "I will appreciate that Kid. Maybe we can get together again some time?"
"Maybe, Belle, should it be at all as good as last time." He was lying as he had no intention of making up with this woman who had seduced him all those years ago; not when he had someone like Annie waiting for him back home.

Jake Russo lay fully clothed on his bed only slightly interested in the channel on the screen, when the knock sounded on his door. He rose lifting the Glock off the bedside table, almost certain that his caller could be no other than Len.

He was right, his unexpected visitor bursting in with "What the hell are you up to Kid?"on his lips.
"Nice to meet you too, Len." Jake closed the door behind the human hurricane, calmly adding, "Can I offer you a drink, however limited the choice may be?"
Len waved a hand throwing himself down in a chair. "No. Let's cut to the chase. How in the name of Jesus H Christ did you think to take down Viconti on an open fairway?"

Jake understood the man's anger, he had a right to be. "Joe believed he could take Viconti when he went for a pee in the bushes. Might have worked, unfortunately it did not."

"So it was Joe, Andy hit. Is Joe hurt bad?" Len's voice was void of concern only of the possibility that the hit on Viconti should have to be called off.

"He'll live. I took him to Doc Jones. Fortunately he still lived in the same place as I remembered."

Len sat forward in his chair. "You what!" Len stared in disbelief at the man across the room. "I told you he would let Viconti know the minute he patched up Joe." Len jumped up, "Christ, Kid what have you done? The Doc will identify you and those two bums with you!".

Jake lifted a hand. "The doc won't be telling anyone of our visit."

Heaving a sigh of relief, Len sat back down. "Honestly Kid I will be more than happy when the hit is made and this is all over."

"That's a false hope Len my boy, for you it will only be the start when you take Viconti's place."

For once Len looked shaken, perhaps for the first time understanding what it meant to be boss, always having to watch your back. As a means of some sort of relief, Len started. "Three days from now all the heads of the various families will gather at Ginns Point. You remember the chalet at Ginns Point?"

Jake nodded. "I used to help with security up there for Canello."

Len nodded, continuing, "Security is already under way, so I think it would be inadvisable to try a hit on Viconti there, should you be thinking of doing so."

"What makes you think I would Len, if as you say the place is alive with guards?"

"It's the very thing you are inclined to do. Hit when least expected. You would need an army to get anywhere near there. There are guards all over the hillsides, including all roads leading up to the chalet."

"Then I will have to think of another venue for the old man, won't I?"

"I sincerely hope so, for you are rapidly running out of time. And you also have an injured man to contend with."

Len rose and Jake said, "That's not all I have to contend with."

Len sank back into his chair, fearful of hearing any further bad news.

"I went for a meal to a place downtown, and by the worst of coincidences ran into someone from the Canello days."

Len stared despairingly at Jake. "No let me guess. Not Belle Franklin?" Len halted, knowing he had no other choice than to ask, "Did she recognise you? Christ, say she did not, Kid."

"Sorry, but she did."

Len was back on his feet. "Then if she did, Viconti will know already."

Jake smiled at the way Len had phrased his words. "Not quite. I convinced her that I was working for Viconti not against him. Also as she seemed sore at what had happened since the night I took down Canello and somehow believed me to be responsible for her fall from grace you might say, I consoled her by promising to come good with a few dollars in way of compensation, should compensation be the correct terminology, here."

Len stood there, his mind in a whirl. "You think she believed you, after all you cost the organisation by taking down their boss? And that Viconti has forgiven you and made you his main man?"

"Guess so, the way she looked at me when realising how close she had come to having Viconti beat up on her for blowing my cover."

Len turned for the door, reluctant to accept the Kid's explanation. "You best be right Kid or we are all in the shit."

Jake Russo left his car in the restaurant's parking lot. Belle should be expecting him and have his table all set for his arrival. Contrary to his last visit the place was quite full. His reserved table in use by a young couple already enjoying their meal. A little perplexed Jake caught the arm of a young waitress rushing passed. "Excuse me, Belle should have a table reserved for me, but I don't see her."

"Neither can I mister. She did not call in sick either. Now she has me doing double shifts."

The young girl shook herself free of Jake's hold. "Now if you will excuse me I have work to do. Should you see Belle, say hi! And thanks for the extra shift, bitch."

Outside, although having agreed to contact one another solely in an emergency Jake somehow felt the need to text his former partner. Something was wrong, either Belle had somehow attempted to screw Viconti, or she in turn had been screwed, whatever the reason, he had to know.

The reason came four minutes later. It simply read. Matter taken care of. L

Sadly Jake knew what that meant. And probably for the first in a long time felt sorry for someone.

Poor Belle, and it was him who was to blame.

Chapter 14

Jake Russo took the rifles out of the car parked in one of the fire breaks. Handing first one to Jed then the lighter weapon to the injured Joe. He himself slung the heavier .50 calibre rifle over his shoulder.

"Up there," he pointed to the hill above. "We should make there within the hour. We are still a long distance away from the first of the guards."

"Are you sure, boss?" Jed asked hitching the weapon on his shoulder a little more comfortable. "Sure, they were nowhere near where we are going, when I took a look- see yesterday." Jake's answer was crisp. "The rocks are too steep at the chalet end, and I am betting the walk is a bit on the long side for them to where we are going from here, but keep your eyes open, both of them.

Jake's estimated time for the climb was within five minutes.

Joe threw himself down exhausted on the short grass, Jake dropping the backpack he'd carried beside him.

"Time for a coffee." Jake opened the backpack extracting the flask of coffee. He handed it to Joe.

"I'll take a look around while you two help yourself, but only to one drink. We will be up here for quite some time."

Leaving the two men behind Jake climbed cautiously to the top of the hill, where laying flat he swept the intervening space between him and the chalet below, halting now and again to adjust the lens of his binoculars. After a few minutes, Jake swung back the glasses, something or somebody amongst the trees had caught his attention. "Gotcha," he whispered. It was the first sighting of the security guards amongst the trees.

Jake returned to his men. "You have had your break, so let's get going."
"Is it far, boss?" Jed asked apprehensively. "I am tired as hell."
Jake drew him a look of disappointment. "Tired at your age? Come on get your ass up there."
Reluctantly Jed levered himself up from the grass. "Have a heart boss, I'm a city fella. When I go high it's usually in an elevator."
"Well unless Joe here volunteers to carry you, you will just have to try, or I might just have you put down seeing as I cannot stand the sight of a dumb animal suffering."
"And boy is he dumb," Joe sniggered.
Jake smiled at that and the tension was broken.

An hour later they lay hidden amongst the tall grass from where they had a perfect view of the chalet some distance below.
"What the hell is that?" Joe could not believe his eyes.
"I put it there yesterday when I came up here. Now get yourself back there amongst trees and leave the rest to me. You both clear on what you have to do?" Both nodded that they understood.

Rising cautiously, crouching, Jake made his way to the edge of an escarpment where he lay down his weapon at the ready.
Jake expertly adjusted the telescopic site bringing the empty line of cars parked outside the chalet closer, then squeezing the trigger watched the nearest cars gas tank

explode, followed by another and another in quick
succession.

Amid the chaos of security men either running for cover or
attempting to pin point from where the gun flashes came,
Jake changed his aim to shatter the windows of the chalet
itself, silently wishing for an air strike to take out these
evil men within.

Letting off a few more rounds Jake was on his feet running
back to his original position throwing himself down to
await the next phase of his plan. It was not long in coming.

One man ran into the clearing halting abruptly at the sight
of the small white cooler in the centre of the open space
and why it had come to be here, his question destined to
remain unanswered by a bullet catching him in the throat.
Almost immediately a second guard rushed into open
ground slowly drawing to a halt at the unusual sight of a
dead man lying beside a small white water cooler, before
he too was hit.

Jake answered a wave from Jed hidden in the trees to his
left, a second confirmation following from Joe on his right.
"A few more and we are finished here," the thought
scarcely having entered Jake's mind before another two
men appeared, these however sensing the trap beat a hasty
retreat back amongst the trees before he could snap off
another shot.

Back pedalling on all fours from his hidden position, Jake
signalled to the others to follow him, believing that the two
who had sensed his trap were not so very far away
amongst the trees.

"Where to now boss?" Jed asked, hitching his back pack on to his shoulders.

"Back the way we came. It takes us in the opposite direction from the road the mob will take back to town."

"Pity we did not get Viconti," Joe moaned.

"You know that was never the purpose of this little escapade Joe, merely to scare the shit out of the big boss himself. Now let's get out of here, we have a ways to go and I do not want those last two guys to know which way we are headed."

Over an hour later, the trio threw themselves down at the top of their climb.

"How long before the big shots leave the chalet, boss." Joe chewed the piece of grass in his mouth.

"Soon. They will not wait to finish their business, not when their assassins are still at bay. I figure they will take the same road down as they came up, and when they reach the crossroads on the edge of town split up and continue on their respective ways home."

Jake stood up. "Come on we do not have much time to spare. Our car is not so far away now, we can reach it in less than fifteen minutes."

Sitting in the back of the car beside Len, Felix Viconti was visibly shaken by what had happened back at the chalet.

"They got two men up the mountainside." It was more of a question than statement from the old man.

"Five back at the chalet should you include those standing by the cars." Len answered staring out of the side window.

"It was me they were after Len."

"Could be, you being the main man and all." Len was bent on adding fuel to his boss's fear. "Maybe you should take a trip until all this blows over and we find out who is behind it Mr Viconti."

"No, Len that would show weakness, and Christ knows what havoc my mob would reek while I am gone."

"Could be you are right, sir, but should that happen we would sure as hell know who is behind it all."

Viconti's sigh held the weariness he felt, perhaps it was time for him to quit, quit before it was too late.

"It is good that I have you Len to rely on. And should I stand down I will sincerely nominate you to the organisation that you take my place."

"Mr Viconti you honour me." Len's voice rose in fake surprise. "What can I say?" Then a little quieter, "But would the Heads accept me? I am younger than most, many having been in the organisation longer than I have."

"They will, should I give you my full support." Viconti patted Len on the knee. "But let's leave it there for the present, do not rush out to buy yourself a villa or two just yet," the old mobster laughed.

"No Mr Viconti" Len answered, while thinking maybe those villas are closer than you think old man.

Only two cars remained from the original convoy the others having left to go their separate ways. Eventually the condo came in sight. A few seconds later Viconti's car had reached the entrance, and the old man blew out relief at safely reaching home while he waited for the driver to open his door.

Now a little more cheerful Viconti pointed to where the gardener worked by the entrance. "I must tell Harry, I want those plants removed. They are too close to the door. All the local dogs pee on them, you have to wear galoshes to reach the entrance," Viconti laughed, and Len laughed with him.

The old man got out and walked towards the entrance calling out to his gardener, who swung round firing two rapid shots into his frail body.

"Christ!" Len howled, stumbling out of the car.

Two security guards ran past him firing at the fleeing figure of the gardener, who by this time was running towards a car slowing down to pick him up.

Jake 'the gardener' reached the slowing car, and running beside it his hand outstretched waited for the door to fly open to let him climb aboard, the driver grinning out at him, and that driver was no other than Jed, then the car sped away, leaving him to face too many armed men running towards him, led by no other than Len himself.

"Recognise the road Kid?" Len asked, sitting beside Jake in the back of the car.

Jake Russo watched the landscape rush past, as if the driver was impatient to have this all over. "Leave the road here, Joe," Jed instructed the driver, his voice no more than a whisper.

Dust blew across the windscreen almost blocking out their vision on this sandy side road.

"Harry taught you how to use a gun here. Remember Kid?" Len's voice bitter at the recollection. "That was before you shot him dead, here in this same place. Now it is your turn Kid. Ironic is it not?" Len smirked, his hand on the door handle waiting for the car to draw to a halt.

Across the sand a little way ahead, bushes, now much taller than the last time he was here, Jake walked beside the three men.

"This is far enough." Len halted. "I think this is the exact spot where you killed my partner, Kid. Is it not?"

"Enjoying yourself, Len?" Jake asked staring angrily at his executioner. "Revenge is not all it's cracked up to be, especially when the reason is nothing other than shit. And this sure as hell is shit."

"Cut the act, and the crap. You cannot talk your way out of this." Len howled at the man he still feared and hated.

"Perhaps not, but deep down you know that your dear departed Harry had double crossed you. Should dear Harry's plan have worked, he would have left you and I to face the music, Canello's music, Baseball on bums, or something similar."

"Cut it out Russo!" Shouting, Len drew away, pulling out the gun from his pocket.

"You will never know how much I have dreamed of this day, Kid. And it has worked out better than I could ever have imagined. I got the great Jake Russo the Kid to take down Felix Viconti and at the same time put *me* in his place." Len looked up at the sky, his eyes glowing, "And now to cap it all, I get to finish it, ironically with your own gun, Kid. Perhaps the very same gun you shot my partner Harry with."

Len cocked the Glock, and Joe and Jed stood back.

"I will give you the same consideration that you gave my partner. We were good partners doing well until you, Canello's prodigy came along and spoiled it. You let Harry look you in the eyes when you took him down, I can only do the same for you, besides I want to see that last look when you are hit with your own gun."

Len raised the cocked weapon, the sound of the shot resounding across the open sandy space, as disbelief in his eyes he sank to the ground.
Jake Russo took the few steps to the fatally wounded man. "You once told me always to watch my back. You forgot Len, a fact that has me thinking that you would not last long as head honcho of the organisation."
Len stared past Jake to Jed who stood with the still smoking gun in his hand. "You were *my* man. Why?"
Jed shrugged. "The Kid made Joe and me an offer we could not refuse."

Epilogue

Jake Russo was almost home, at least to Kent, the place he had come to call home these past five years. Here was all he knew and loved, especially Annie. He could not wait to be with her again. He exhaled a long breath of satisfaction. No more hits, no more excitement other than selling cars, and the few dollars brought in from the motel.

The Viconti job was his last. For a moment he let himself dwell on those last few days. He had failed, having underestimated his escape after bringing down the old man, and it was Jed's quick thinking that his driving away was the only way of saving him that had led Len to believe that the two men were still faithful to him.

Road signs ahead told any unfamiliar traveller that Winley was to the left, the right to Kent.
Jake stared almost lovingly at the sign. Now that he was free again should he pop the question, ask Annie to marry him? He had little doubt that she would. He had not let her know of his coming, he wanted to leave his home coming a surprise.

Troubled, involuntarily Jake slowed his car. Was it at all right what he was asking of the woman? He a killer, a hitman, an assassin. He thought himself free, but nothing could be further from the truth, the law would never give up on him. So far he'd been lucky, there being no real evidence to suspect or convict him, but this could change overnight. So was it fair to this lovely innocent girl? Should she not deserve to be told the truth? And should he do so, would she accept him for what he was, nothing other than a killer?

Perhaps it best that he walk away, leave her to meet a sound regular guy one she'd be proud of, not having to stop, fearful every time she heard a police siren. But could he bring himself to walk away from the woman he loved? The woman who promised to wait for him, and he her?

He was almost at the sign now. Which way? Two lives depended on his decision. Left and out of Annie's life, or right, to the one he loved.
With a cry of frustration and near despair, Jake Russo, aka The kid, gripped the steering wheel tighter.
The End

Printed in Great Britain
by Amazon

17377492R00148